UNCORRECTED GALLEY PROOF
Not for resale or distribution.

My Super Sweet Sixteenth Century

Rachel Harris

Entangled Publishing, LLC
2614 South Timberline Road
Suite 109
Fort Collins, CO 80525
Visit our website at www.entangledpublishing.com.

Edited by Stacy Abrams
Cover design by Liz Pelletier

Print ISBN978-1-62061-135-7
Ebook ISBN978-1-62061-136-4

Manufactured in the United States of America

First Edition September 2012

To my beautiful, brilliant, boisterous daughters Jordan and Cali.
I hope you always go after your dreams.
And to my amazingly supportive husband Gregg.
You are my rock.

Chapter One

I'm trapped.

I concentrate on the monitor in front of me and scan through the in-flight entertainment, attempting to tune out Jenna. Like that's even possible. When my dad's bubbly fiancée gets this excited, I swear sometimes only dogs can hear her.

We've been on this plane for over six hours. I woke up less than an hour ago, cramped, cranky, and carb-deprived, and yet the woman insists on being perky. It's as if she were born with caffeine in her veins.

"Cat, do you know what this means?!?"

I quirk an eyebrow at Dad but, judging by his all-consuming interest in the newspaper, his stance of neutrality is in full effect. To tell you the truth, it's not his impartiality that hurts. It's knowing that by staying out of it, what he's really doing is taking her side.

And moving further away from mine.

I settle for a crappy re-run and decide to throw the evil step-witch-in-training a bone. I lean forward and look across the aisle, catching a glimpse of her flying fingers on her BlackBerry—thank goodness they have inflight WiFi, or she might've actually wanted to bond. "No, tell me, Jenna. What does it mean?"

"It means your party is practically a shoe-in for the show!"

My party. Right. As if anything about this is for me. If Jenna really cared about me, you'd think she'd have clued in to the fact that anything involving crowds, paparazzi, and scrutiny isn't exactly my thing. She refuses to grasp that while I might be a daughter of Hollywood, it doesn't mean I'm a product of it. If anything, this party is for *her*.

Jenna's too excited by her coup to notice my lack of reaction. She leans over Dad and gushes, "The buzz on this is absolutely unreal. Your party is going to be the biggest, flashiest event I've ever put together!"

Yay, me.

I turn back to the television and pick up my headphones.

Unfortunately, that does nothing to deter her. "You can even sketch caricatures of the guests as they come in the door if you want." She flashes a brilliant smile, like she's doing me a huge favor. "Adds a fun, kitschy element to the whole thing, don't ya think?"

No, I don't think. I'm an artist, not a street performer.

She kisses Dad on the cheek and then rubs her thumb over the coral lipstick stain, and I watch him turn to mush. He's so whipped. "Order me a Diet Coke if the cart thingy comes by, 'kay?" Jenna says. "I'm off to brave the bathroom line!"

I shake my head as she haltingly maneuvers down the aisle and stumbles into a woman's lap. Jenna turns on her hundred-watt grin, tosses her poufy blond hair, and apologizes profusely. Then she plops herself on the woman's armrest, abandoning all thought of bathroom trips in lieu of getting better acquainted with her new bestie.

Whatever. At least her ADD works for me, I think as I slide into her vacated seat, lay my head against Dad's shoulder, and inhale the familiar scent of his spicy aftershave and Armani cologne. He wraps an arm around me and I snuggle closer. It's quiet moments like this when I can imagine things are back to normal. Before he fell in love with someone completely wrong for him.

Dad kisses the top of my head. "Thank you."

I lift my head slightly, not willing to move out of his embrace just yet, and shoot him a puzzled look. "For?"

"For letting Jenna throw you a Sweet Sixteen. You may not believe it, but she has the best of intentions."

Sure she does. I glance forward to see her slap the armrest and let out a high-pitched squeal. The only intention Jenna has is having her event-planning business showcased on MTV. Date someone famous, get his daughter on television, and generate mad buzz for your business—not bad for nine months of work. I glance back at Dad. Why can't he see how fake she is? It's like ever since she came into the picture he's had blinders on, only seeing this giggly blond happy person—who is *nothing* like me. If he loves her so much, how can he possibly still love me?

"Jenna had one when she turned sixteen," he continues. "She said it was, and I quote, 'The highlight of her adolescent experience.'"

He rolls his eyes and grins, and the pressure in my chest

lessens. He hasn't changed. We're still us, even with her around. Then his forehead wrinkles and he shifts uncomfortably, and that guilty look creeps back into his eyes.

Crap. Here it comes.

"Peanut, I know you're always trying to take care of me, but I'm the grown-up. And it's my job to look out for you. I want you to have at least *one* normal childhood experience."

I snort. "Normal. Right." With a teasing grin, I lean back a little and lift my eyebrows in disbelief. "Dad, I hate to break it to you, but we live in Beverly Hills. And while having your birthday party and private life broadcast around the world for entertainment purposes may be an unfortunate reality for media-obsessed brats, I don't think anyone would call that behavior normal."

Dad chuckles, and I lean closer with a confident smirk. "Besides, when have we *ever* done anything like the rest of Hollywood?"

And the defense rests, I think, sitting back with a nod. Dad can't argue with that logic. If it weren't for our zip code and my fancy over-priced education, you'd never know we had money. Although he's a well-known film director and has a handful of Golden Globes, Dad has this thing about "normalcy." I've never missed a day of school in my life, and he rarely takes on projects during the summer. That's time for family and vacations, but none of that "private jet to remote locations" stuff for the Crawfords. Nope, we go to good old Disney World and the beach, with the occasional stop at a film set in Canada to spice things up. We don't even have a maid or a cook.

Dad squeezes me tighter. "You're right, we're abnormal. But I still think it's a good idea." My head lolls against my seat and he smiles. "It's a party; it'll be fun. Plus, I'm already doing a major suck-up job bringing you to Italy. Doesn't that earn me any negotiating cred?"

I have to admit, if everyone has a price, a trip to Florence would be mine. I've been obsessed with my Italian heritage—the only thing I accept from Mommy Dearest—and the Renaissance ever since I saw Bernard van Orley's *Madonna and Child with Apples and Pears* painting in fourth grade. Since then, I've inhaled every art book and novel on the time period or on Italy that I can find.

As bribes go, the trip is a good one.

Still, there's no way I can let Dad off the hook that easily. What he's asking of me is huge. Maybe things would be different if I was just a normal girl from the Mississippi countryside or the Cape Cod beachfront, or if people didn't take one look at me and assume they knew my whole life story. If I could just be me, Cat Crawford, without any expectations or preconceived notions, then maybe I'd be bonding with Jenna over napkin samples and color swatches right now. But that's not reality. So I shrug, affecting the confident, blasé image I've perfected for school and the media, and move back to my own seat.

I immediately reach in front of me for my backpack. Just holding it makes me feel better—more in control of my crazy life. I peruse the contents: my makeup kit and toiletry bag; my wallet, camera, iPod, and funkadelic-purple iPhone; my art supplies and color-coded binder filled with tour packages and historical information; and finally, my reading material, including the copy of *The Hunchback of Notre Dame* I'm reading for English. I brought it to work on whenever I needed a Jenna-break.

By the time this trip is over, I'll be a freaking Victor Hugo expert.

I pull out the book and zip my bag before leaning down to slide it back under the seat. As I sit up, I spot a familiar woman's face out of the corner of my eye and freeze. My hands slick with sweat. My heart pounds, and the roar of the jet engine beneath me intensifies.

It's just a picture, Cat, I tell myself. But it doesn't help.

Splashed across my seatmate's tabloid is a beautiful smiling face and yet another jilted lover with the headline, CATERINA ANGELI DOES IT AGAIN.

"Another one bites the dust."

The words are out of my mouth before I can stop them. The owner of the tabloid takes a break from her engrossed reading to sneer at me, but then a hint of recognition dawns on her face. She quickly turns to compare the picture of my mother on her cover to the downgraded, non-airbrushed, soon-to-be-sixteen-year-old version next to her.

I want to sink into my seat and look away, pretend I have no clue why she's staring, but I can't. So I force myself to meet her gaze head-on with a confident smile. Casually, I turn back to my book, open to the dog-eared page, and pretend to read. I feel the woman's eyes on me—watching, waiting for me to do something scandalous—and fight the urge to fluff my coffee-colored hair or gnaw off a nail.

Soon enough she'll stop looking at me, expecting to see my mother. She'll grow bored, go back to her gossipmonger ways, and forget all about me.

They always do.

Chapter Two

Firenze. I look out my hotel room window and gaze at the rolling green Tuscan hills, the twisting Arno River, and the beautiful Ponte Vecchio. The world-famous Duomo, nestled amidst a sea of russet roof tiles, looks close enough to touch. I'm about as far away from Hollywood as I can get. I lean my head back, close my eyes, and breathe.

La vita è bella.

Lady Gaga interrupts my reverie and I motorboat my lips. The chick may be a one-woman dynamo when it comes to style, and her songs are totally catchy, but my *Poker Face* ringtone doesn't exactly fit the tranquil setting I have going on. I crack an eye open, sigh, then trudge over to my phone.

"Buongiorno," I say in greeting.

Yeah, I'm all about the Italian.

"Is the room to your satisfaction, *Signorina* Crawford?"

I hear the smile in Dad's voice and grin in return. Holding

my hands out wide, I spin in a circle. Thanks to his newly engaged status—and the guilt over the whole throwing me an unwanted Sweet Sixteen bit—Dad abandoned his tightwad ways and splurged for adjoining suites. Our hotel is an honest-to-goodness, real-life Renaissance palace, complete with breathtaking frescoes covering the walls of my room.

I'd say it meets with my approval.

"Meh. It'll do."

Dad laughs. "Well, I'm glad to hear it. I'm sure you're settled in already." I look around, noting the dresser containing my clothes organized in perfect rows, the dry-cleaning bags hanging neatly in the closet, and the empty suitcases tucked out of the way on the top rack. He knows me well. "Jenna's itching to get going already and I'm sure you are, too. How about we meet downstairs in, say, five minutes?"

My smile fades. I shoulder my backpack and grip the phone tighter. "Actually, Dad, I was hoping you'd let me explore on my own this morning. Before you say no, I've already looked into everything." The key here is to prove I've done my homework, and that I'm a completely responsible human being. "There's a three-hour, English-speaking guided tour leaving from the Piazza Strozzi in about half an hour, and the concierge already gave me detailed directions. It's only a ten-minute walk from here."

My voice comes out calm and confidently level, despite my painfully scrunched-up face and death grip on the phone.

It's impossible to put into words how important this is to me. And it's not just because I need a break from Jenna, although I totally do. But coming to Italy and exploring my heritage, my only *good* connection to my mother, has been my dream since forever. I really need to ease into it on my own.

"By yourself, huh?" Dad pauses and I hear Jenna talking in the background. He covers the phone and I hold my breath. I walk over to the shiny gold wall sconce and trace the delicate curves, bouncing on my toes and moving my backpack to the other shoulder. Finally, he gets back to me. "Jenna and I discussed it." He's big on presenting this united front, as if Jenna has an interest in my well-being or whatever. "And we agree you can go as long as you promise to meet us back here at two o'clock. That should give you plenty of time—"

"No problem!" I do a happy shimmy and kiss the foot of a cherub on my frescoed wall. "I'll be waiting in the lobby no later than quarter till two, I promise."

There's a pause on Dad's end and I hear the muffled *click* of a door closing. "I know you need this, Caterina."

I stop gyrating and wait for the other shoe to drop. He only uses my full name when he's about to get mushy. Or when he wants something. But then, in exchange for an entire morning exploring Florence on my own, the man can have whatever he wants.

He clears his throat and continues in a lower voice, "When you come back, we'll grab lunch, go do some shopping, and then have a nice dinner together. As a family."

My eyes close and I sink against the wall. *As a family.* The idea of giving me a close-knit family, like something out of one of his movies, has become an obsession with him. Dad and Jenna aren't even married yet, and he's already trying to cast Jenna and me into this perfect little mother-daughter scenario. I know my less than enthusiastic performance has been a disappointment, but I just can't help it. I don't trust her as far as I can throw her, and the fact that she seems so eager to be all buddy-buddy just makes me more suspicious. I already have a mother, and one sordid maternal relationship is more than enough.

But I still hate disappointing Dad.

I count to five and exhale a slow breath. "Deal." I hear his grateful sigh over the line and open my eyes, blinking repeatedly to staunch the flow of tears building and threat-ening to erupt. Why can't things just go back to the way they used to be? "Thanks for letting me do this, Dad. I love you."

"I love you, too, Caterina." His voice is soft and cracks a bit at the end. He coughs. "Now, be safe, okay? You *are* going to have your cell phone with you, right?"

I pat away the tears, careful not to mess with my makeup, and straighten my shoulders. "You know it. Fully charged, with the extra battery pack ready to go. Please, did you really think I'd go anywhere without it?"

"Excuse me, what was I thinking?" Dad laughs and my shoulders relax, letting go of some of my *disappointing daughter* guilt. "Go have fun, Peanut."

We hang up and I kick into overdrive, straightening the rumpled comforter and running to check my appearance. While it's unlikely that paparazzi followed my family to Italy, the unfortunate truth is you just never know. They're like an infectious rash you can't get rid of.

When I glimpse my reflection in the gilded mirror, I cross my eyes and gag. The little flying I've done in the past has never agreed with my complexion and today's excursion has proven to be no exception. Not having time for the full palette of colors I always have on me, I grab my makeup bag from my backpack and pull out the essentials. Mascara to my skimpy lashes, eyeliner to rim my uninspired brown eyes, and concealer to the annoying zit that crept onto my chin overnight. Then I pump the wand of my coral lip gloss and coat the oversize mouth my mom is most noted for, yet somehow looks completely wrong on my smaller face.

Sighing, I return my bag to my overstuffed backpack, knowing I can always do touch-ups later, and then heave it onto my shoulder. The thing is heavier than the pancake makeup Jenna wears, but I really don't have time to rummage through it now—I'll barely get to the piazza in time as it is. After a cursory glance around the room, I grab my large dark sunglasses and hotel key from the nightstand and book it down the curved staircase of the hotel.

On the bustling cobbled street, I sidestep a shiny candy-apple-red Vespa and breathe in the scent of sunshine, espresso, and perfume. A smile breaks across my face—this is what I've been waiting for. It feels as though I'm walking onto one of Dad's movie sets and that none of this is actually real. Not the group of boys kicking a soccer ball in the alley or the bubbling fountain serving as a bench for some of the most beautiful people I've ever seen. Of course, they *are* competing with the surrounding American tourists in their wide array of T-shirts, white socks, and unflattering khaki shorts. Typical, cliché, and regrettably, realistic. I stifle a laugh and pick up the pace, making it to the Piazza with only two minutes to spare.

Slightly out of breath, I take a moment to size up the group waiting for the tour to begin. Our guide is a polished woman with mahogany hair and a sunshiny lemon-yellow dress. She has white-rimmed sunglasses and scarlet pumps, an interesting choice for a walking tour. Her loud hoot of laughter immediately reminds me of Jenna. I wiggle my shoulders and continue my appraisal of the group.

A family of four stands off to the side, huddled close together and looking completely out of their element. The little girl clutching her dad's leg is probably no older than eight or nine, and their teenage son has ear buds in and an iPod clipped to his jacket. He's got the whole scruffy, skater boy look going on. He catches me gawking and I quickly turn away.

Way to spaz, Cat.

From the corner of my eye, I catch the conceited grin on Skater Boy's face, and I roll my eyes. This is why I don't date. Well, this and the fact that the guys who do approach me are either wannabe actors just trying to get a meeting with Dad or asshats who expect me to act like my mother. Really, who needs birth control when you have parents like mine?

A cute elderly couple rounds out the rest of our group. The woman's serene smile makes my heart hurt for my grand-parents, reminding me of the summers I used to spend at Nana's house in Mississippi, tucked away from the rest of the world. It was the only time I could pretend I was normal.

But when I glance back at our small group, I realize that isn't true. Not one of these people has given me a second look. It's like I can actually feel the weight leaving my shoulders.

"Attenzione!" Our guide beams at us and points to the golden-brown stone palace behind her. "This is the Palazzo Strozzi," she tells us in highly accented English, and I breathe a sigh of relief. Besides a few key phrases I've picked up in my reading, none of which will be helpful in any type of real-life situation, my Italian is limited to *prego, pasta,* and *pizza.* "It

was begun in the year 1489 for Filippo Strozzi the Elder, a rival of the famous Medici family, who wanted to create the most magnificent palace in Florence. It was inspired by the Palazzo Medici, but unlike that palace, this one is a completely free-standing structure."

I shield my eyes as I peer up at the enormous building. The rough stone façade adds weight to the massive structure, commanding even more of a visual presence in the piazza. What blows my mind the most is that this was actually a house for one family. And not even a royal one. While Beverly Hills certainly has its share of over-the-top homes, the Italians in the Renaissance knew how to do it right.

Our guide—Paola, I read from her name tag—gives us a few minutes to explore the area before we leave for the rest of the tour, and I slide my digital camera out of my bag. I don't have time to sit and sketch all these buildings now, but I can cram my memory stick with inspiration for later. Following the other members of our group through the building's rounded entrance, I snatch a half dozen shots just of the stone work before turning to capture the pockets of people milling about inside.

Although it's crowded and the palace is surrounded by street traffic, the courtyard feels peaceful. Quiet. In contrast to the warm October air and the sun beating against the pavement outside, the interior courtyard is cool. I lean against one of the tall stone columns and close my eyes.

Behind my veiled lids, I imagine this house is mine and I'm the Italian daughter of a wealthy Renaissance merchant. I picture myself gliding down the stone steps and across the secluded space in a long, flowing golden gown, my hair up in braids twisted around my head. My days are spent sewing or reading, living among the artisans of the time. At the age of sixteen, I'm already considered an adult in the eyes of many.

I'm certainly not forced to host a stupid party I don't want.

A hand touches my shoulder and I open my eyes to the woman from our group, the one who reminds me of Nana. She doesn't seem to speak English but she motions to the street and I nod. I lean my cheek against the cool, smooth stone one last time and then follow her out into the busy piazza.

Our group congregates around Paola and the flag she holds before taking off at a dizzying pace. Over the next two and a half hours, I pack more facts into my brain than I did studying for the PSATs and load up my camera as the rest of the tour melds into a series of Italian sights, sounds, and smells.

After a brief stop and sugar rush at a gelato shop, Paola leads us to the Accademia. Home to Michelangelo's *David* sculpture and the reason I took this tour. For years, I've dreamed of coming here, seeing up close the artwork and masterpieces I've considered friends, and I have to pinch myself to prove it's real. If my art teacher Mr. Scott could see this, he'd flip.

I pass the crowd of art students on the ground sketching, wishing I could join them, and stand in front of *David*. The statue towers over me. I study the detail in his face and neck, his knees and feet. I stare forever at his hands. It's as if his fingers could flinch at any second. He was carved over five hundred years ago, yet the detail work remains unrivaled.

It's strange. I always knew people were people, regardless of time, but seeing the craftsmanship before me, in person, it's like an exciting wakeup call. Throughout history, while day-to-day life has changed, humanity hasn't. Renaissance people had the same talents, abilities, creativity, passion, drive, hopes, and fears we have today.

Or at least close enough.

Paola walks up and gives me the evil eye. As if waking from a dream, I blink and look around to realize our group disbanded and the mob around the statue has grown. She points to the exit and I take one last glance at *David*, knowing I'll be back.

I follow Paola out into the warm Tuscan air and watch with an almost giddy feeling as she waves good-bye and disappears through the crowded Piazza di San Marco.

I am alone in Florence.

A quick check to my watch confirms I have an hour before I need to be back at the hotel, and I plan to enjoy it.

A couple of guys zip by me on bikes as I turn down a side street, wandering and exploring, following the crowd and my internal navigation system. I end up at an outdoor market and slow my natural stride to match the lazy pace of the other patrons. Stalls are busting at the seams with leather jackets, purses, and belts, and I make a mental shopping list of all the goodies I plan to come back and buy. At an outdoor delicatessen, a young boy working behind the counter offers me a sample of biscotti and it literally melts in my mouth.

The street sign for Via Sant Antonino is ahead, and even though it's only been fifteen minutes, I decide to head back to the hotel. It's probably best not to push Dad to the limit on the very first day. Plus, if I come back early, maybe he'll give me a get-out-of-jail-free card on that *family* dinner later.

Fat chance, but hey, it's worth a shot.

I round the corner and a dark army-green tent catches my eye, its front flaps fluttering in the breeze. It seems odd—a tent in the middle of the street—but I continue past until I hear a woman tell her friend over the clanging of church bells, "I thought they'd gotten rid of all the Gypsies."

My ears perk up and I stop. Maybe it's Victor Hugo's influence—Esmeralda, the badass gypsy in *The Hunchback of Notre Dame,* is my favorite character in the novel so far—or the whole When in Rome—er, Florence—mentality, but I decide to be wild for once.

In forty-five minutes, I'll be having lunch and finalizing plans for a lavish, extravagant, over-priced, stupid, *unwanted* birthday gala where I'll be forced under a microscope for all the world to criticize. I want—no, *need*—to do something just for me.

Something private and very, very un-Cat-like.

I pull back the flap and enter the gypsy's tent.

• • •

Inside, it's dim with only a few lit candles illuminating the space. The flap closes behind me but for the effect, it may as well be a steel door—the outside noise is completely muffled. I take a step and gravel crunches under my sandals, sounding all the louder in this spooky set-up.

I've officially walked into the Twilight Zone.

"Hello?"

I stretch my hand out and feel a ledge. Opening my eyes wide, I struggle to read the framed sign perched atop some sort of intricate shelving system. It says to place any bags or belongings on the top shelf, and to take off my shoes and slide them into the tray provided.

I really don't get how Steve Madden gladiators will interfere with a psychic reading, but whatever. I'm being wild.

Tiptoeing farther inside, following the trail of dotted candlelight, I continue to be amazed at how large the space feels. It's a freaking tent, and not even a big one at that, yet I feel as though I could walk forever. One side is completely lined with shelves, and from the flickering flames of the candles, I can see rows of teacups, labeled vials, unlit candles, crystal balls, and stacks of cards.

As I drift toward the back of the tent, the smell of patchouli incense tickles my nose and I see a small card table with a black silk sheath draped over it. Resting in the middle is a large sapphire-colored candle, its flame a spotlight on the woman sitting behind it.

Her entire face is covered by purple veils; only her eyes are visible.

Creeptastic.

"What answers do you seek?"

I jump. Not because I didn't see her mouth move or the fact that she spoke English. But her voice is not at all what I expected. It's youthful, cautious, and…Russian?

I lean closer to get a better look but all I can see are the layers of veils covering her head and mouth. And those eyes. Even from this slight distance, they are hypnotic. A combination of ancient wisdom and sparkling humor, as if she's peering into my mind and laughing at what she sees. My scalp tingles and a shiver of unease dances down my spine, but I refuse to leave. I've already come this far.

The woman, or I guess I should say girl, lifts an eyebrow and it disappears behind a veil. I realize she is waiting for an answer but for the life of me, I can't remember the question. I blink a few times and rack my brain, my eyes never straying from hers.

"You fancy a reading, *tatcho*?"

Her blunt question and flat, tired voice shake me out of my trance and remind me this isn't real. If it wasn't for the occasional funny beep of tiny foreign cars, this could totally be happening in some back room in West Hollywood. Not that I believe any of this hocus pocus stuff anyway. The only destiny I believe in is the one I can control. So I shrug and say, "Yeah, whatever you usually do, I guess."

The gypsy flicks her wrist, causing dozens of bracelets to *clank* in unison, and motions to the chair opposite her. She continues to stare at me from behind the table, her head slightly tilted, her hazel eyes narrowed. Finally, she nods and walks over to one of the shelves, her layers of bright multicolored chiffon skirts swishing around her feet. She picks up a teacup.

I wonder if I should mention that I don't really dig tea.

"What is your name?"

Part of me is tempted to tell her if she were a real psychic she'd know it already, but somehow I doubt that'll go over too well. "Cat."

She pauses mid-sit and lifts her head. "Cat?"

Her disbelieving tone irks me. I straighten my shoulders, put on my usual mask of aloofness, and say, "Caterina. You need a last name, too?"

Although I can't be sure, I think I hear her snort from behind the veil, which just annoys me even more. It's impossible to get a handle on this girl. The gypsy shakes her head and begins preparing the tea, and I pretend to relax back in my seat.

A nervous energy buzzes through my veins. Maybe this wasn't the best idea I've ever had.

Holding the pearl teacup by its delicate handle, the gypsy pours hot water from a kettle on a nearby hot plate, and then stirs in a heaping spoonful of tealeaves from a tin. Neither of us speaks while it steeps. She just sits across from me, her eyes boring into mine. I try to glance around the tent but continue to be drawn back to her gaze, like she exudes some type of magnetic force field. Eventually, my eyes grow accustomed to the dark and I'm able to see her more clearly. They are strangely beautiful, like a luminous marble, amber colored with specks of russet, jade, and charcoal.

It's spooky. But I'm completely transfixed.

The spell is broken when she reaches for the cup. She blows on it, holds it out, and says, "You are right-handed, so you must take this cup with your left. As you drink, relax and clear your mind. Try not to think. If something does continue to come to mind, however, hold onto it. Meditate on it. Make sure to leave a small amount of tea at the bottom of your cup and try not to consume too many of the leaves. When you're done, hand it back to me."

There seems to be an awful lot of rules just to drink some tea and make up a fake fortune, but I'll go with it. I take a sip. The tea is hot, and the floating leaves are icky and tickle my mouth, but I drink. I try to keep my mind clear like she said, but for some annoying reason Jenna keeps popping in. Visions of her laughing and constantly trying to give me a hug assault me, and then are replaced with equally disturbing ones of my mother. Fuzzy snapshot images from when she was actually around and then clearer, sharper ones from the big screen.

Despite my every attempt to do or think otherwise, my mother continues to appear.

In my effort to stop the movie playing in my head and push away all the chaotic emotions those two women bring, I nearly drink the entire cup of tea. Luckily, I catch myself and hand the delicate cup back. Definitely want to avoid incurring any Gypsy wrath. I wipe my mouth and pretend not to be eager to hear her response.

Okay, so maybe I'm the tiniest bit superstitious.

She swirls my cup three times, then dumps the last bit of the tea into the saucer. She keeps the cup overturned for a few seconds before flipping it back over and peering inside.

I tap my fingers on the table and ask, "See anything good?"

The gypsy nods. "*Arvah.* I see a tent."

"A tent? You mean like the one we're in?"

She nods again. "A *tsera*—a tent—is a symbol for adventure. You may find yourself doing something completely different soon. Perhaps travel is in your future."

Hmm. A tent like the one we're in and traveling in my future. Pretty convenient, considering I'm a tourist. Aloud I say, "Adventure, huh? Like emancipating myself and relocating permanently to Florence?"

She lifts an eyebrow and I wave her off. "Kidding, obviously."

I get up from the table and realize the tent has gotten smaller. No, that's silly; my eyes must have adjusted to the dim lighting. Either that or this chick has some seriously freaky tea.

I walk back to my bag and as I stretch to reach into the front pouch to get my wallet, I twist around. "How much for the, uh, session?"

The gypsy's eyes grow wide and her brows disappear behind

the veil again. I look down, expecting to see a tarantula or some other crazy creepy crawly to justify her being so freaked, and see the small tattoo on my right hip exposed. I drop my arms and yank down my shirt.

She bolts out of her seat and flies toward me, looking intently at the cute top now covering my body art. "May I?" she asks hesitantly.

I bite my lip and think. I never show anyone my tattoo. Considering my age, getting one wasn't exactly legal, especially since I didn't have Dad's permission. But more than that, it's personal.

A reminder.

But the girl seems so fascinated, and it's not like I have to share its meaning or anything. If she's a real psychic, she'll know. Very slowly, I lift the hem of my shirt to uncover my upper right hip. Her fingers flex as if she intends to brush them over my stomach and I flinch. Gingerly, she draws them back.

"The painted pear."

Chapter Three

The gypsy's voluminous outfit of veils tickles my arm. We're the same height, so I have no problem looking into her eyes. The skin around them crinkles and if I thought she looked intense before, it was nothing compared to this enthrallment. She's practically humming. I lower my shirt again and say, "Uh, yeah. It's from my favorite Renaissance painting. *Madonna and Child with Apples and Pears*?"

I'm normally not one to turn my statements into questions, but the girl is kind of freaking me out.

She nods and then claps her hands. "The *ambrol*. The Renaissance. *Misto*!"

I feel my eyebrows scrunch together as I slowly follow her to the back of the tent where she's flitting about. I know I should probably just leave, but I can't stop watching the scene playing out before me. It's as if someone flipped a switch—all reserved gypsy mannerisms have completely been thrown out the window. Or in this case, out the tent flap.

The girl twirls and dances over to a shelf containing rows and rows of unlit candles. "It is time," she says, darting a glance back toward me, a Cheshire cat smile on her face. "I have waited years for this *divano*."

She runs her fingers across the orange candles, then the white, and hesitates over the yellow before landing on the purple and nodding. She grabs a bejeweled jug and motions me back to the table with a wag of her head.

"Please, stay but a moment more." Her smile withers when I hesitate with one hand on my bag. "There will be no charge."

If living in LA has taught me anything, it's that nothing is ever free. I check my watch. It's one thirty. It'll take me twenty minutes to get back to the hotel from here, which means I have ten minutes tops.

But I'm intrigued.

I walk to the table and sit on the edge of my seat. Her smile returns and she sets her supplies down. "You may call me Reyna," she says in a noticeably thicker accent as she carves *Caterina* onto one side of the candle. I want to tell her it's Cat—my self-involved mother may have named me after her, but only Dad's allowed to utter my given name—but what's the point. This will all be over in a few minutes and I'll never see this girl again.

Reyna writes something else on the other side, but I can't make it out in the candlelight. Then she picks up the sparkly jug and pours what appears to be oil onto the candle before setting it down on a mirror and lighting the wick. I jump at the sudden burst of light. The dancing flame, along with the reflected glow, causes elongated shadows to fall across the table.

Strange shapes appear within the inky outlines and I struggle to convince myself it's just my overactive imagination rearing its ugly head again.

I have definitely seen one too many movies.

Staring into the flames, Reyna chants, "Powers that be, powers of three, let Caterina's destiny be all that I see."

She repeats it two more times before grabbing my hands and closing her eyes.

Nothing happens and I assume whatever voodoo stuff she tried to do failed. Surprise, surprise. I go to get up, and then the table begins to shake.

Reyna's cool fingers snake up and grasp my wrists.

I try to wrench them away but Reyna's grip tightens as she pulls me forward and throws her head back.

Suddenly the flame snuffs out and the room goes black.

Every sense I have goes on red-alert as I try to remember any of the moves from the self-defense class Dad made me take. I can see the headline now: DAUGHTER OF HOLLYWOOD MURDERED BY NUTCASE GYPSY.

She frees my wrists and I cradle them to my chest even though they don't hurt. A queasy feeling churns in my stomach. My skin prickles and there is a subtle yet undeniable roar in my ears.

I sense Reyna moving around in the dark and my muscles clench, ready to bolt. She strikes a match and a spark ignites. When the large candle is relit, Reyna is standing over me, eyes glittering. I spring from my chair, my hand at my throat.

"Dude, are you trying to give me a heart attack?"

Reyna ignores my gasps for air and nails me with an eerie stare. "Caterina, a great adventure is in store for you. Be sure to keep your mind open to the lessons ahead."

She nods toward the front of the tent, almost dismissively. I stand there disbelieving—and to be honest, more than a little frazzled—waiting for more. Surely she's going to explain what all *that* was about.

Or not. Instead of giving any semblance of an explanation for the creepy parlor trick I just witnessed, Reyna just continues to stand there smiling, bouncing on her toes.

Okay, then.

With a shake of my head, I move to the front of the tent. "Well, thanks. For the free reading. That was…interesting."

I grab my bag and slip my sandals back on. As I pull my sunglasses back on, I keep waiting for her to say something, anything, but she remains silent.

This chick is two French fries short of a Happy Meal.

I stop just inside the tent, a hand on the front flap, to look at her one last time. Even from this distance, Reyna's eyes visibly dance with emotion. I give a stilted wave and she nods again, but as I turn around she whispers, "*Latcho Drom*, Caterina."

With chill bumps racing down my spine, I pull back the flap and step outside.

• • •

My first thought as I take in my surroundings, squinting at the bright sunlight permeating my shades, is that I must've been in the tent for a lot longer than thirty minutes. My next thought is that Italians are crazy.

The street is inexplicably filled with reenactors, dressed as if they're at a Renaissance festival and taking their jobs way too seriously.

I stand there blinking, watching a donkey-drawn cart full of produce roll past me down the narrow road. The clattering of the cart's wheels on the cobblestone echo off the buildings and all of a sudden, I am hit with the powerful stench of animal feces.

Lovely. Definitely time to head back to the hotel.

Stepping away from the tent, I feel soft fabric brush across my leg. Absently, I look down and freeze.

I'm wearing a flowing golden gown.

What the heck?

Flipping my sunglasses onto my head, I whirl back around to interrogate Reyna, but instead of the tent I just stepped out of, I see a goat. A freaking goat. Both the tent and Reyna are gone.

What was in that gypsy tea?

Mystified, I think back to the last half hour and try to make sense of what's happened. All around me, people are dressed in similar period outfits, without a single badly dressed tourist in the bunch. The buildings look the same but cleaner, and somehow everything seems brighter, the colors sharper. There are no rumbling engines to drown out voices or the rasping *click* of cicada.

I wander absently down the road, past reenactors hawking food from makeshift stalls, searching for any type of reflective surface to look into—perhaps a side-mirror of a car or a shiny window—but the *polizia* must have cleared the streets for the weird reenactment. Maybe it's a national holiday. How that explains my wardrobe change, however, is completely beyond me.

I spin around, disoriented, and my backpack slaps hard across my back.

Normalcy.

I'm not crazy. I have my backpack, my white-knuckle grip on sanity. I stoop down and tear into it, grateful it's loaded with so much crap. I unzip my makeup case and pull out my compact. When I glimpse my reflection, I do a double take.

The first thing I notice is that my zit is gone.

Hallelujah for small miracles!

Then I notice the scrubbed face. Every lick of makeup that I painstakingly applied a few hours ago is gone. I like to think of the face as just another canvas to paint on, and right now, mine is completely blank. It's like I'm auditioning for a Neutrogena commercial. Tilting the mirror farther and sliding off my shades, I see my hair is twisted on top of my head in a braided crown, a vibrant red ribbon threaded through it. Definitely not the way I fixed it—I stopped doing ribbons in kindergarten.

Maybe I'm dreaming.

I pinch myself. Hard. "Freakin' A!"

Nope, not a dream.

Enrapt in the enigma that is suddenly my life, I rub my arm and stare at my backpack, the one thing that still makes sense. I don't hear the man dressed like a crazed Shakespearean fanatic until he is standing right in front of me. He touches my hand and looks at me with concern. "Signorina D'Angeli?"

My spine tenses and my teeth clench, but I paste on a sunny smile. Someone was bound to recognize me or see the resemblance eventually. I yank my hand back and open my mouth to inform him he's wrong—that I'm not my mother—but out comes, *"Vi sbagliate."*

Holy crap!

Do I know what I said? I think for a moment and realize I

do. I'd said, *"You are mistaken."*

Since when do I know Italian?

He gives me a puzzled look and, with his cane, motions toward a carriage that is sitting on the side of the narrow road. I look at the people traipsing about and realize I've become the center of attention—as if *I'm* the weird one!

My worst nightmare is coming true, standing in the middle of their scrutiny with no place to hide. Having one parent in front of the camera and the other behind it, you'd think I'd relish the attention. Or at least be used to it.

I hear their muffled whispers and understand every Italian word. Every witty comment made at my expense.

It's like my brain is automatically translating.

I bunch the soft fabric of the dress in my hand and then reach up to feel the ribbon in my hair. I lightly skim my fingers over my chin and feel my lack of zit. I take in the costumes of the crowd, the stench of the animals, and the Italian I can now speak and understand. And suddenly it hits me.

Reyna must have pulled some kind of gypsy mojo.

Maybe this is one of those nifty "change your life" magic scenarios like in the movies. I mean, mostly I'm still expecting to blink and be right back in the midst of overpriced, gaudy tourism, but for now, the gypsy-time-warp explanation is infinitely better than thinking I've lost my mind. As I decide to go with that option, I feel my frantic tension melt away.

The growing crowd seems to notice my change in demeanor and begins shooting one another amused looks, but I don't care anymore. A smile stretches across my face. Evidently, I was wrong earlier; Reyna *is* a psychic mind reader, because if this is her special brand of bibbity-bobbity-boo, than she made my exact daydream from earlier in the courtyard come to life.

The long gold gown, the braided hair, the Italian merchant's daughter, the time period. I am in Renaissance Florence.

I stare dumbly at the ground, the words and reality sinking in.

I'm in Renaissance Florence!

Cane Man clears his throat and points toward the carriage again. I glance at my surroundings with new eyes and suddenly remember Reyna's words. It's as if they float in the air around me. *Caterina, a great adventure is in store for you.*

A maniacal laugh escapes, and I don't even try to stop it. The man shoots me a look of terror and I wave him off. Reyna was right, this is an *adventure*, and there's no way I'm letting it pass me by without reveling in it. Gypsy's orders.

Part of me wishes Dad could be here, too. He'd probably come back with killer ideas for a new historical or something. But being without Jenna for twenty-four whole hours (or I'm assuming, anyway, since that's how long fairy-tale magic usually works, the whole stroke-of-midnight thing)? A mini-vacay from being the third wheel in my own pseudo-family? Yes, please. Sign me up for that kind of gypsy voodoo.

Nodding at the man, I take a step toward the carriage. There has to be some type of timer set on how long the magic will last, and I don't want to waste another second. His shoulders visibly relax and his anxious expression clears.

Then he shoots a pointed look at my backpack—obviously not the usual Renaissance accessory.

To distract him, and to figure out exactly what I'm dealing with here, I ask him in Italian, "Excuse me, but can you tell me what year it is? For the life of me I just can't seem to remember at the moment."

The man's anxious expression creeps back and I stifle a laugh. He hesitates, as if he's hoping to see I'm joking, and then replies, "It is the year of our Lord 1505. Are you ill, Signorina?"

I laugh and throw my arms around his stiff shoulders. The year is 1505! Michelangelo finished the *David* in 1504. He was still in Florence, along with Leonardo da Vinci and Raphael, in 1505. The artists at the heart of the Italian Renaissance, my idols, are walking in the very same city I am at this very moment. I look around eagerly, half expecting to see one of them pass by with an ancient paint set and easel.

The man steps back, seemingly scandalized by my overzealous behavior. I'm thinking hugging servants isn't exactly par for the course in the sixteenth century, but I'm too giddy with excitement to worry about details. I take the man's hand and practically drag him back to the carriage. People around us continue to stare, but I just smile and wave. Let them look; I don't care.

I'm in Renaissance Florence, baby!

Chapter Four

Outside my small window, it's as if someone ripped a page from my history book and brought it to life. The inside of the coach smells musty, but I lean out of the open window and the warm aroma of fresh baked bread fills the air. Uniformed guards stand at regular intervals, perched beneath colorful banners in front of familiar ancient buildings, and nod as we roll past. Hordes of people, dressed in a wide variety of period clothing, shop in open-air markets comprised of makeshift tents and stalls. Peasants hobnob near aristocrats, vying for the freshest fruits and vegetables, and the streets are chaotic as patrons scream over the clamor of sellers calling out their wares. A herald gallops alongside the carriage, proclaiming the news of the day.

Even though I know I'm in the midst of gypsy magic, I still can't believe it's real.

Sitting opposite me is the man I assume is my chaperone for

this journey. He hasn't said a word since we climbed onboard the carriage, but I catch him stealing glances and shaking his head. Damage control is obviously in order. If I want to enjoy this trip to the past, and not be thrown into the loony bin or cast aside as a cultural ignoramus, I'm going to have to call upon the acting genes I inherited from my mother and play the role I've been given.

Luckily, I've picked up a thing or two about the process from visiting Dad's sets, so I know the first thing any actor worth her salt does when prepping for a role is create a backstory and then conduct research. The backstory will have to be filled in as details become available, but here's what I know about the Renaissance: It began in Florence in the Middle Ages and spread throughout Europe. Crazy talented artists like Michelangelo, da Vinci, Raphael, and Botticelli exploded during this time. And last but certainly not least, a little-known playwright was born. A man named William Shakespeare.

From my carriage window, I watch period costumes parade by and thank the stars that fashion improved from the drab frocks they wore in the Dark Ages. But period trendsetters are still creating quite a few faux pas. Men have on colored tights and puffy shorts—though honestly, it's hard to complain about the yum-a-licious views of their well-toned legs—and the women aren't much better, sporting sickly white makeup and bright, scarlet cheeks.

I'm in the middle of trying to remember how close Verona, the setting for Shakespeare's *Romeo and Juliet*, is to Florence when the carriage rolls through the arched doorway of a four-story, tan stone building and stops in the middle of a lush courtyard.

And just like that, all thought of role preparation is forgotten.

My chaperone steps out of the coach and turns to take my hand. He guides me down and I stroll in a trance-like state to the center of the space where a marble fountain sits. The gentle trickle of water coaxes me closer and I walk up the delicately sculpted steps to peer over the edge.

I have no idea why we stopped, why we're here, or even where *here* is—but it's gorgeous. My hand snakes into my backpack and I pull out a quarter. Before tossing the coin into the watery depths, I close my eyes.

Let this not be a dream.

Chaperone Man clears his throat behind me. I turn my head to see him giving me the same weird pointed look again, and I stifle a laugh. I really need to do a better job of being more sixteenth-century-like.

I take a seat on the top step and lean against the cool stone, breathing in the scent of wet earth and flowers from a nearby garden. Carved columns and sculpted arches frame the courtyard along with countless rounded windows. The same peaceful feeling from the previous palazzo rushes over me.

A moment later, the slow build of click-clacking forces me to stand. I turn with a sigh as a simply dressed servant rushes across the stone floor. She bows at my feet before turning toward Chaperone Man and asking for my name.

"Pray tell your master that Signorina Patience D'Angeli has arrived."

The servant scurries away, I assume to announce my arrival, and I consider this newest development.

Patience. Is that like an actual name? More importantly, is that seriously what they believe is *my* name? Even in the beautiful Italian language in which my chaperone spoke, the name is horrid. It figures the universe would pull this kind of cosmic joke. Having a cool or exotic name, like Margherita, or Bella, or Anastasia would be too perfect. Instead, the powers that be stick me with boring, old, goody-goody *Patience.*

Sounds like a girl who knows how to party.

A chirping voice above interrupts my annoyed internal rant, and I peer up to see a dark head scamper past an open window. The servant returns and motions us toward a huge stairway.

Suddenly I'm nervous. I let the two of them walk ahead, realizing I don't know anything about the people who live here. I don't even know if Patience is supposed to know them. A masculine voice floats from inside the house and my breathing escalates.

What if they already have expectations of me, like everyone else in my life?

My heart hammers in my chest but before I can get too carried away wondering how I should act, a man descends the stairs with open arms. He has salt-and-pepper hair and wrinkles around his mouth and eyes, the kind you get from years of smiling. He steps in front of me and envelops me in a hug.

"How beautiful you are, Patience. You are an honor to your father and mother, Signore rest their souls."

I pat his back awkwardly and rush to process the incoming information like puzzle pieces. This family is rich. The man of the house—besides having no concept of personal space—is obviously kind. A definite plus. And apparently, my parents, or Patience's parents, are dead.

The chaperone trudges past us, carrying a huge black trunk in his arms. He nods at the man still hugging me and carries the load up the stairs.

The owner of the house finally steps back and points to himself. "I am your uncle Marco. I am sure you do not remember me. It has been many years since your family moved to London, but I once held you in my arms." He tightens his lips into a straight line, and looks up to the sky for a moment before continuing. "The loss of my brother and his wife is great, but it is my honor to welcome you into our home and family."

I open my mouth, unsure of what to say or how to respond, and am saved by the pitter-patter of several pairs of feet on stone steps. Anxious, I straighten my shoulders, preparing to meet the rest of the welcome wagon. I stand on tiptoe for a glimpse and a jolt of fear shoots through me.

Behind my uncle, my mother approaches.

I blink. Same dark hair, dark eyes, and beautiful face. But there *is* one striking difference, and that's what allows me to begin breathing again. Plastering this woman's face and shining in those dark eyes is an authentic smile—and there ends the uncanny resemblance. That particular expression has never graced the face of Mommy Dearest, aka Caterina Angeli, the temptress of Hollywood.

If anything, this woman's smile reminds me of Jenna.

The Caterina/Jenna mismatch pulls me into another hug. *Great, I'm surrounded by a family of huggers.*

She shakes me back and forth and kisses both cheeks. "What a beauty! Oh, look at you!" She leans back and grabs my chin to scrutinize my face. I struggle to look away from her intent gaze but she has a ninja grip. "Oh, how I have eagerly awaited this day!" Then she giggles and throws her arms around me again.

"Pray, Mama, give my cousin some air. Do you wish her to suffocate on the first day of her arrival?"

My aunt laughs, unwraps her arms from around my neck, and then throws them around the girl beside her. The girl rumples the skirt of her celadon gown in one hand, fidgets with the flowers in her auburn hair with the other, and offers me a nervous smile. She appears to be about my age, maybe a little younger, and is astonishingly beautiful—the kind of girl guys back home would drool over and girls would hate, if not for her obvious awkward shyness.

The woman squeezes the girl's shoulder. "You are right, that would not do at all. Patience, please excuse my exuberance. I am your aunt Francesca, and this is your cousin Alessandra. And this," she says, pausing to grab a young man's hand and pull him forward, "is your cousin Cipriano. You are a most welcome addition to our family."

Alessandra and Cipriano. Two fancy, Italian names—both complete mouthfuls. I decide to christen them Less and Cip, and move onto appraising the boy before me. He's a few years older than I am, and while he seems friendly enough, he definitely takes after his more reserved dad. He nods at me, and his dark hair brushes the shoulders of his cobalt blue doublet. He's cute in an aloof, boy-next-door sort of way.

I scan the smiling faces before me. Besides a few strange glances at my backpack, they certainly have the whole welcome committee thing down. But they can't be for real. No one just invites a complete stranger into his home, right? I mean, I know they think I'm their niece, but I could be anybody off the street...and I kind of am.

Ever mindful of my role, however, I nod at the perfect little family unit in front of me. "Thank you for your kindness. It is greatly appreciated in this time of sorrow. But if you do not mind, I am quite tired after my travels."

Heh, how's that for acting on the fly? I'm totally nailing this old-world gig.

Aunt Francesca's face crumbles and I stare wide-eyed. Having avoided female emotional drama for most of my life, I'm clueless as to how it all works. Was it something I said? Should I apologize or, since I'm supposed to be English, offer a "spot of tea"?— I dart a worried look at the girl, Alessandra, but before I can stress too much, Aunt Francesca thumps her hand against her chest.

"Oh, dear, I am so sorry. Please, come inside." She grabs my hand and begins pulling me up the stone steps. "Your exhaustion is to be expected. You have endured a long journey."

Longer than you know.

The rest of the family follows us up the stairwell that leads to an elegant second floor. I try to take in the impressive high ceilings, dark wood furniture, painted walls, and tapestries, but suddenly I have difficulty just keeping my eyes open. Gypsy magic must take a lot out of a girl.

Aunt Francesca pulls me down a long corridor and stops before a thick, heavy door. When my uncle pushes it open, I have to squint at the sensory overload. Frescoed walls in a dizzying display of geometric shapes seem to jump out at me, colorfully and loudly begging me to run my hand along the bumpy plaster. I blink to adjust my eyes and touch the wall, letting the texture tickle my fingers. The black travel trunk my chaperone carried up sits beside a painted chest in the corner of the room that completely dwarfs it. I wander over and feel my eyes practically bug out again at the delicate biblical scenes and images, each crafted in meticulous detail. It's like having a mini Sistine Chapel right in my own bedroom.

Across the room, near a large open window, is an elaborately carved, dark oak table and matching stool, both inlaid with an intricate mother of pearl design. A gold comb and brush set rest on the tabletop next to a small round mirror. And pressed against the back wall and swallowing up most of the floor space is a massive four-poster bed, complete with suspended royal blue velvet curtains looped in knots.

Besides the sparse furnishings, a few tapestries, and a family crest on the wall, the room is empty. Yet it feels more luxurious than most of the finest hotels I've stayed in.

And I thought the room back at the hotel was impressive.

My jaw drops as I take it all in, and Aunt Francesca smiles. "We will put away your belongings in here," she says, placing her hand on the painted chest, "but it is my intention to indulge you now that you are with us. I insist upon you having the finest fabrics, done up in the latest Italian fashions." She sits down on the chest and stamps her feet rhythmically. "I am so pleased to have another girl in the house to dress!"

My uncle sidles up to my aunt and places his hand on her shoulder. "Come now, dear. We have all the time in the world to play dress up. Patience is not going anywhere." He looks back at me and winks, and I immediately decide I like him. "In the morning, the three of you may talk of fabrics and surcoats, and all sorts of women's matters. But this night, we shall let the girl rest. Now, Patience, is there anything you require before we leave you to catch your breath?"

I shake my head and give him a grateful smile. "No, I'm good."

My uncle furrows his forehead and Alessandra crinkles her nose. "I, I mean, I fair well. Thank you, Uncle."

The confusion washes from their faces and I exhale in relief. We stand around staring at each other, them smiling politely, me waiting eagerly for them to leave. My uncle takes a step toward the door and then, just as I'm feeling I have a handle on this whole time travel thing, my body takes over…and I break into a curtsy.

Now, I've never curtsied before in my life—and certainly don't know when it's appropriate to do so in the sixteenth century—but if I had to judge, based on the raised eyebrows, this is not one of those occasions.

Oh well. I can blame it on jet lag. Er, carriage lag.

I pull myself back up and stretch my arms out in an overly exaggerated fake yawn. "I trust that I shall fall asleep the moment my head hits the pillow," I say, forcing an awkward smile.

Luckily, they get the hint. The family files out one by one, Alessandra hanging back at the end and studying me with a tilted head. I keep that pathetic excuse of a smile on my face, and subtly nod toward the doorframe.

She lowers her eyes and grins. "It is lovely to have you with us, cousin. I pray that you rest well."

I nod in response, no longer trusting my body and mouth not to betray me, and she bounces out of the room. With a sigh, I crumple against the closed door, finally alone in my Renaissance bedroom. My backpack falls to my elbow and I reach inside, grabbing my iPhone and turning the power off— no sense in draining the battery on a lifeline to normalcy. Then I thump my head against the solid wood door and rest my eyes on the family crest mounted across from me.

D'Angeli.

I continue scanning the rich artwork, glancing at a tapestry of a bunch of angels in a room similar to mine, and then bolt upright.

Angeli.

My mother's name.

Slowly, I cross over to the crest and trace the letters of the family name with my finger. The resemblance between my mother and my new aunt is eerie. Add to it the fact that I'm here, and there's no way it's a coincidence the two last names are so similar. At some point, someone must have dropped the beginning *D,* thus creating the Americanized version Angeli.

Which means, this family doesn't just believe I'm one of them…I really am. Just very, *very* far removed.

I just hugged my ancestors!

The reality makes my head spin.

As I try to make sense of the latest twist, a scene from an old show I saw not too long ago flashes in my mind. I'd been flipping through the channels in my bedroom, avoiding the love fest between Dad and Jenna in the living room, and stumbled across *Quantum Leap* on the Syfy channel. While I only caught a few minutes, the premise completely sucked me in. The main character was a scientist who gets stuck time traveling throughout history, temporarily taking the place of other people to right various unknown wrongs.

Squeezing my head, I backpedal until my knees knock against the bedframe. Could that be why Reyna sent me here? I mean, I'm obviously still in my own body, but maybe this isn't just a twenty-four-hour joyride through history like I'd thought.

Maybe this is one huge quantum leap to take Patience's place and undo some kind of life-altering wrong?

I free-fall onto the colossal, lumpy mattress and throw my arm over my eyes, blocking out the nauseating geometric shapes splattered on the walls. A few hours ago—heck, a few *minutes* ago—this whole gypsy-trip thing seemed like a great excuse to leave my life behind, even if it was just for a day. But now, things are getting real. And scary.

And monumentally confusing.

If this is a real family—*my* real family—then where is the real Patience D'Angeli now?

I kick off my shoes and cover myself with the soft, sapphire coverlet, my heavy lids rebelling against the onslaught of possibilities. I'm too tired to even take off the pound of clothes I seem to be wearing. But right before I pass out, one final thought manages to creep into my exhausted brain.

If Reyna did send me here for a specific reason, a reason I don't know anything about, how will I ever get back?

Chapter Five

A rooster's incessant crowing yanks me from a ridiculous dream about geometric shapes playing leapfrog. I yawn and snuggle deeper under the coverlet, trying to grasp the remaining wisps of beautiful sleep. Then the annoying form of poultry outside my window crows again, and I huff.

Who let a freaking rooster get so close to our hotel? Somebody's *so* getting fired.

I throw off the covers, crack my eyes open in defeat, and stare at the hypnotic painted wallpaper.

It wasn't a dream.

Yesterday's events come rushing back and I look down at my golden gown. Guess I can scratch hitting the shops with Dad and Jenna off my to-do list. I purse my lips and absently run my hand along the soft fabric. The fact that I'm still here also proves my Renaissance vacay wasn't just a day trip.

I draw in a shaky breath and try not to panic.

Part of me knows this is the coolest thing that's ever happened to me, but it's also terrifying. If this is all real, and the magic didn't end at midnight like in the fairy tales, then I'm completely flying blind.

Why didn't I make Reyna explain what was going on?

I rub my forehead and play back her last words like a repeating track: *Be sure to keep your mind open to the lessons ahead.*

Great. So this isn't a pleasure trip after all. I'm supposed to learn something. A lesson, like in some teenybopper show. I stare at the door and wait for Miley Cyrus to come barreling in, singing off-key about our pasts being the key to our futures. Just what I need, more focus on my past. I grab the pillow and throw it over my head.

This is what I get for being wild.

I never should've walked into that gypsy tent. I should've just gone to the hotel, gotten my bonus points for being back early, and let Jenna extol the virtues of public scrutiny. At least then, I'd know what I was dealing with—a future stepmother gung-ho on ruining my life—and not some elusive lesson to learn.

At least there's one silver lining. If there *is* a lesson buried in all this, then learning it must be my ticket home...and if that's the case, then when I go back is completely within my control.

That I like.

It's not that I don't miss Dad already. I do. I also miss air-conditioning. But if I can somehow hang around just long enough to also miss my Sweet Sixteen, or have them cancel it, that wouldn't completely suck, either.

A short rap on my thick, heavy door startles me, and a

young servant girl enters the room. "Pardon me, Signorina."

I shake my head and blink. Despite realizing this isn't a dream, my sudden ability to understand and translate Italian is still a shock to my spinning brain.

The girl closes the door behind her. "The mistress has asked for you. She will be breaking her fast soon and insists you join her."

At the mention of food, my stomach rumbles. I think back and realize the last thing I ate was the biscotti sample in the market yesterday. I jump out of bed and quickly remember something else I haven't done since then.

Use the bathroom.

I look around the room, expecting to see a chamber pot or some other disgusting device, anything that makes sense or looks familiar from my history books, but fail to find even that. My legs start to shake and I bounce from foot to foot. From the corner of my eye, I catch the servant smirking. I narrow my eyes. There's something familiar about her.

She raises her hand and points to a small door I hadn't noticed before. "The garderobe. If you need to relieve yourself."

Garde-what?

I fly across the room and open the door. The over-whelming stench of sewage hits me, and I slap my hand across my nose and mouth. But the sight is glorious. Inside this miniscule closet is a small bench, with a hole cut into it to create a primitive toilet. I can practically hear the Hallelujah chorus. I hike up my dress, sit down, and feel the sweet relief.

When I'm finished, I return to my room feeling ten pounds lighter and see a bowl of water, several small cups, and a towel waiting for me. The servant girl motions me over. She cocks her head when I stare blankly at the strange mixture, then goes through the process of showing me how to brush my teeth with my finger and this weird homemade paste that tastes like sour honey. I keep thinking about the lovely travel toothbrush and toothpaste set waiting in my backpack. I just knew my neuroticism would pay off one day. While the girl is here, I'll refrain from bucking the system—but I totally plan to sneak back up later.

After washing, she points to the stool and I sit down. She untwists the braid I slept in and starts detangling the rat's nest on my head. As she works, I realize we've barely spoken.

"I'm Patience," I tell her with only a hint of revulsion at the dreadful name rolling off my tongue. "What's your name?"

She pulls the brush through a particularly stubborn mass of knots and when she answers, her voice barely floats over the rhythmic raking of the brush. "Lucia."

I nod toward the window. "Looks like a beautiful day today."

Silence.

I guess she isn't much for small talk, which I completely understand. I'm pretty much a loner myself…though that wasn't always the case.

A memory flashes from when I was seven years old, back when the world was rosy and I actually let people close. My best friend, Ella, and I used to be glued at the hip, especially after my parents' divorce. But then came the summer after I turned eight, when Ella moved and Mom hit the papers with yet another scandal. Classmates stopped accepting sleepover invitations, and suddenly I was no longer invited to theirs. After a while, it just became easier to pretend I didn't need anyone.

Closing my eyes against the icky onslaught of emotions and swallowing past the lump in my throat, I let Lucia's relaxing brush strokes turn me into a pile of goo.

Sadly, she eventually sets down the brush. She wraps a gold net around the back of my hair and places a jeweled wreath crown on top for the finishing touch. I rotate the small mirror she hands me around my head, admiring her work. While it's still a shock to see myself sans makeup, I have to admit I'm digging these period hairstyles.

Lucia pulls me to my feet and tugs off my gown as if we're not practically strangers. I fling an arm across my chest while she strides to the bed to rifle through clothes. I get that things are different here than what I'm accustomed to, but I'm still a little scandalized. She picks up a white linen shirt from the assortment of garments laid out and hands it to me, raising an eyebrow as I attempt to grab it from her fingers while continuing to cover all my lady parts.

I yank the scratchy wide-necked top over my head, along with the matching long sleeve linen gown, complete with fitted waist and full skirt. It's very plain, but I'm just happy to be clothed again. The last thing she hands me is a beautiful hunter green silk gown. "A surcoat," she calls it.

I slide the luxurious fabric over my head and smooth it over my hips, wishing I had a full-length mirror. The gown really is more like an outer coat, with the bottom cut open in a V-shape to expose the white linen skirt underneath. The bodice of the surcoat has a white crisscross pattern and the neckline sits right above my shoulder. It is sleeveless, resting on my shoulders and on top of the linen sleeves, which are trimmed in delicate lace at the wrists. I slip my feet into a pair of mules.

Despite the layers of clothes and the stuffy room with no A/C, I feel elegant. Regal. Especially when I compare my ensemble to Lucia's simple white gown and brown surcoat, accessorized with a stiff white apron and white bonnet. It has to be hard helping others get dressed in fancy clothes and rich fabrics while having to wear something so plain.

A stab of guilt hits, but then my stomach rumbles. Loudly.

The girl smirks again, giving me another surge of déjà vu, and wordlessly waves me toward the door. I nod in appreciation and run into the hallway before remembering I have no clue where to go.

"Um, could you point me in the right direction?"

She nods and steps in front of me, guiding me down the rug-covered corridor. The sound of happy, chirpy voices lets me know I'm getting close, as does the smell of fresh baked bread. I quicken my steps and nearly plow into Lucia's back when she stops short outside the room.

"Thank you," I tell her as I breeze past, heading straight for the sideboard displaying toasted breads, jars of marmalade, and thick slices of ham. My mouth waters.

"Patience!"

At first, I think my aunt is telling me I have to wait before hungrily tearing into the spread. But then I remember that it's my stupid name.

"Yes, Aunt Francesca?" I ask, picking up a plate and piling it high. *Break fast, indeed. At least I got that part of the time period down.*

"Good morning, child! We were just discussing the day's schedule. I hope you rested well, because today begins your introduction to Florence!"

Why is it my destiny to be surrounded by sunny morning people? I carry my overflowing plate to the table and sit across from Alessandra. She looks up; gives me a sweet, genuine smile; and then darts her eyes back to her plate. A light blush works its way up her cheeks. She is completely adorable.

"Yeah, I slept gr…very well." *Frick, this is hard.* I grab the small, gold fork, prepared to stuff my mouth before it can mess up again, and do a double take. The tines are short and straight, with no curve at all. I turn it over in my hand. How weird.

I lift my eyes and see both my aunt and Alessandra staring at me strangely. I guess they are used to the medieval fork shape. I quickly drop my hand and straighten my shoulders, playing off the momentary lapse in my façade. The most important thing I've learned over the years is that confidence is half the battle. If you project a certain image with confidence, people tend to believe it.

My aunt shakes her head and then smiles brightly. "Today Alessandra and Cipriano are going to escort you to the piazza and help acclimate you to your new home. Then tonight we shall attend a party hosted by your uncle's business associate." A rare frown appears on her face. "The family is quite horrid, but the food should be agreeable. And it is our duty to attend."

Alessandra has continued to watch me through squinted eyes but at this last bit, she sighs. She leans forward and whispers, "Antonia is most unpleasant. She thrives on causing others to feel inferior."

Well, yippee. Sounds like I'm in store for a barrel of laughs tonight.

Although I appreciate my cousin's warning, I'm not worried about old Antonia. I live my life by the wise words of

Eleanor Roosevelt: no one can make you feel inferior without your consent. It's why I don't really do the whole boyfriend or girl-bonding thing. I mean yeah, life would be easier if I had someone like Ella again—but it'll just be one more person who'll eventually leave.

My aunt gets up and flits about the room as if she is bursting with energy and needs to get it all out. I continue stuffing my face while I watch the lively display, wondering how it's possible the two of us are related. Even though we *are* family, and she believes I'm Patience, she literally opened her home and life to a complete stranger. It's as if she doesn't know how cruel people can be, or worse, doesn't care. How can she live her life with such blind trust? She certainly didn't pass that trait along in the gene pool.

She floats to the other side of the room, stopping to fuss and fluff Alessandra's hair and flash me a brilliant smile. She also has that maternal affection thing down.

Obviously, she failed to pass that trait along, too.

• • •

The Piazza Mercato Vecchio is teeming with people. It's like the mall of Renaissance Florence. Not only is it a great place to shop—anything you could possibly want, from food and flowers to clothes and tools, can be found here—but it's an excellent place to people watch.

Cipriano stays a few feet behind us as we stroll through the crowded streets. He's nice enough, and takes his role as chaperone and protector very seriously, but he seems so intense. I lean closer to Alessandra and whisper, "Is Cip always so glum?"

She wrinkles her nose at my choice of nickname. "Cip?" She follows my eyes to her brother and the light bulb turns on. "Ah, yes. Mostly, though his spirits are much lighter when he is among his friends."

Alessandra tilts her head and looks at me, and a glorious smile breaks across her face. She links her arm through mine and pulls me closer. "I have not had many friends myself, and I am ever so pleased to now have a sister."

I nod and smile, keeping my mouth shut. I haven't had a lot of friends, either, but the difference is I'm not exactly itching to break that record—as tempting as it can sometimes be. But telling this sweet girl that would be like kicking a puppy.

At the corner of Via del Corso, a man pulls a slab of roast pork off a spit and bites into it. In the next stall, a vendor offers a group of women slices of bright red fruit. Everything looks fresh and delicious and unbelievably mouthwatering. I slow my stride, about to ask for a sample, when Cipriano screams, "Lorenzo!"

The sudden exclamation from my silent cousin successfully diverts my attention from my greedy stomach.

I watch as he breaks into a jog down the road and stops in front of a guy facing away from us. Cipriano laughs as he pounds him on the back in a manly guy-hug. This family is all about the hugs. From the corner of my eye, I see Alessandra look at me, then at the boys, then at the ground with a frown.

Suspicious.

With a hand on my hip, I squint to get a better look at whoever made her so flustered. All I can see is curly blond hair and broad shoulders, and an outfit like all the other guys walking around the crowded piazza. But seeing as how she didn't get all twitchy before, I figure something has to be up. Distracted, I ask, "Who's that dude, Less?"

A group of women stops in my line of vision. Unable to see around them, I turn back to Alessandra. A weird look is on her face. I meet her stare, then hear my own words play back.

Two verbal gaffes in one sentence—so much for my nailing the old-world gig.

Alessandra's forehead scrunches. "Your manner of speaking is quite strange at times. I have yet to travel to London, but it must truly be an unruly place."

Her lips purse as she continues to stare, then, as if realizing what she said, her jaw drops and her eyes widen. A pinky glow blooms on her cheeks as she grabs my arm. "Oh, Patience, my sincere apologies for my ill manners. I do not know what came over me, but I assure you I did not mean to offend."

She looks so horrified I have to fight a smile. Not only is it impossible to imagine her ever trying to hurt anyone's feelings, but her "unruly London" comment kinda gives me an out. For whatever reason, Alessandra's natural innocence is severely cramping my ability to continue the Patience charade. I'm forgetting to keep my walls up—something I *never* do—but with her excuse, I might as well embrace it. Plus, if I go with it, I may even get her to stop looking like a sappy Hallmark commercial.

"None taken," I say as formally as I can. Then with a smirk, "Now, are you gonna tell me who the dude is that made mild-mannered Cipriano run like a banshee or what?"

The pained look washes from her face and is replaced with one of complete shock and confusion. She shakes her head and laughs. "I do not know what a *dude* is, but the *gentleman* in question is Lorenzo, Cipriano's best friend." She glances back at the boys, now visible again. "He is an impressive artist, and he comes from one of the wealthiest families in all of Florence."

She had me at the impressive artist part. "And I take it he's cute, too. Is he like your beau or whatever?"

Alessandra jerks back like I just suggested she prance around the square naked or something. "No! I believe I understand your meaning, and Lorenzo is certainly *not* my suitor. He is like a brother to me—the three of us grew up together."

I quirk an eyebrow, understanding there has to be more to the story, but fall in step beside her as she resumes walking. As we near the end of the row, I finally ask, "If you're not into the guy, then what's the problem?"

At that same moment, a rich, deep chuckle hits my ears. My stomach involuntarily clenches and my gaze sharpens on the back of this mysterious Lorenzo.

Alessandra sighs. "That is the problem." She places her hand on my arm, holding me in place, and solemnly looks me in the eyes. "You must be careful, Patience. Lorenzo is beautiful, and it is not uncommon for a girl to walk away from meeting him with a piece of her heart left behind. But he is just eighteen, and not yet ready for marriage."

I roll my eyes and laugh, then realize she's serious. Smacking my lips, I nod. "Yeah, I assure you, there's no danger on my end. Trust me. I'm not exactly looking for marriage myself." *Because that would be crazy-town.*

What I don't tell Alessandra, what I haven't told anyone, is the other reason I'm certain to be free from any danger. The truth is I've never had a boyfriend. Or even a date. There's a taunting lyric from one of Dad's favorite seventies songs that pretty much sums things up: *Sweet sixteen and never been kissed.*

Yep, that's gonna be me.

Alessandra wrinkles her nose as if she doesn't believe me, but she removes her hand. We close the distance and Cipriano flashes me an open, honest to goodness, lighthearted smile. Finally, my stern cousin looks like a normal teenage guy. This Lorenzo must be some kind of miracle worker.

"Lorenzo, this is the cousin I was telling you about."

Slowly the guy turns and I fall head first into the richest chocolate-brown eyes I've ever seen. He blinks and long, luscious lashes feather across his bronzed cheeks. I can feel myself gawking, just like I did with Skater Boy yesterday at the Piazza, but I physically can't drag my eyes away. Lorenzo doesn't smirk or act all conceited like the other guy, either. He simply stares back, his eyes casually skimming over me, causing my skin to warm and break out in a whole body tingle.

Time seems to stop, and the sounds of the market mute. Alessandra was right. This boy is beautiful.

And he's looking at *me.*

Lorenzo's full, peach-colored lips form a devastating smile, exposing one slightly crooked tooth. He kneels down in front of me and takes my hand in his.

"You are an angel, a vision sent from Signore."

His eyes twinkle with amusement and alarm bells ring in my head. Even though I can't help the zing down my arm—come on, in *any* language that's a smooth line—I straighten my spine and pull on my hand. But his grip tightens.

Obviously, this guy is a player and used to girls falling at his feet. Unfortunately for him, I'm not gonna be one of them.

Lorenzo stands and plants a kiss across my knuckles, a move straight out of a romance novel. He winks, undeterred by my lack of swoon, and with his free hand, runs his fingers through his curly golden locks.

Inwardly my heart goes a little wonky, but it doesn't mean anything. Experience taught me long ago how fickle that particular bodily organ can be.

Determined to get control of the situation, I yank my hand back and wipe it on my skirt. "Thank you for the compliment," I say, and then feeling Alessandra watching me, I flash a confident smile. "I hear you're good friends with my cousins."

Those perfect lips of his purse, as if he can't fathom why I'm not a puddle of drool by now. He nods slowly. "*Sì*, I have known them both since we were babes." Then that twinkle thing happens in his eyes again as he leans forward and lowers his voice into a stage whisper. "But I fear Cipriano will have to explain himself for keeping *you* a secret for so long."

I curl my lip and scoff. Now that I have his number, the lines are *so* not working on me.

My gaze sinks to his mouth.

Nope, not at all.

Cipriano shakes his head. "Lorenzo, I have not kept her a secret. You know she has only just arrived from London. However, had I known you would attack her like a bird of prey, I might have considered keeping her in seclusion."

I do a double take at the joking smile on Cipriano's face. This simply cannot be the same guy I met yesterday.

Lorenzo's gaze slides over my face and I stuff down the warmth in response. He turns to Cipriano and laughs, and then parts his lips to toss back a reply. Before he can, an unsmiling older woman approaches and interrupts him.

"It is time we take our leave."

Instantly the playfulness vanishes. Lorenzo nods once, keeping his head down until she steps a few feet away. Alessandra touches his shoulder and Cipriano shakes his head. "Things still unpleasant at home, I see."

Lorenzo nods again and gives a tight-lipped smile. "I expected nothing less."

When he turns to me, his face is softer than it was before and my breath catches. But then a nanosecond later, the player comes back. "Patience, I must leave you now, but I *will* see you again." He bites his lower lip and raises his eyebrows. "Of that, you can be sure."

Lorenzo grins before turning and walking over to the glacier-like woman, falling in step behind her. I watch him disappear into the crowded market and ask, "Was that his mother?"

Sweet Alessandra actually grunts. "Yes, a most unfortunate situation." She shakes her shoulders then turns to me with bright, curious eyes. "But he certainly seemed enamored with you. Pray tell, have you become another victim to Lorenzo's charm?"

Flicking the net around my hair, I snort. "Not hardly. I mean, he was cute. I guess."

"Cute?" Alessandra says with a laugh. "A word used for pups. I believe our Lorenzo may have finally met his match."

Cipriano rocks back on his heels, mouth pinched, and saunters down the path, clearly not comfortable with the thought of me hooking up with his friend. At least one of my cousins is thinking straight. And soon, Alessandra will figure it out, too.

This is one girl who refuses to be added to Lorenzo's extensive list of groupies.

Traipsing over to a nearby stall, I close my eyes and inhale the sweet smell of the merchant's roses. In the darkness, a flash of vulnerability on Lorenzo's face after his mother showed up flickers, and my betraying stomach does a somersault. In disgust, I lift my head.

Who knows, I think as I stomp behind my cousins on our way back home. *Maybe I'll even prove it to my stupid, giddy hormones.*

Chapter Six

The D'Angeli carriage rolls through the cool dark streets of Florence, the flickering torches on the passing palaces providing the only source of light. Inside the coach, shadows dance across my family's faces from the lantern hanging above.

It's the perfect setting for a ghost story.

"Antonia is a miserable wretch," Alessandra mutters, fidgeting with the folds of her skirt.

"*Sì*, her mother is not much better." Even in the dim light, I can see the deep frown lines etched on Aunt Francesca's face. "I have known the woman for quite some time, and I fear her viciousness has passed on to her daughter."

I'm glad the darkness of the cab hides my cowardly sinking into my seat. I may talk a big game, but seeing my aunt so rattled is freaking me out. I haven't known her long, but one thing I've already learned is if there's *any* possible kindness in someone, or a silver lining in a situation, she'll mine that baby until it's discovered.

Maybe tonight *will* be as bad as Alessandra's making it out to be.

My aunt leans across and places her hand on mine. "We must remember, girls, that regardless of our hosts' actions this evening, it is our duty to treat them with respect, according to their station. You must bring pride to your family name."

Uncle Marco clears his throat. "It cannot be as bad as you make it." He looks around the coach, expecting assurance—in his guyness, completely not understanding the subtle art form that is women's cattiness—and not receiving it from any of us. He tries again. "Tonight is a party, after all. There will be plenty of things to distract us from Stefani female spectacles. In fact, I am quite confident that our own Patience will be the star of the evening."

The star of the evening?

I swallow hard and take a breath before asking the dreaded question. "Uncle, how many others will there be tonight?"

"I am not certain. Along with our family, and our host family, the Rynaldi and the Cappelli families are both expected to be in attendance." He turns to Aunt Francesca and gives her a weighted look. "As well as an important business associate, Signore di Rialto."

My aunt's eyes widen as my brain replays the word *important.* Alessandra slides her arm around me and whispers in my ear, "Lorenzo is a Cappelli."

Great. So now I'm expected to be the belle of the evening in the midst of mysterious important people and, regardless of how hard I'm trying, I'm a complete cultural idiot. I have no clue how to act, what utensils to use, or what topics to bring up.

Are women even allowed to start a conversation?

I hate feeling like I'm under a microscope, and now, to top it all off, Lorenzo's gonna have a front row seat to watch the insanity.

Awesome.

Our carriage stops in the courtyard of another stone palace. Countless torches fill the air, lighting the square like a red-carpet premiere. All around me, servants bustle about. One of them comes to greet us, leading us up the stone steps and into the equally bright second floor. I scan the crowd of standing guests, pretending I'm not searching for Lorenzo, and catch his eye from across the room. The right side of his beautiful mouth lifts into a sexy grin.

Good heavens, I'm in trouble.

Alessandra playfully bats my arm and gives me a knowing look. I straighten my shoulders, ignoring her infectious giggle. Despite what she thinks, one look from Lorenzo—a smile he probably practices for hours in the mirror—isn't about to change my mind. In fact, it only proves my theory. The boy's a player.

I steal another glance and find him watching me intently.

And he's extremely dangerous.

I continue my inspection of the room, where enormous portraits of sour-faced men stare back at me. Rich, expensive rugs cover the length of the hardwood floor. The entire room exudes haughtiness. I know people like this in Beverly Hills, people who think showcasing their money makes them superior. It never does. It just makes them look like pompous jerks.

A stunning girl around my age approaches from the other

end of the gaudy hall, giving me the once over with a barely contained sneer. The skirt of her crimson gown brushes the floor with each sway of her hips, and as her feet bring her closer, I register the pure venom in her annoyingly beautiful brown eyes.

This must be the infamous Antonia.

A much older man walks beside her, his dark hair curling over the collar of his russet doublet. As they walk, Antonia leans toward him territorially. Possessively. Almost as if the man's her *date* instead of her father.

Uncle Marco speaks up. "Patience, it is my pleasure to introduce you to Antonia Stefani, the daughter of our hosts for the evening." I force a smile on my face in greeting. She doesn't return it. "And this," he continues, indicating the older man beside Antonia, "is Signore Niccolo de Rialto."

Ah. The *important* associate. I don't know if it's customary to shake hands, curtsy, or what, so instead I do a little head bob. "Lovely to meet you both."

Light blue eyes the color of blown glass shine back at me. "The pleasure is all mine, Signorina D'Angeli," Niccolo says, wrapping his warm hand around mine. He squeezes my fingers and a slow smile steals across his face.

Antonia's sneer grows into a full-fledged, hostile glare.

Well, that's awesome.

I take my hand back and look from one to the other, then to my uncle for some kind of help. What did I do this time?

Thankfully, Antonia's mom picks that exact moment to herd us into the dining room. I pull Alessandra aside and slow her stride, allowing the rest of our group to walk ahead of us. "Okay, what is Antonia's deal? Seriously, that girl looked like she wanted to toss me out on my ass."

Alessandra sighs. "I told you she was a wretch."

I follow her into the spacious dining room and nod. "Yes, you did. And I shall never doubt you again."

Keeping my head down to avoid any other awkward encounters, I find my way to my seat and ponder this latest development. Antonia is definitely the concept of *mean girl* personified, but something tells me her contempt for me is more personal than that.

I sit down, distracted by my thoughts, and study the candied fruit on my plate. When I eventually lift my eyes, I run right smack into Lorenzo's chocolate ones.

"I did say we would meet again, though I must confess, I did not think it would be this soon." He rests his elbows on the table and leans closer, his player grin twitching the corners of his lips. "But I will be sure to remember this fortuitous moment in my prayers."

The boy is good; I'll give him that. But I can stay strong in the face of such delicious temptation. The only reason he's even acknowledging my existence is because I'm fresh meat and didn't fall all over myself at the piazza earlier. He's just like every other guy out there, intrigued by a challenge. But this is one he won't conquer. I'm from the twenty-first century; I'm smart enough not to fall for his Renaissance game.

I nod politely, refusing to engage in the flirtatious repartee. Musicians carrying strangely shaped guitars enter the room and begin serenading us. I watch them perform as they encircle our table, fully aware that Lorenzo is watching me. Of their own accord, my eyes dart back to him. His eyes, glowing in the table's candlelight, dip to the neckline of my surcoat and leisurely work their way up my neck to meet mine. He winks and my breath catches.

Traitorous hormones.

A servant reaches over to place a cup on the table in front of me and I grab it from her hands, tossing the liquid back to wet my parched throat.

And immediately begin choking.

With a shaking hand, I try to put the cup down and end up spilling wine all over myself. The minstrels stop playing. I catch Lorenzo's concerned gaze and nearly die of embarrassment. Well, that and lack of oxygen. My eyes water from the burning inside my nose, and I struggle to stop sputtering. My throat aches. I pound my chest and glance around to see all eyes focused on me.

My uncle was right—I *am* the star tonight. The evening's *real* entertainment.

With hot tears running down my face from choking, I manage to rake in a ragged breath. And another. I cough again and then breathe deeply, my head hanging low like a rag doll. I exhale in shaky bursts and look up to offer my audience a wan smile.

Alessandra puts her hand on mine. "Cousin, are you ill?"

I dab at my soaked surcoat as a servant refills my cup, and then laugh half-heartedly. "No, I'm fine. Thank you. The wine just went down wrong, that's all."

Shaking my head weakly, I focus my gaze on my lap, waiting for conversations to continue and everyone to forget this ever happened.

From the other end of the table, Antonia asks, "Is our refreshment not to your liking?" My head snaps up at her scathing tone. She smiles condescendingly, and then turns toward the other guests. "Perhaps our newest Florentine prefers London wine to our own."

I hear Alessandra's sharp intake of air and feel my own blood boil. Who does this chick think she is? Everyone seems poised, waiting for my response. Lorenzo nudges my foot under the table. My aunt looks over Alessandra's head, an unspoken plea in her eyes. Uncle Marco's head is down, looking at his plate.

And Niccolo, my uncle's *important* associate, is right beside him, focused on our exchange.

Great.

It's not too late to salvage this. I count to five and clear my throat. "No, Antonia, I assure you the local wine is delightful. I just expected water in my cup and took too big of a sip. My apologies for disrupting the meal."

Feeling the weight of everyone's stares, I grab a pear slice and sit up tall. Even though I hate myself for doing it, I look at Lorenzo, needing to feel some type of assurance. His eyes narrow slightly in question, but the smile that breaks across his face seems genuine. My insides warm.

And then Antonia opens her mouth again.

"Water?" she asks, her shrieking voice like nails on a chalkboard. "Are you insinuating we are trying to harm our friends and guests? Do you dare insult the Stefani family at our own table?"

Say what?

My head jerks back as if she slapped me, and I look at Lorenzo with wide eyes. His nostrils flare and his lips draw together in a tight line.

"Antonia, do you dare insult a *guest* at your own table?" he asks in a commanding voice. "Perhaps I am mistaken, but I did not hear Signorina Patience imply any devious actions at all. She simply misunderstood. And perhaps London water is safer than our own here in Florence. Are *you* insinuating you know more about her homeland than she does?"

Oh, snap!

That shuts her up. Antonia's mouth puckers and she shoots me a look of disgust. After a beat, the minstrels start playing a lively tune, perhaps to cover up the palpable tension at the table, and I give Lorenzo a grateful smile.

I can't believe he just did that. Along with his Romeo persona, he must just have a thing for saving damsels in distress. It would totally fit with the whole fairy-tale hero vibe he tries to project.

The glacier-like woman from the piazza leans in and whispers something in his ear, and just as before, the light and joy he seemed to radiate completely goes out. He nods once stiffly, then starts eating, keeping his head down. The woman turns her attention to me, targeting me from across the table with a lethal stare. I throw my head against the back of the wooden chair.

If looks could kill, I'd be a barbequed pineapple.

• • •

By some miracle, I make it through dinner and now I'm just waiting for the blessed words, "It's time to go home." All I want to do is take off my damp dress, curl up in bed, and try *not* to replay my fantabulous choking exhibition over and over.

Standing to the side of the room, I watch Uncle Marco say

his good-byes to Niccolo. They both glance in my direction and I clench my fists. All I can do is hope I didn't completely ruin their business arrangement.

Aunt Francesca sidles up to me and laces her arm around mine. "I am proud of you."

I turn to her, shaking my head. "Proud of what? My ability to cause a scene and spaz out with nothing more than a cup of wine and my sparkling wit? You're right, I am quite talented."

A peel of laughter erupts from her throat before she catches herself. She darts her eyes around the crowd and tightens her mouth to hide her smile. "You have such a wondrously strange vocabulary, Patience, but you amuse me greatly." She hugs me closer and presses a light kiss on my cheek. "I am so glad you have come to join us. Our lives will be richer and merrier because of it."

I don't know what to say to that. I blink. "I'm glad I'm here, too," I say, meeting her gaze for a moment before looking down at the ground. It's strange, feeling completely accepted, especially after such an embarrassing performance. What's even stranger is having these words of affection come from my mother's doppelganger.

My aunt starts walking and I fall in step beside her, our arms still linked. "What I meant was I am proud of you for controlling your tongue. It is not easy in the face of such antagonism."

First the mushy words and now a compliment. I literally don't know what to do with myself. Alessandra joins us, taking her place on my other side, and we walk out of the dining room, our skirts swishing in unison.

"Tonight's party was the most interesting one I have ever

attended, cousin." Her eyes sparkle with amusement. "And witnessing Lorenzo put Antonia in her place was a rare treat indeed."

"Yeah, it's a shame the night's over. I had a whole second act planned. Maybe next time, right?"

"Over?" Alessandra asks with a quick look to her mom. "Are we not staying for the music and entertainment?"

"Of course we are, daughter. A guest should not leave until dismissed by the host, or they have a pressing engagement like Signore di Rialto. Unless Patience truly is ill?" She turns to me, concern wrinkling her forehead.

It's so tempting to lie. If I say I'm sick, this horrid night can end. The D'Angeli clan will pack themselves into the carriage, head on home, and I can safely avoid any additional embarrassment. But I don't want to lie to them. They've been nothing but nice, especially the two worried women standing on either side of me. They don't deserve that.

Plus, if I were *really* being honest with myself, I wouldn't mind hanging around with Lorenzo a little longer. On a strictly platonic level, of course. He did defend me, after all.

"No, I'm fine," I say, forcing a fake smile on my face. "I can't wait to see what else they have planned."

We follow the group into the Grand Sala, a room boasting several carved dark wood chairs and a harpsichord. I recognize it from the movie *Amadeus*. Instinctively, I start searching for Lorenzo and find him near the roaring fireplace, talking with Cipriano.

But his gaze is connected with mine.

I take a faltering step and trip, and a slow smile crosses his face. Alessandra grabs my arm, pulling me forward.

"You can deny your feelings all you like, dear cousin, but you cannot fool me. We are blood relations, and I can decipher your thoughts as if they were my own." She smiles wickedly and lifts her eyebrow, daring me to deny my interest. "Come, let us join the gentlemen, shall we?"

I attempt to calm the fluttering in my stomach as we walk across the room. Lorenzo bites his lower lip and lazily watches us approach, which only makes the butterflies go more berserk. I sigh. Cipriano looks back and shakes his head.

"Cousin, you are making it impossible to hold a conversation with my friend. I fear you have completely bewitched him." He grins and playfully punches Lorenzo on the shoulder.

Determined to get a hold of the situation, I throw my shoulders back and smirk. "Maybe it's just that your conversational skills are lacking, dear *cousin.*"

Both boys stare at me for a moment and then break into raucous laughter, eliciting a round of disapproving glares. Alessandra's mouth drops and she turns to me. "You must teach me to speak with such a cunning tongue. Clearly, you have a gift."

I smile, imagining sweet Alessandra tossing out verbal barbs. "It takes a lifetime of practice."

A dinging of crystal causes the crowd to quiet, and I look to the front of the room where Signora Stefani and Antonia stand.

"Friends and guests, we are grateful for your presence this evening. My own Antonia has agreed to begin this night's entertainment. And," she says, casting her eyes at our small group, instantly making me nervous, "it is our shared hope that the younger Signore Cappelli will grace us with his accompaniment."

Lorenzo's lips twitch as he tries to hide a confident grin. He glances at me and nods. "It would be my pleasure, Signora Stefani."

He walks to the front of the room, passing close enough behind me to slide his fingers along the back of my hand, and tingles shoot up my arm from the simple touch. The crowd claps politely as Alessandra and Cipriano lead me to the empty seats near my aunt and uncle.

And I try not to hyperventilate.

It's not that a guy's never touched me before. I held hands in junior high—back when that was the epitome of hooking up—and even slow danced at school dances.

It's just that no one's ever made my pulse rate go all supernova.

I put my hand over my heart, trying to calm its erratic beat, as Lorenzo places his on the wooden keys of the harpsichord. Antonia leans in close and whispers in his ear, and a pang of jealousy hits my stomach. Then the music begins.

Despite my disdain for the girl, I have to admit she knows how to work a room. She stands before us, completely in the spotlight—well, so to speak—and seems to thrive. She oozes self-confidence and doesn't appear to be afraid of anything. Her singing is flawless. The two of them perform together as if they've done it a million times, and while I'm envious of their obvious connection, I'm also extremely happy it's not *me* up there.

At the end of the song, Lorenzo stands, bows to Antonia, and then leads the applause for her. With reluctance, I join in with the rest of the crowd, lightly tapping my fingers together. But when she smiles and turns to acknowledge Lorenzo, I clamor to my feet. I whoop and even break out with a whistle.

Then I realize everyone is staring at me. Again.

"They certainly are lively with their admiration in London," Antonia says with a smirk, and I fight the intense urge to wipe it off her face. "Perhaps they are equally so in their performance."

She pauses, and I get the tunnel vision sensation of a camera zooming in as the villain lowers the boom.

"Patience, will you do us the honor of singing next?"

The evil glint in her eye tells me she knows exactly how this is going to go down. I look to my aunt's and uncle's delighted faces, realizing from the reading I've done that it's an honor even to be asked. Girls in the past loved displaying their talents for large crowds, but there's one small problem. I can't sing.

I'm always reading books about girls who are terrified of singing and supposedly can't do it at all, but then end up stealing the show. That's not gonna happen here. I have a voice made for silent musicals. It's not pretty.

I look to Alessandra and then my aunt, begging them with my eyes to get me out of this, but they just smile encouragingly. Alessandra gives me a not-so-gentle push, and then I'm standing in front of the room. Awaiting my latest failure.

Lorenzo places his fingers on my elbow and even the zing of electricity isn't enough to distract me. He leans in and his curls tickle my nose. "What shall I play for you?"

I snort. I don't know any classical music, especially not any with words. I could attempt opera, but that would just break the lovely crystal and glass the Stefanis have going on in the room. I'm gonna have to wing this.

"To be honest, Lorenzo, I don't know any Italian songs. Maybe I should just sing by myself." At least that way he'll be spared from association with this suckfest. "Why don't you go ahead and take a seat?"

I beam at him, pulling out the smile I've perfected for the paparazzi, and then turn around and freak out at the wall. What on earth can I possibly sing? Something tells me they won't appreciate Lady Gaga, and My Chemical Romance could potentially get me thrown outside the city gates. It has to be slow, calm, and non-future-like.

Then it hits me. Last year, Dad took me to a production of *Les Misérables* and I fell in love with the whole story. Around the middle of the play, the character Eponine sings a haunting song, "On My Own," which I downloaded as soon as I got home. It's raw, and beautiful, and sounds old. The story is even set sometime in the past. Even though it'll be in English, and they probably won't understand a single word, it's my best shot.

I turn back to the audience and scan their confused faces. Lorenzo smiles and I quickly look to my aunt. There's no way I can watch him while I do this.

Someone coughs impatiently and I realize I can't delay the inevitable any longer. With spaghetti legs, I take a breath and open my mouth. The first line tumbles out barely above a whisper.

Alessandra squints. *Louder,* she mouths to me.

I nod, raise my voice, and completely overcompensate. The next note is so shrill and loud it even startles me. I wince, and so does she.

My heart is hammering so loudly in my ears that I can't even hear my own singing. I fight the urge to run from the room, knowing—as hard as it is to imagine—*that* will shame my family even more than this horrendous performance.

Eventually, after struggling with a few more notes and

sliding up and down the entire vocal scale, I manage to find a middle ground. But it still isn't pretty. Glass doesn't break and the guests don't go running out screaming into the night, but their pinched faces and the laughter shining in Antonia's eyes lets me know it truly is as bad as it sounds to my own ears.

I can't even force myself to look at my uncle. Thank the stars Niccolo left before *this* disaster. Whatever business arrangement they had would've been as tattered as my pride right now.

Alessandra smiles in solidarity and I want to kiss her. I stumble on a lyric, close my eyes, and try to find a happy place.

Why can't the Gypsy-magic send me back right now?

Finally, after what feels like an eternity, the song ends. I sigh in relief, taking a moment to enjoy the silence, and start preparing for the judgment. With head held high and shoulders back, I attempt to look confidently out into the audience.

You could hear a pin drop.

Slowly, the applause begins. It is *way* less enthusiastic than Antonia's, but I know I don't deserve even this meager effort. Somehow, the lack of obvious ridicule only deflates my false confidence, and with tears pricking my eyes, I lower my head and rush back to my seat. I brush past Lorenzo, refusing to meet his gaze. I'm sure whatever interest he had in me has been squashed like a bug.

Antonia's gotta be loving this.

"Thank you, Patience, for your performance." At Antonia's words, I look up, waiting for her to go in for the kill. "I am sure it was not easy being asked to do so without preparation, and while you are still acclimating yourself to Italy. Pray, excuse my discourtesy. That was lovely."

I blink, and then actually rub my eyes. She doesn't appear to be mocking me. Her face is serious. Well, this is unexpected.

"Thank you, Antonia."

She nods, sits back down, and Alessandra and I exchange looks of bewilderment.

After three more *l-ong* performances, the night finally comes to an end. I follow Alessandra out of the room, keeping my eyes on the ground. If I can manage to walk to the carriage without face-planting, I'll be ecstatic. At the door, we stop to thank the Stefanis for their "graciousness."

"You simply must hold a ball on Patience's behalf, Francesca," Mrs. Stefani says, her nose held slightly in the air. "Introduce her to *Italian* society."

Antonia's fake smile crumbles and she turns to me, her gaze scrutinizing me from head to toe. "I sincerely doubt Patience is ready for something like that, Mother. A baby must first learn to crawl, after all."

As much as I don't want a fancy shindig held in my honor—um, hello, trying to escape my Sweet Sixteen drama was the whole reason I ended up here to begin with—I almost wish my aunt would host one, just so I could put that sour expression back on Antonia's face. Obviously, she doesn't like sharing the spotlight. Lucky for her, I have no interest in doing so.

My family starts our descent down the stone steps toward the courtyard. When I spot our carriage waiting at the far end of the square, I barrel past Alessandra, my only thought of ending this night. I've almost made a clean getaway when a hand snakes out of the darkness.

"I am sorry we did not get to talk more this evening," Lorenzo says, stepping into the dim corner of the courtyard.

He's so close I can feel his breath skimming across my hair, and I shiver. "Cipriano is going to arrange a day in the country for the four of us tomorrow, a get away from all the noise and *interruptions* of the city."

All I can do is stare up at him. How, after that horrendous performance, is he still remotely interested in me? Is his overinflated ego that stubborn?

He gazes down at our joined hands and begins rubbing slow circles on my palm. In the dark, with the moonlight causing his golden curls to shine, he almost looks like an angel. The right side of his mouth kicks up.

A *fallen* angel.

A soft laugh escapes Lorenzo's lips. "Patience D'Angeli, you fascinate me." He shakes his head as if he can't believe it, and his eyes travel across my face.

I actually forget how to breathe.

He leans down and kisses the hand he's holding, and then lifts his eyes to scan the area. We're alone. He stands and presses his lips against my forehead. The seconds meld together as I struggle between needing to push him away and wanting to pull him closer. I take a breath and push my hand against his hard chest.

He steps back, grinning, and says, "Until tomorrow, I shall see you in my dreams."

The words act like cold water.

Ladies and gentlemen, our player from the piazza has returned.

I shake my head as he ducks back into the darkness. During the entire interlude with Lorenzo, I hadn't said a single word. I didn't push him away, act aloof, or tell him the truth…that I'm really not fascinating at all. I was a brainless robot, completely under his spell.

"Patience?" Alessandra's voice rings out into the night, jolting me to reality.

Giving myself a mental shake, I yell back, "Coming!"

I slide out of the shadows, disgusted, and as I stride toward my waiting family, I try to ignore the happy butterflies dancing a jig in my stomach.

Chapter Seven

The next morning, I wake up before Lucia comes to my room. I sneak a quick tooth brushing with my illicit Crest and ransack my bag for other contraband items. After washing my face with dermatologist-approved soap, scrubbing my body as best I can, and applying deodorant, I almost feel like myself again.

Having accomplished so much on my own, I decide to venture into my huge trunk of clothes. It's like a little girl's princess dream come true. There are dozens of surcoats, in just about every conceivable color you can imagine. I grab one and then toss it aside for what is beneath, each dress more gorgeous than the next. It's when I'm in the middle of digging through the assortment—completely surrounded by fabric—that someone knocks at my door.

Please don't be my aunt, please don't be my aunt, I beg the universe, looking at the mess I've created. Another cultural mistake. I'm sure the average, everyday Renaissance girl isn't fascinated by her huge silky wardrobe. In fact, she's probably used to it.

"In a minute!" I call, grabbing as many dresses as I can and stuffing them inside the painted chest. The door opens and I quickly turn, caught red-handed with a dozen surcoats in my arms.

Luckily, it's Lucia. She's dressed in the same outfit as yesterday, plain brown with a starched white apron and matching bonnet, and I'm hit again with how unfair her life must be. She doesn't seem to be that much older than I am, yet she's forced to help me get dressed in these luxurious clothes every day. It has to suck.

Suddenly an idea comes to me. I scamper across the floor, leap over the last pile of surcoats, and grab the buttery yellow one on top. With a grand flourish, I present it to her.

"For you," I say, proud of myself. Lucia looks at me in confusion and I add, "To thank you for your service to the D'Angeli family."

When she doesn't grab the dress from me in uncontainable joy, I snatch her hand and try to place the dress in it, assuming she's just being shy. But when she fervently shakes her head and wrenches her arm from my grasp, I get the feeling that perhaps I've missed something. Lucia backs away from me until she hits the wall, as if I'm holding a poisonous snake instead of a silk surcoat.

Okay, not exactly the reaction I was going for.

"Is something wrong?" I ask, trying not to sound angry. Maybe manners have changed, but where I come from it's pretty rude not to accept a gift.

She nods and her face tenses. "Do they not have sumptuary

laws in London?"

Again with the historic lingo I don't know. I have no clue what sumptuary laws are, much less if they were a part of London's legal system. "Um, no?" I answer, trying to keep the confusion out of my voice and failing miserably. I drop the dress to the ground, my plan an obvious failure. "Why? What are they?"

In reply, she looks at the ground and points toward the table and stool. I tramp across the room, wondering if I'll ever get an answer from my silent servant, and plop down. In my peripheral vision, I see her raise an eyebrow at the smear of blue and white paste still clinging to the washbasin.

Oops.

Lucia runs her fingers through my hair and all annoyance flies out my open window. It isn't until my eyes are closed in pure bliss that I get my answer.

"Sumptuary laws keep commoners from imitating the aristocracy." I stay silent, trying to understand, and she explains further. "They could arrest me for wearing my mistress's surcoat."

My eyes bug out and I sit straighter. "*Arrest* you? Are you serious?"

"*Sì,*" she answers, pulling the brush through a mass of tangles.

That is crazy! I can't believe how messed up things are in the sixteenth century. No wonder she looked at me as if I were giving her a death sentence instead of a dress. Here I was trying to do her a favor, and instead ended up looking like an inconsiderate jerk.

"I can't get anything right."

First the fork incident yesterday at breakfast, then the wine debacle at dinner, not to mention the countless verbal mistakes I've made over the last two days, and now this. I'm a walking advertisement for Idiots R Us. Hot tears sting my eyes and I blink fast to keep them from falling.

"You did not know," she says softly.

I shake my head and her hands tighten around my head to hold it in place. "That doesn't matter." I snort. "Back home in, uh, London, my parents were well-known. Especially Mom. Before we'd even met, people would have made up their minds about me. I don't have the luxury of making mistakes like other people. I have to be perfect."

As soon as the words are out of my mouth, I clamp it shut. My cheeks burn. I don't know what possessed me to tell her that. She might feel familiar for some reason but the truth is she's a complete stranger, and I just spilled my guts.

The brushing stills and I wait for the lecture, the "you need to get your act together" and "everyone has it rough" speeches. I tell them to myself every day. I know I have a dad who loves me and I'm lucky to come from such a wealthy family.

It doesn't make the rest any easier to live with, though.

"Pardon me for saying so, Signorina," she finally says, her voice soft but strong, "but you are no longer in London."

It takes a moment for the meaning of her words to sink in. I stare into the small round mirror thinking, *Yeah, no duh, lady*, and then it hits me. Replace London with Los Angeles and the point is people don't know me here. And they don't know my parents. Here, in Renaissance Florence, I don't have to combat Mom's reputation and failure with my perfection. I can just be me.

Patience D'Angeli.

...

The vigorous rocking of the carriage over the deep ruts in the road lets me know I'm not in Kansas anymore. Gone are the cobblestone roads, crowded markets, and noisy patrons. The Tuscan countryside is a whole other world.

We pass a man in a short brown garment plowing his field with an ox. A variety of farm animals stroll along either side of our coach, and mop-haired children chase each other with sticks. The tree-filled landscape is interspersed with rolling hills of wildflowers, just like the mural at my favorite Italian restaurant in Malibu, *Grissini*—only much better because this is *real*.

I shake my head and lean farther out of the open window, a content sigh escaping my lips. Alessandra giggles and I turn to see my fellow travelers exchanging amused looks at my expense, but I don't mind. It's hard to care about anything— much less silly propriety—in this kind of setting.

Our driver steers the horses to the right, and we follow a well-worn path through the olive trees to a clearing. I snag a shiny leaf and inhale the clean scent of flowers and sunshine. Birds are singing and chirping happy tunes, and in the meadow before me, vibrant red poppies explode against the deep jade of the grass and the lush gold of the wheat fields.

You just can't get this kind of scenery in Hollywood.

The coach stops and before I can worry about how a proper young sixteenth-century lady would act, I jump out and run for the fields. I throw my arms wide, skimming my fingers along the passing flowers, and laugh.

This is what freedom feels like.

Ever since this morning's epiphany with Lucia, all I've been able to think about is living without the worry of judgment constantly pressing down on me. Here, in this ancient world, I'm not just free from unwanted parties and ridiculous future stepmothers. I'm actually free to become the Cat I've always wondered about and wished to be.

The thought is both thrilling and terrifying.

Alessandra shoots past, giggling like crazy, and I glance at the boys strolling leisurely behind us. Lorenzo shakes his head and flashes a devastating grin, and my mouth goes completely dry. I exhale and drag my eyes back around. Just because I can be a new me here, it doesn't mean I should go falling for the local hottie. I just have to keep repeating to myself: *He's a player, he's a player, he's a player.*

Alessandra turns and runs backward, never missing a step. She lifts her hands in the air and shouts, "You cannot catch me, fair cousin!"

Her playful energy, much like her smile, is infectious. Laughing, I shake my head and cup my hand over my mouth. "Challenge accepted!"

I hike up my long skirt and her squeal rings out across the countryside. We run across the crimson poppy field and through a meadow filled with wild daisies, the intoxicating aroma of fresh flowers filling my head. The warm sun seeps into my skin and as a cool autumn breeze whips loose strands of my long brown hair across my face, I smile what might possibly be the most authentic smile ever to cross my face.

In two long strides, I cover the remaining distance and tackle Alessandra to the ground. "Oomph!"

She rolls me off her and gives me a playful push. "Your

mother," she says, pausing to catch her breath and straighten her skirt, "must have descended from the goddess of Victory."

I draw a ragged breath and shrug. "Nah, I'm just that good."

Alessandra wrinkles her nose, but then smiles brilliantly. She begins gathering daisies into a pile as Cipriano plows into Lorenzo's back a few feet away. I watch them both nosedive and disappear into the overgrown flowers, laughing and taunting each other. As my throat grows thick, I realize I'm envious of their easy friendship.

"Goddess Victoria." I turn at Alessandra's teasing tone to see her holding a crown of daisies. "Victor of our race." She places it on my head and bows hers in solemn mock-adoration. Then she giggles and quickly makes one for herself. "Now we shall match."

I swallow past the increased thickness in my throat and lower my eyes slightly. "Thanks."

My eyes sting and I actually feel the pressure of tears building behind my nose. I blink, shake out my hands, and make the mascara face, trying to get myself together.

What is up with me today?

Luckily, the boys provide a distraction. Cipriano's dark head pops up to my right, his hands fisted on his hips. "I want it known," he declares to no one in particular, "that I *let* Lorenzo win. To do otherwise would have been impolite, as he is so obviously enamored with our cousin."

Blood rushes to my cheeks—even though I know I'm nothing special to Lorenzo—and I brace myself for the typical guy response. Denial, mocking, maybe even a sexist comment in response to Cipriano's taunting. But when Lorenzo stands to dust himself off, he just grins. "Your benevolence is most appreciated, old man."

Then he looks at me.

I fight the slow grin wanting to creep across my face as he walks over, stray shards of grass clinging to his curls. His flirtatious gaze grows darker as it trails over me, from the crown of my head, over my freckle-dusted nose, to my too-large mouth. The muscles of my stomach clench, then release, then clench again. Even though my hair's a hot mess, my face is completely bare, and I'm flushed from both running and his blatant appraisal, I've never felt more beautiful.

And that's a problem.

Lorenzo plops down and brushes the ribbons of hair away from my mouth, never taking his eyes off mine. Heat ripples throughout my body as his thumb grazes my lower lip.

If I don't distract myself right now, I may do something really stupid—like tackle the poor boy. So I shake my head and turn to Alessandra. "Y-you know," I stammer, my annoying voice all girly soft. I cough, sit up tall, and try again. "You know, this place is amazing. I mean, I've seen movies—or, um, plays— with settings like this, beautiful meadows filled with flowers, but I've never actually seen one in real life."

I look again at the scenery, trying to freeze it in my memory so I can preserve it in paint when I get home, and glance back with a smile. Cipriano squints at me, and too late, I remember I'm supposed to be from London. If BBC's *Pride and Prejudice* is any indication, that city and the neighboring ones probably have tons of little wooded pastures and meadows to romp around in.

Maybe I'll get lucky and they'll ignore that comment like they do all my other screw-ups.

Alessandra leans forward and claps her hands excitedly, her eyes glowing with a light I've never seen before. "Oh, pray, Patience, tell me about the theater in London! Is it as wonderful as I imagine?"

All blood seems to leave my face and my jaw drops. I think I'd have preferred them to question me about the meadows.

Way to go, Cat. Open mouth, insert foot.

"The theater?" I repeat ever so brilliantly.

My knowledge of ancient English theater begins and ends with Shakespeare, but while he did spring up during this period, I don't think it was until a half century from now. And the idea of what could happen if I tell them about a play—or anything really—that hasn't happened yet completely boggles my mind.

The weight of this situation suddenly crashes into me. It's not just my life, or even the real Patience D'Angeli's life, I'm messing around with here. I can potentially change, to its detriment, world history.

"I don't know," I say, nervously knotting a daisy stem. "You've seen one play, you've seen them all. Right?"

Lorenzo lowers his chin and narrows his eyes at me in question. I flatten my lips and look away, wondering what I'm going to say and how I'll pull this off.

Alessandra sighs. "I adore the theater."

Then she smiles, gets dreamy eyed, and seems to forget all about her question. I slump forward in relief.

Her eyes shift to a space off to my left as if she's watching a play only she can see. "Witnessing the birth of a new identity, the uninhibited laughter and tears of the audience, the thunder of applause breaking all around me—it is truly an experience to behold."

The passion blazing from her pores is like a postcard from home. A pang of homesickness hits my stomach and it tightens. Dad is just like her, loving the entire movie-making industry and craving the frenetic energy and creative process so much that he can't comprehend my aversion to his chosen profession. What he doesn't seem to understand is that when your life feels like one big acting job, it doesn't exactly make you eager to prolong the charade when you don't have to.

But if I ever felt the way Alessandra obviously does, nothing could keep me away.

"Have you ever done it?" I ask, a vision of her as Queen Titania in *A Midsummer Night's Dream* so vivid in my mind that it's hard to imagine it's not real. But Alessandra's eyes grow wide in horror and the boys snicker. I tilt my head and wrinkle my nose in confusion. "Perform, I mean?"

"No," she says slowly, her eyes growing wider by the second. "Have *you*?" She rapid-crawls over to me and smacks her hands against my arms. "Your father allowed you, a *female*, on the stage? Did the church know?"

Think fast, Cat, think fast.

"Of course not," I reply, rolling my eyes in what I hope is an "I was just kidding" way and not an "I think you're crazy-town" way. "You just seemed so into it that I assumed the rules were different here in Italy, that's all."

Alessandra's shoulders sag and she shakes her head solemnly. "I am afraid not. Women are allowed on the stage, but the church is so fervently against it that not many participate. They equate female performers to promiscuous courtesans, and the desire for applause to immoral behavior." She bites gently on her lip and flashes her doe-eyes at me. "Patience, do you believe it is sinful to want to be on the stage, even if it is but a dream?"

I stare into her wide, imploring eyes and feel my walls melt. Somehow, without me realizing it, this beguiling girl wormed her way into my heart and forced me to feel protective of her. And now, she actually has me wanting to risk a friendship— something I haven't really wanted since Ella.

I smile and shake my head. "Less, I don't think you have a sinful bone in your body."

She seems to grow taller before my eyes, beaming as the familiar blush spreads on her neck.

Cipriano sits up and begins plucking petals off a nearby flower. "You do not dare disagree with the church, do you, cousin?"

"No, but I don't think it's wrong to have dreams, Cip. And I also don't see anything wrong with a little game of pretend among friends." Energized by my new plan, I stand up and brush the grass from my skirt. "Less, when you have these dreams of the stage, what it is you imagine?"

She looks down bashfully and lifts a hand to play with the crown on her head. She casts a nervous glance at her brother, who watches with his trademark reserved cool. "My secret wish, in my heart of hearts, is to shuck for but a moment my role of dutiful daughter and become someone wicked." The blush extends to her cheeks and she sinks back inside herself. "It is a frivolous dream, I know."

"P-shaw," I say, waving her excuse away and looking around for props. "The heart wants what the heart wants. Think of it as a simple experiment."

I figure teaching them an entire unwritten play or story could maybe result in some future cataclysmic alteration, but little harm will come from just one or two tiny scenes. I send the boys back to the carriage to get the picnic basket Cook sent along with us, and I ask Alessandra to gather a bouquet of daisies. When the boys return, I snag an apple from the basket and quickly explain to my new troupe of actors the concept of Snow White.

"So, the evil queen disguises herself as an old hag and convinces Snow White to bite into the poisoned apple. When she does, she falls into a deep sleep. The seven dwarfs come home and find her, but they think she's dead, so they lay her out in the woods in a glass coffin. Then the prince arrives and, overcome by her beauty, gives her true love's first kiss, and she wakes up."

Spellbound, Alessandra asks, "And then what happens?"

I shrug. "They all live happily ever after."

A smile breaks across Alessandra's face as she hears the clichéd phrase, possibly for the first time. She jumps up and grabs the apple. "I will be the evil queen!"

"Yeah, that's what I figured," I tell her with a laugh. "And I'll play Snow White." I turn to the guys and realize that one of them will have to play the prince.

And kiss me.

Now, this is huge, because even though it'll be staged, it will still be my first kiss *ever*. I can pretend until I'm blue in the face that I'm not attracted to Lorenzo, but there's no way I'm letting this chance pass me by. Besides, kissing my cousin? Ew!

"Cip, you can play one of the dwarfs." Cipriano shifts uncomfortably on his feet and twists his mouth back and forth. I put my hand on his shoulder and say, "Listen, all you have to do is pretend to be upset that I've choked the big one, lay me down on the grass, and put the bouquet of flowers in my hand. Easy-peasy, right?"

His head jerks back. "Choked the big one? *Easy-peasy*? Do all Londoners speak in this bizarre manner?"

My heart hammers as I realize just how comfortable I've let myself get today. Relaxing the act in front of Alessandra is one thing, but doing it in front of Cipriano and Lorenzo is completely different. And maybe even dangerous. When I'm home, back in my own century, I *never* let my guard down. How is it that I'm forgetting myself while I'm here? What is it about these people?

I open my mouth to explain, having no clue what I can possibly say that will make sense, and Cipriano shakes his head.

"You certainly keep life interesting, cousin. And while your expressions are quite unusual, I believe I understand them. And yes, it shall be *easy-peasy*."

He tugs a strand of my hair and smiles. My body unfreezes and I laugh, relieved, at the silly term rolling off his proper-Italian-speaking, sixteenth-century tongue. He plucks up the bouquet and scans the area, and after a few steps, he points with the flowers in his hand to a patch of grass. "This will be the place."

Still smiling, I nod in agreement. "It's perfect."

I turn to the rest of my cast and Alessandra starts waggling her eyebrows with a smirk. Faking nonchalance, I wave a hand at Lorenzo. "And I guess you can be the prince."

He takes a step forward and rakes his hand through his curly locks. "And I shall give you true love's first kiss," he says, his voice a low rumble.

Lorenzo's chocolate brown eyes find my mouth and he

smiles devilishly.

My breath catches and the sound of the ocean roars in my ears. My body temperature skyrockets. I lift my hair in a ponytail off my neck in an effort to cool myself, and I lick my suddenly parched lips.

He steps toward me as if it were an invitation.

Poking him in the chest, I say, "Whoa, buddy. True love's first *staged* kiss. That means all you're getting is a chaste peck, Buster."

Behind him, Alessandra shakes her head and snorts.

Lorenzo places his warm hand over mine and lowers his head to look deeply into my eyes. The edges of my world go fuzzy.

"I would never dishonor you," he tells me softly.

Then he steps aside and I have to shake my head to clear it. *Alessandra.* I need to focus on Alessandra.

As I watch her prance around the meadow, apple in hand, a thought occurs to me. Maybe *this* is why Reyna sent me here. Maybe this is the lesson I'm supposed to learn—finding a useful outlet for my uniquely dysfunctional family heritage.

It's at least worth a shot.

The four of us go over the scenes again and I explain the concept of blocking. After I lead them through a quick dry run, we're ready to go.

"Action!" I call.

Alessandra walks toward me with a pronounced limp and a sneer upon her otherwise adorable face. Her voice is harsh as she says her lines, and I have to remind myself that while I've seen the movie countless times, this is all new to her. But the way she embodies the role, reveling in the evil hag's vicious laughter when I bite into the apple, you'd never know it. As Dad would say, the girl's a natural.

And she isn't the only one owning her performance. For all of Cipriano's usual seriousness—or maybe because of it—he brings an honor and dignity to the dwarf part I highly doubt was ever there before. He hobbles around and carries me effortlessly toward the spot he chose, stepping back with great sadness. He may be over the top with the emotions, and his actions are a bit stiff, but I'm enjoying watching him through slitted eyes so much I almost forget the ending.

Until Lorenzo kneels over me.

Of course, with my eyes half closed, I sense him before I see him. I feel the heat radiating off his legs, inhale his woodsy male scent, and hear his quickened breathing. My own breathing stops, along with time itself, as his calloused hand gently cups the back of my neck and tilts my mouth toward his. Warm breath fans across my face. And then, finally, his firm lips press against mine.

Lorenzo's kiss is surprisingly gentle, almost hesitant, as if he's holding himself back—not exactly what I expected from a guy like him. But I've waited almost sixteen freaking years for this, and I'm going to savor the moment. Ignoring my own previous warning about it being staged, I thread my fingers through his hair, anchoring him to me, and kiss him back with abandon. His lips taste sweet, and every nerve ending in my body screams in excitement.

I can't help thinking, *It's really happening.*

Lorenzo's lips curve into a smile and I crack my eyes open to see him staring at me. His eyes feather closed again and he lightly skims the back of his hand across my cheek as he presses another soft kiss against my mouth. His tongue flicks out and glides over my lips, and all the air leaves my lungs. Then he releases me.

I lean forward, eyes still closed, trying to find his mouth again. When I only feel the cool air, I open my eyes to see him staring at me hungrily. He slides his hand down my arm and interlaces our fingers, then gently guides me to my feet as he announces the ending line in a rough voice. "The princess has awoken."

We hold each other's eyes for three full beats. Then Alessandra's gleeful laugher rings throughout the meadow and she rushes toward me, throwing her arms around my neck. I fall into her and release a shaky breath, grateful not only for the support for my wobbly knees, but the mask of her curtain of veiled auburn hair. A few more seconds gazing into Lorenzo's eyes and he'd have seen the roiling emotions that are coursing inside me flit across my face.

I squeeze Alessandra tighter. "You were wonderful," I tell her, closing my eyes against the full impact of all the new feelings of the day. "Just as I knew you would be."

She dances in my embrace, bouncing on her toes. "I am forever in your debt for this glorious experience!"

Peeling her arms from around me, I stand back and smile at her never failing exuberance. "Watching you out there was more than enough. Really, it's the stage's loss."

Lorenzo picks a flower and hands it to her. His fingers graze my arm. "A greater actor could not be found in all of Christendom. Shall we enjoy a late afternoon snack and make merry in celebration?"

Alessandra positively glows at our joint affirmation, and when

Cipriano stops her for a hug and whispers in her ear, I swear it's as if she swallowed a fluorescent bulb.

I cop a squat on the ground as Cipriano unpacks our basket of fresh white bread, tangy cheese, and a leather satchel of wine. He hands me a silver, jeweled goblet and I meet Lorenzo's gaze over the rim. Without thinking, I run my tongue across my bottom lip, tasting him again, and he winks.

Alessandra pokes me in the ribs and wiggles her shoulders with a grin. She leans over, breaks off half the bread, and does the same with the cheese. "Brother, what do you say we go for a walk over to that cypress tree across the meadow?"

Cipriano scrunches his nose in confusion, and she pouts and jerks her head in my direction. If my cheeks get any hotter, I swear they'll self-combust and burst into flames. I flatten my lips and widen my eyes at Alessandra, but she bats her eyelashes innocently. Cipriano's face finally clears in understanding, but his mouth twists in contemplation as he eyes Lorenzo.

After a moment of wordless communication between the two friends, he nods. "We shall walk to that tree, sister, which is in obvious sight from here. Clear, unobstructed view of the entire meadow. The perfect choice for sightseeing."

Lorenzo smirks and punches him playfully. "The art of subtlety is not one of your many gifts, my friend. Rest assured not a finger will be placed upon Signorina Patience. You have my word."

Stupid regret pools in my stomach. *Good*, I tell myself. *Been there, done that. Who needs a repeat performance?*

An annoying inner-voice answers back, *Me! Me!*

As if he can hear my inner dialogue, Lorenzo kicks up the right side of his mouth in a grin. I examine the heavy white bread in my hand, watching through hooded eyes while he scoots to a safe distance beside me.

"Cipriano sure knows how to overreact," I tell him, relying on the blasé, comfortable persona I've worn for so long. I know today's supposed to be the first day in recreating myself in a new image, but this boy makes me way too nervous. Baby steps. "As if anything would happen between us anyway."

Lorenzo sighs and squints at the cypress tree now covering my cousins. "Cipriano has much on his shoulders, so you must not judge him too harshly. He leaves for Milan in only a few short months and is concerned for his sister, and now for you." Lorenzo turns to look at me. "He believes he is leaving you both unprotected."

"Leaving?" I ask. This is news to me. "Why's he going to Milan?"

Lorenzo's head jerks back, obviously surprised I don't know. "He has been learning the family business so he can establish their presence in Milan. As you are aware, the D'Angeli family has posts in the port cities of Florence, London, and Venice, allowing an unencumbered three-way trade route. Cipriano's presence in Milan, a city praised for its well-crafted armor, will only increase the familial wealth."

I turn my head and meet my cousin's gaze across the meadow. No wonder he's serious so much of the time—I can't imagine having that kind of responsibility on my shoulders at his age. He's only twenty years old, yet he's about to move to a foreign city by himself without a cell phone, e-mail, or even an Internet connection.

Cipriano lifts his chin in acknowledgment and I smile back, seeing him—seeing the hardships all the young people go through at this time—through new eyes. He turns to Alessandra, continuing their conversation, and I turn back to Lorenzo.

His head is thrown back, watching the clouds drift across the sky. The Romeo persona he usually hides behind is gone, and in its place is an open, younger, more vulnerable-looking Lorenzo. One that instantly feels more dangerous.

"Your uncle trusts his son," he says, instinctively feeling my gaze, not taking his off the sky. "Believes in him and supports him. You do not know what I would give to experience that for one day from my own father." He sighs and closes his eyes, the light autumn breeze ruffling his hair. "He would love nothing more than for me to follow in his footsteps and take up our family business as Cipriano is doing. But I am not a banker." His eyes snap open. "I am an artist."

We sit quietly, his words echoing between us. I've tried to keep the topic of my own past out of this experience, not knowing anything about Patience's previous life or what will happen *when* I magically transport back to the future. But right now, I need Lorenzo to know I understand where he's coming from. We may not have that much in common, but this I get.

I scoot closer and lay my hand on top of his. "I know exactly what you mean."

He tilts his head and narrows his eyes in question.

Here goes nothing.

"My father—" I hesitate. I can't say that my dad wishes I had an interest in our "family business," too. Women in the sixteenth century weren't really invited to join the work force. I shift my feet under me and try again. "I mean, I don't know exactly how you feel, because I can't take up our family business, but if I *could*, my father wouldn't have understood my passions. Uncle Marco, either. It's hard to explain to someone who doesn't have an artist's spirit how it completely consumes you."

His eyes widen eagerly and he slides closer toward me on the grass. Our knees touch, and although there is a bazillion layers of fabric between us, ripples of awareness shoot out to my limbs.

"You are an artist?"

I decide to let the shock and awe in his voice slide, and I nod. His face breaks into a breathtaking smile and I lose myself for a moment in just how gorgeous this boy really is. He scrunches his mouth, which just makes me think about kissing it again, and guides my finger to point at the sky, pressing his chest close behind me.

My eyes flitter closed and I feel my body start to sink against him.

"What do you see?"

At his awe-filled whisper in my ear, my eyes open and my spine straightens. I blink to focus. "Clouds?"

I hear the soft chuckle under his breath and instantly feel stupid. This is a test. An artist's test. A test I am going to pass with flying colors.

"I meant to say that I see an azure sky with wisps of magnolia colored clouds," I clarify, a smug smile creeping up my face.

"Very good," he says, his voice still a sexy Italian whisper. "My father would look up and see nothing more than commonplace blue and white. He has no imagination."

Proud that I proved myself imaginative, I sit taller.

Then Lorenzo asks, "What about shapes? What objects do you see in the clouds?"

This test is harder. I let my eyes relax as I gaze above, hoping and praying I'm not as closed off as his dad. I've always loved art. It's the one place I can make a name for myself—the one area I can just be me, without the mess of who my family is. But I've never really stopped to see the beauty in everyday things like cloud formations.

As I watch above, shapes suddenly pop out at me and a grin creeps up my face. I haven't stared at clouds since I was a kid, but he's exactly right. This is art. I clear my throat. "Well, right there—that one? That is a huge clock tower, and to the left below it is an elegant arched bridge." Despite myself, I snuggle back into his hard chest and sigh. "I love bridges."

Lorenzo stiffens behind me and I look up to see him staring intently in Cipriano's direction. I remember his promise not to touch me and go to move, but he snakes his arm around my waist, securing me against him. And for once, I don't feel the need to move.

As if nothing happened, he carries on. "They are quite beautiful," he says, his whisper huskier now. I swallow and close my eyes as he presses his nose between my shoulder and neck, grazing my skin ever so softly as he inhales deeply. "However, you missed the cherub floating down the celestial road."

I laugh at the smile in his voice, knowing I passed his test after all. "Had to see if you were paying attention," I say, then crack open an eye to see if I spot a cherub anywhere.

I don't.

Squinting, I lean forward, totally obsessed with finding this hidden object now. It's like the world's biggest, most annoying

Where's Waldo? A long, tan finger crosses in front of my line of vision, zeroing in on a cluster of clouds in the distance that completely looks like a baby angel.

I shake my head and grin, then take a few moments to see what else I can find in the ever-changing skyline.

When I turn back, Lorenzo's gaze drills into mine, his usual lighthearted demeanor suddenly gone.

"Patience, I must know." He pauses and glances down to find my hands. He clasps them in his own, and his pleading eyes swing back to mine, instantly making me nervous. "Do *you* believe I am a dreamer? You are lit inside with a fire and passion, unlike anyone I have ever known—I know you will speak the truth. So please, tell me, am I just a fool chasing dreams, wanting to be an artist?"

The softness and vulnerability in his face jolts me. This is the real Lorenzo. Not the player I met at the piazza or at Antonia's dinner. That guy's a front, a mask. A way of hiding who he really is from the rest of the world.

Something I know a little about.

Lorenzo squeezes my hands in his, and I take a deep breath. The weight of his question is almost crushing. We're talking about a man's future here—banking or art, two very different life paths.

I've never even seen Lorenzo's work—he has supplies back in the coach to sketch the countryside, but so far I've kept him too busy with impromptu plays and cloud watching—so the only thing I can go on is word of mouth from Alessandra and his poetic descriptions of the sky a few moments ago. But still, I know an artist when I see one. And while I'm certainly not the poster child for standing up to your parents, somehow this feels more important than an unwanted birthday party.

Slowly, I shake my head. "No, Lorenzo. You are not a fool."

He relaxes visibly and a grateful grin graces his mouth. The kind of grin that can only come from sharing your soul and not having it rejected. And it twists my stomach.

What would that be like? To chance opening up to him, letting Lorenzo into my own secret world and inner demons, and trusting him—trusting *anyone*—enough to strip myself of my defenses. The desire is powerful and tempting.

But I can't. Not just because I've never done it before, but because, in this case, telling him my truth wouldn't just be risking rejection. I could be thrown into the loony bin.

But he can at least know my real name.

"Lorenzo, would you do me a favor?"

That confident grin of his comes back full force as he leans in eagerly. "Anything you desire is yours."

I roll my eyes at this corny line, but this time, I smile while doing it. Squeezing his hands, which are still holding mine, I say, "Back home, my friends called me Cat." At his perplexed expression, I try to explain. "It's a nickname, and I know it doesn't make any sense, but I would really love it if you'd call me that."

I bite my lip and wait for his reaction, not really understanding *why* I need to hear my real name in his husky baritone voice, only that I do.

Lorenzo releases my hands and tucks a strand of hair behind my ear. "It would be an honor to do so, *Cat.*"

The sound is just as glorious as I expected.

• • •

When the sun begins to fall behind the hills, we pack up our belongings and head back toward the carriage. We decide to take the scenic route, following a foot-worn trail through the woods. As the shelter of the trees envelops us, the sound of crashing water makes its way over the incessant clicking and buzzing of insects. Eagerly, I pick up the pace until I push aside the last tree limb and stand before a breathtaking waterfall emptying into a small shaded pond.

My body sags in longing, and all I can think about is how long it's been since I've immersed myself in water. I took a shower before I got on the plane for Florence, but since then the best I could hope for is a sponge bath.

I kick off my shoes. "Last one in is a rotten egg!"

Alessandra's arm juts out, slapping me hard across the chest. "You do not honestly mean to go into that filth, do you?"

At the sound of her frantic voice, I tear my eyes away from the refreshing waterfall. "It looks perfectly clean to me, Less. Besides, I haven't had a bath in ages. It'll be fine, come on."

I try to take another step but this time Cipriano stops me. "Public bathing is believed to contribute to the spread of the plague."

This gives me pause. I get where he's coming from. I do. The intellectual, sixteenth-century-acclimating, *Patience* side of me completely understands what he's saying. But the girly, twenty-first-century-missing *Cat* side of me just sees a makeshift shower.

And that side wins out.

"Listen, I hear you, but it's perfectly fine. If you don't want to join me, you don't have to. I understand. I'll just meet you back at the carriage. I won't be long, I promise. But I hate to say it—I'm going in."

It takes a few more minutes to convince them I'll be okay, minutes I spend eagerly hopping from foot to foot in anticipation. Finally, they walk off and I dash to the pebbled edge, stripping clothes as I run. I slip into the shallow pond and swim to the center of the rushing frothy foam.

The cool water rushing over me is like a balm to my soul, and while it's colder than my normal showers back home, the feeling of sweat and grime washing off me is worth the price of admission. My only regret is that I didn't bring my backpack so I can wash my hair properly, but at this point, I'll take what I can get.

I slide my hands through my hair to slick it back, inhaling the scent of rich earth and sweet flowers. A constant stream of movie scenes plays in my mind, and I imagine I'm a young Brooke Shields in *Blue Lagoon*. A shadow falls across my arm, followed by a darkening of the sky in general, and I assume I've lost track of time worse than I thought. Then the rumbling of thunder passes overhead.

Quickly, I step out from under the deluge, searching the sky for cracks of lightning, and plod through the water to my clothes, scattered among the moss-covered rocks and tree limbs. Another rumble groans above and I scan the swaying tree line for random peeping toms before making a run for the linen shirt nearest the edge of the pond. The fabric sticks, and as I struggle to get my arms through, I hear a rustle in the trees.

I freeze, my head and one arm through the shirt. I try to stretch my hearing, past the sound of my own pounding pulse, for any unexpected sounds. The wind has picked up now, the leaves swishing wildly. Maybe it was nothing. Then I hear the pop of a twig and a muffled curse, and my stomach drops. I yank the top down with trembling hands. "Who's there?"

I open my eyes wider, looking for any sudden movements. I tiptoe to the rest of my clothes, pulling them on without blinking.

Why did I think this was a good idea again? Surely sickos and perverts existed in the Renaissance. Why did I insist on my ability to handle being alone? With my eyes scrutinizing every dancing leaf and eerie shadow, I don't see the rock in my path. I trip.

"Crappy, crappy, crap, crap," I repeat through clenched teeth, grabbing my throbbing toe. Hundreds of ants feel as though they're crawling along my skin, and not just from the pain—but also from fear. "Please," I beg the shadows. "If anyone's there, just come out."

About a foot away, I hear more rustling and a figure steps forward.

It's Lorenzo.

"I only meant to make sure you were safe…," he says, taking another step. "But then I heard the storm." He pauses and even in the shadows, I can see his cheeks flushed in embarrassment. "My apologies for causing you any fear."

Tugging my rose-colored surcoat farther over my hips— ensuring all my parts are nicely covered—I watch Lorenzo shift his weight from foot to foot and crack his knuckles. Obviously, he's flustered; an emotion I can only assume is new for the lover boy of Florence.

He takes a third step, pulling his bottom lip between his teeth. His gaze shifts to the waterfall, then quickly back to me. "Do you forgive me?"

It's tempting to draw this out, to pretend I'm deeply concerned over how much of an eyeful he got and demand he make it up to me. But honestly, I'm too busy being relieved there wasn't a band of crazy weirdos waiting in the trees.

I nod. "Yeah, I forgive you. But don't ever do anything like that to me again. You scared the snot outta me."

Lightning streaks across the sky, followed by a thunderous boom. Rain starts falling on the canopy of trees acting as our umbrella, the beat of the drops on the leaves and branches a strangely beautiful symphony—but one I want to get out of ASAP.

I wrinkle my nose and throw my hands over my head, stepping in front and letting him follow as we dash to the carriage. Although I know it was just him watching, I'm still freaked from the whole "possible creeper in the woods" scenario, and this weather situation is doing nothing to quench it. I wring out my sopping hair, despite the torrent that is sure to hit us when we escape the woods, and attempt to peel the now see-thru white linen gown away from my damp, sticky body. As I do, I remember my tattoo.

Fear grips me as I pull the surcoat tighter over the transparent undergarment. Surely if Lorenzo saw the telltale sign of my nonconformity during his so-called patrol mission, he would've said something. Well-bred girls don't exactly sport body art during this time.

I toss a nervous smile over my shoulder, looking for any hint that he suspects something. What I get is worried looks up at the sky, now completely covered with swollen black clouds. Clearly, he's got things on his mind—and my tattoo and what it may represent isn't one of them. I turn back in relief.

My secret's safe.

For now.

Chapter Eight

As it turns out, I was right about losing track of time under the waterfall. When Lorenzo and I finally made it back to the coach, it was nearly sundown. And that's when I discovered an interesting tidbit I had not yet known about Renaissance Florence: the city has a curfew, along with ten guarded gates that get slammed shut at sunset. Apparently, if you're found wandering the streets inside the gates after curfew, you get to spend the night in jail. And if you find yourself outside the gates when they're bolted, you're stuck up a creek until sunrise.

Another noteworthy detail is that being locked out isn't that big of a deal, as there are plenty of inns outside the walls where the newly homeless can stay until morning. While this alone isn't shocking, what *is* crazy is that with all the rules and regulations about society and sumptuary laws, and keeping classes in their places, the owner of the inn we stopped at had no qualms about giving us a room for the four of us to share.

I, on the other hand, have qualms galore. And they all center on one hot boy that'll be sleeping on the floor next to the very bed I'll be in, most likely dreaming of him.

Fan-freaking-tastic.

I glance over at Lorenzo as he works, eyebrows scrunched in concentration. I know that expression well, having seen it on just about every other student in Mr. Scott's classes the last two years, and occasionally on myself when I attempt a self-portrait. Eyes and mouths are the trickiest things for me to get exactly right, too.

Lorenzo looks up and grins, then puts his head back down, hand flying across the paper.

Our driver, acting as our chaperone since Cipriano and Alessandra are at dinner downstairs, shifts uncomfortably from his perch near the door. I offer him a smile. I *would* offer him a seat, but besides the one mattress, the only other option is the floor.

"*Cat.*" Lorenzo's voice is laced with exasperation, but hearing my name still sends a secret thrill through me. He knows to only use it in private, but I doubt our crabby old driver is gonna say anything.

I turn my face back to Lorenzo and correct my pose. "Sorry." I pause. "Again."

His lips tense and his strokes appear to gain momentum, and a stab of guilt hits me. It's not that he's taking too long. I'm an artist—I understand how much time these things can take. My inability to sit still has nothing to do with him, and everything to do with *me*.

Growing up, whenever my mother did something scandalous, I could almost guarantee there'd be a few paparazzi stalkers sitting outside my house or my school, waiting to get the most pathetic picture they could find. It took me years to stop buying the magazines and tabloids, obsessing over the comments and criticism about my appearance.

And that was just a group of strangers looking at a crappy picture—not a hot guy that I'm kinda/sorta/okay a lot into, sketching me in intricate detail with a pen.

"It is almost finished."

Stifling my sigh of relief, I smile encouragingly. "I know it's gonna be amazing. I can't wait to see it."

That part is true. I'm dying to see Lorenzo's work in any form, even if I am the subject.

He looks up from the page and we lock eyes. His drawing hand stills, and his teeth sink into his lower lip as his eyes roam over me. Even from this distance, several feet away, I can see they're darker. The same dark chocolate shade they were in the meadow, when his eyes trailed over me like this before. And just like then, I *feel* beautiful.

When Lorenzo brought his art supplies up from the coach with him and suggested I pose, my jaw nearly dropped to the floor. So did Cipriano's. I was imagining Rose and Jack from *Titanic,* and while obviously he hadn't seen the movie, I think Cipriano was pretty much picturing the same thing. So when Lorenzo and I both didn't want to go down for dinner, Cipriano made our driver come up to "guard my virtue." But honestly, he should've trusted his friend more. I'm posed leaning across the bed, one arm bent to support my weight, my head slightly tilted.

And I'm fully clothed.

But then again, the way Lorenzo's looking at me over his sketchpad, and the way my insides are turning to complete mush as my skin forms a third-degree burn, maybe we did need that virtue protection after all.

"Ahem."

We break eye contact and I grin at our driver, who rolls his eyes. Lorenzo looks at the sketch, takes a step back, and then rubs his neck. He swallows and his Adam's apple bobs with force. He folds his arms across his chest and says, "It is complete."

As soon as the words leave his mouth, he looks as if he wants to take them back. But I jump up, wiggle my joints, and haul butt to his side before he can change his mind. Giggling at his look of terror, I jump over the ransacked picnic basket and skitter to a stop in front of the picture.

My hand flutters to my mouth.

I take a step closer, admiring his technique, the use of contrast and his hatch marks, and as I stare in amazement at the girl in Lorenzo's ink portrait, I learn two things.

The first is that if beauty truly is in the eye of the beholder, I want the world to see me the way he does. Every flaw, every imperfection that I hate about myself has been made beautiful through his eyes and with his hand. The sketch manages to both look like me and like a gorgeous stranger at the same time, but I know it's not his creative interpretation. It's how he honestly sees me. It's as obvious as his signature in the corner, in the way he composed it, the way he used the strokes, the areas he highlighted.

I trace the page with my fingers, not wanting to touch the ink but needing to feel closer to the work he's created.

Lorenzo coughs and shuffles his feet.

"Lorenzo, you *need* to be an artist."

He stops all his nervous gestures and searches my eyes. He grins. "You are pleased with it, then?"

A slow smile creeps up my face and I nod. "Very much so."

Then the pit of my stomach completely drops out below me. My pulse races and my spine locks in fear as I finally admit to myself the other thing I've learned from staring at Lorenzo's artwork.

I'm starting to fall for him.

• • •

"I *told* you he was an impressive artist," Alessandra whispers in my ear, crawling over to my side of the hay-stuffed mattress. "That day in the piazza, before you even met, I told you, did I not?"

I stare blankly into the darkness and nod weakly. "Indeed you did."

She leans in and plants a kiss on my cheek. "And I am always right. Now I bid you good evening. I shall dream of evil hags and magic kisses tonight." She giggles and rolls back to her side of the bed, leaving me alone in my upside-down world.

Alessandra did tell me Lorenzo was talented. She even warned me to be careful, letting me know from the beginning how girls have a habit of falling all over themselves when it comes to him. And when I told *her* I wasn't interested, and set out to prove I'd be the one girl immune to his player charms, she laughed at me.

Maybe Alessandra's part gypsy, too.

My stomach flutters and I instinctually place my hand over my sliced pear tattoo. Letting *anyone* besides Dad get close to me was never a part of my life plan. I've seen what it does, the pain it can cause. But now it's happening anyway, and not just with Lorenzo. Alessandra, Cipriano, my aunt and uncle... Loving each of them is like an earthquake—I can feel it; I know the destruction it'll leave behind, have witnessed previous aftermaths; but I'm powerless to stop it. And the worst part is I don't really want to.

Turning onto my side, I shove my hands under my head and replay the last sixty or so hours of my Renaissance life. This experience is making me lose myself, forgetting who I am and where I came from. Earlier today, the idea of becoming the Cat I always wanted to be was exciting. New and different and harmless. But after only one day, it's already causing casualties.

I wiggle one leg on the lumpy mattress, trying to smooth down the bunched-up hay under me, and scratch the other one. I'm trying not to think about how clean these sheets really are or what kind of things could be living inside the mattress. But then maybe thinking of invisible bed bugs can distract me from what waits for me in the morning.

When I open my eyes tomorrow, there's every chance in the world that I'll be back in my plush clean bed in the hotel room, back in my own time. This afternoon I helped Alessandra live her dream, and in the process rose above a few of my mommy issues. I embraced what may very well be the only good thing about Caterina Angeli besides her Italian heritage—her theatrical side. And maybe that's all I needed to do. Maybe the powers that be will shrug and say, "Eh, good enough. Off you go now," and transport me back to the twenty-first century, back to the land of shopping malls and technology and lots and lots of smog.

My throat closes and I swallow past the pressure. I know

that's where I need to be. My life is there, my dad is there, and who knows what havoc I can create if I stay here too long. But the thought rips at me, leaving a jagged, brutal hole. I have family *here* now, too. A kind—if somewhat quiet—uncle and an exuberant aunt, both of who welcomed me into their home and lives without question. But even more importantly, I have two cousins who've actually become my friends, and I'm gonna miss them like crazy if and when I do go home.

Not to mention Lorenzo.

I squeeze my eyes shut at the tearing sensation inside my chest, and throw my arm out, letting it dangle off the mattress near the spot where Lorenzo laid down hours ago. Just holding it somewhere over his sleeping body helps the ache lessen by a degree.

Then a strong hand clamps over mine, and my eyes pop open. I can't see him in the darkness, but I feel him as he interlaces our fingers and gently squeezes. The hole inside me closes and a warm peace fills me instead.

Holding onto Lorenzo's hand like an anchor, I scoot closer to the edge of the bed, closer to him. And as his fingers begin to draw lazy patterns on the back of my hand, coaxing me to sleep, I grip his hand tighter in mine, scared to death it'll be empty in the morning.

Chapter Nine

I awake the next morning, fresh from a dream of Lorenzo's lips, and find his hand still clamped around mine. I grin as I take in my sixteenth-century surroundings and place my other hand on top of his, sandwiching it between mine. Keeping him attached to me as long as I can.

Last night, before I fell asleep, I promised myself that if I woke up in this uncomfortable bed, I'd make the most of every minute I have left. No regrets. And if that means letting people close to me, having friendships, and exploring whatever feelings I have for Lorenzo, then so be it. It's not like I have delusions that it can last.

One day, I *am* going to wake up, or somehow magically transport back to my own century, and leave all of them behind. And until that day comes, I can either do what I've always done—push people away and guard my heart like Fort Knox—or I can choose to use this impossible situation to experience what I can't back home. And then hold onto the memories when I'm left alone again.

The first glimpses of daylight break through the small window, but I'm the only one awake. Cipriano's sonorous musical stylings are still going on across the room, and next to me Alessandra's soft sighs and smacking lips let me know she's knocked out, too—dreaming of food or kissing, I'm not quite sure.

I bite the inside of my cheek and contemplate climbing down beside Lorenzo. Not to do anything scandalous, just for a little cuddle time. Another memory to file away. But the second I get the nerve to throw a leg over the side of the bed, Alessandra's eyes pop open—probably saving Cipriano from a mild coronary.

"Morning!"

Along with killing my game, her high-pitched bubbly voice serves as a wakeup call for the guys, too. Cipriano springs to his feet and throws on his doublet, ready to roll. Lorenzo, on the other hand, takes a more casual approach to the waking process. He languidly gets up from his prone position, rolls his shoulders, and yawns. Then he stretches his toned arms over his head and his thin linen shirt rises, exposing a strip of smooth washboard abs.

Yum.

Cipriano heads downstairs to talk with our driver, and Alessandra saunters to the window, tossing me a pointed look and a suggestive waggle of her shoulder. With medieval rules of propriety, this is as close to privacy as we're gonna get. Lorenzo and I stare at each other.

Gnawing on my lip, I look up at him through lowered lashes,

suddenly feeling shy for the first time in my life. I've always been uncomfortable with scrutiny and hated any kind of focused attention, not to mention what a total and absolute spaz I am around guys—but I've never been *shy*.

Or I should say I've never been shy before I met Lorenzo. There's just something about this guy that makes me completely abandon my belief system, and instead act as giddy as those annoying twits in chick-flicks—and approximately twice as dopey.

Lorenzo rubs a hand over his messy curly hair and gives me a sleepy grin. "Good morning."

I feel the pull of a huge old cheesy smile plastering itself on my face. "Good morning yourself."

His gaze dips to my hand, the one he held all night, and I feel heat spread up my arm and straight to my cheeks. We are only a foot away from each other, a few little steps, but it feels like an ocean apart after last night. I tuck my hair behind my ear and glance down briefly at the floor before forcing my gaze back to his. Lorenzo takes a step closer. Then the door to our room swings open.

Cipriano marches in, rubbing his hands, and then stops abruptly, narrowing his eyes at the two of us. The distant ringing of bells floats through the open window and he announces, "The gates of the city just opened."

Choosing to ignore the big brother/protector vibe rolling off Cipriano, I look around our empty room and realize we don't really have anything to pack. Alessandra grabs the now-empty picnic basket, Lorenzo gathers his art supplies, and I carefully roll my picture. With a last look at the room, I follow the group down the stairs and into the waiting carriage.

At the city's gates, we fall in line behind a row of farmers, bringing their vegetables and crops to sell in the crowded markets. The sun is still creeping over the landscape, painting the sky in rich shades of orange, pink, and purple. I love this time of day, when God uses the sky as his own personal canvas. I've never really been that religious—the only time I've been to a service is when my grandparents took me in Mississippi—but the sky at sunrise and sunset has always been my church. I rest my head on the open window, soaking up the beauty and wishing I'd brought my camera for a covert shot, and Lorenzo's foot nudges mine. Without looking over, I know he's watching out his own window, marveling the same way.

Once inside the gates, our carriage rolls through empty cobbled streets, void of the usual chaotic hustle and bustle I've already grown accustomed to the last few days. From across the coach, Lorenzo rubs his foot alongside mine. I shake my head in a silent laugh, my eyes never straying from his, and smile like an idiot for so long my face actually starts to hurt. Cipriano grunts and jabs Lorenzo with an elbow, wearing his responsible guardian role with flair as he darts his eyes between us. And next to me, Alessandra grins and looks about as happy as Jenna when she, well, does pretty much anything.

At the Cappelli palazzo, our carriage rolls to a stop and Lorenzo climbs down, making sure to hook his fingers in mine before he gets out. I ride the rest of the way on the bumpy roads with the feeling of floating.

As our coach rolls through the arched doorway of my current home, I suddenly wonder whether Aunt Francesca has been worried. Locked outside the gate until now means no word was sent that we were safe at the inn. Alessandra waves away my concern.

"Ours is hardly the first excursion caught on the other side of the gate. Our extended stay may not have been expected, but it was not cause for alarm."

Sure enough, when we walk up the stairs, breakfast is waiting for us, along with a smiling, calm Aunt Francesca.

Well, as close to calm as she gets, anyway.

She ushers us into the room and kisses each of our cheeks as we make a mad dash to load our plates. "I want to know everything that has happened since I last saw you. Did you have many adventures in the countryside? Were the inns full, or was it easy to obtain a room?" She pauses for a nanosecond and waves her hands impatiently. "This house has been too quiet in your absence. I need details!"

The three of us look at one another, wearing matching grins as we think about our impromptu production, my scandalous waterfall swim, our getting caught in the rain, and my making us miss curfew.

"It was just another day in the country, Mother," Cipriano says, before biting into a large hunk of bread. He chews and swallows, then adds, "And as for obtaining the room, it was easy-peasy."

Aunt Francesca's forehead and nose wrinkle in extreme confusion, and Cipriano catches my eye across the table and winks.

I hide my laugh behind a cough and look down to my plate, impressed. Not only did he remember the expression, he even used it right. I know I need to do a better job of watching my mouth and trying to blend in, but I can't help being amused at the idea of my expressions catching on and finding their way into classic literature. A snort escapes as I imagine Heathcliff in *Wuthering Heights* saying Hindley "choked the big one."

After breakfast, we all split up. The rest of the house off to do whatever it is they do to amuse themselves without television, computers, or video games, and me to my room to relax with my creature comforts from back home. It's not that I haven't enjoyed hanging out with my relatives, but I'm a loner by nature and need some quiet time.

Back in my room, I carefully place Lorenzo's drawing in my chest, then sink to the floor for my backpack. I glance over to ensure the door is closed, and then dive inside for my iPod. I shove in my ear buds and hit shuffle, and as Rihanna blares in my ears, I throw myself across the bed and flip open a battered copy of *US Weekly*.

Skimming over the *Who Wore It Best* section and the Hollywood gossip that's completely wrong and out of date anyway, I stop at a write-up about Dad's latest blockbuster. The picture is from last month's premiere and it shows him with his arm around Jenna. In the corner of the picture, if I squint, I think I can make out my right elbow.

This *isn't* a complaint. The fact that I avoided the paparazzi shot may make it the one and only time I've been okay with Jenna squeezing me out.

I look back at Dad's happy face and a jolt of homesickness shoots through me. For the first time since all of this started, I stop and wonder what's going on back home. When I left, did time freeze, or is he frantically searching for me in the future? Has Jenna flipped her pancake because she can't ride my coattails onto MTV?

Does he even miss me?

As soon as I think it, I know it's unfair. Of course Dad misses me. If time is ticking along normally back home, then he's probably out of his mind with worry—and feeling guilty for letting me go off on my own.

Wanting to stay here is selfish. My feelings for Lorenzo and my relationship with my cousins are nothing compared to my relationship with my dad. Until recently, it's always been the two of us against the world—almost quite literally, when you throw in the tabloids.

But as guilty as I feel for whatever it is he's going through right now, I honestly have no idea how to get back. It's not like there was a Handbook to Gypsy Transportation waiting for me upon arrival. The only clue I do have is to keep my mind open for some kind of lesson, whatever that means.

Dad's face continues to beam up at me from the page as the weight of guilt presses down, heavy and stifling. I rip out my ear buds and shove everything back into my bag, struggling to breathe as the dizzying walls seem to close in around me.

I've spent the past few days doing nothing but think about adventure, boys, and kisses, while Dad's been stuck in the future, wondering if I'm even alive. The thought nearly doubles me over, and I run to the garde-robe. As I lean close to the hole, my free hand clamped over my mouth and nose to block the horrific smell, I remember how happy I was to wake up this morning, still here.

I am a horrible, horrible human being.

Eventually, my queasiness subsides and I hobble back to the bed on shaky legs.

There's nothing I can do to get home quicker, short of begging the universe for a crib sheet on this elusive lesson to learn—and staying here, clinging to a bedpost and feeling guilty to the point of nausea is not gonna help me get back to Dad. I need to focus on something else. I need to find a distraction.

I need to get out of this freaking room.

I race to the door and throw it open, but hesitate in the hall with no idea where to go. Ever since I arrived, I've had an Alessandra-sized shadow with me at all times. I guess I could go up to her room, but she has an eerie way of reading me too well. The second she opens her door, she'll ask what's wrong. And what can I say?

Um, yeah, Less, you know all those weird and crazy things I keep saying and doing? Turns out, I'm not nuts—I'm just from the future, and right now, I'm really feeling homesick. By any chance, do you know of any gypsies hanging around here?

For some reason, I don't think she'd react to that very well.

Nope, I'm on my own. I glance to the left and then to the right, wondering which direction I should take. Turning left will lead me to the main living areas of the house: the dining room, the atrium, and the stairs down to the courtyard. And on the right lies the great unknown. It's been almost seventy-two hours since I first set foot in this ginormous mansion, and I've yet to take the grand tour. Now seems to be as good a time as any. I go right.

Not counting the ground floor and courtyard, the palace is three stories tall. As I wander down the never-ending hallways, my arms wrapped tightly across my chest, I manage to only get turned around a few times—which is saying something, considering each floor has pretty much the same décor. Brightly painted frescoes are everywhere, adding vibrant color and warmth, and thick, luxurious tapestries make the expansive rooms seem more intimate. Beautiful, soft rugs whisper beneath my feet and long, silk, scarlet damask curtains hang in every room. The whole house really is an artist's dream, and I run my hands along the cool stone walls covered in thick plaster, trying to muster up the appropriate amount of enthrallment.

Melodic trickling from the courtyard fountain drifts through the countless open windows, and I lean against one overlooking the street. Inhaling the delicate sweetness of the iris garden on the sill and watching the flowers dance in the autumn breeze helps the pain in my chest to lessen — until I look down and see two boys engaged in a mock duel with swords. An image flashes of a similar scene from one of Dad's military action films and I push away from the window.

On the third floor, I get odd looks from the servants. This is where the kitchens and servant quarters are located, supposedly because it's the most convenient for dispelling the heat. That may be true, but I still think it seems *inconvenient* to have to carry all the food down two whole floors. But what do I know? I'm no space planner.

Peering inside the kitchen, I spot a dark head. I rush inside, hurrying past the huge fireplace and the worktables where the cooks are preparing our mid-day dinner, looking for Lucia.

If I can actually get her to talk, maybe she'll be the diversion I need.

Dozens of servants dart about the room, all of them dressed in the same drab uniform Lucia wears, but I don't see her among them. What I do see is a slab of meat on a spit turning above a three-legged pot in the fireplace and people cutting vegetables, sifting flour, and kneading bread. One of the cooks grinds herbs with a mortar and pestle, and in the corner, I spot one of those contraptions used to churn butter.

As much as Dad loves to cook, I doubt he'd enjoy it with this ancient set-up.

Despite the high ceilings and row of windows, the kitchen is a sweltering sauna. Frustrated and sweaty, I escape into the hall and nearly run over a servant carrying a huge woven basket, piled high with fresh linens.

"Whoa," I say, reaching out to keep it from falling out of the girl's arms. "Didn't watch where I was going. Sorry about that."

"Patience?"

I pluck the basket out of the girl's arms and look into Lucia's shocked eyes. "Hey! I was just looking for you. Need some help?" I wrap my arms around the basket and glance down the hall, looking for a laundry room.

"No," she whispers, snatching it back. "And you should not be up here."

I stagger back at her open hostility and fold my arms. "I was just trying to help. You don't have to be so nasty."

Lucia's furrowed brow relaxes. She sets the load on the ground, looks around, and motions with her head for me to follow her down the hall. Annoyed with her snippiness, my inability to get away from memories of home, and severe boredom, I tromp behind her. We stop beside a wooden staircase.

"It is not right for you to help servants," she tells me in a hushed voice. "Your aunt and uncle would be displeased."

I prop my foot against the stone wall behind me and close my eyes. This day is not turning out the way I'd expected after waking up holding Lorenzo's hand. To be honest, it kinda blows. But I can't blame Lucia for looking out for me, even if she does insist on doing so in her own rude-mannered way. "Fine, I'll go. But I want brownie points for trying to help a sister out."

Lucia shakes her head, but I see her lips twitch as I turn toward the stairs with a huff. "Patience," she calls after I take a step, and I look back, hopeful. Maybe she'll give me the distraction I need after all. "We shall meet in your room shortly to prepare for dinner. Do not tarry."

I sigh and roll my eyes. *Please*, I want to tell her, *Cat Crawford's never been late for anything in her life.* I live with precision and punctuality—or at least I did before I came here, the land of no watches—but the pointed look Lucia tosses my way tells me she doubts that.

Whatever. It's not as if she knows anything about the *real* me.

I stomp down the stairs, still thinking about home, and decide I may as well start the tour all over. I can't exactly flip on soap operas or anything.

Exploring the first floor again, I trudge through the atrium and pause to study the log-cabin appearance of the wood ceiling. When I look down, my eyes fall on a hallway I somehow missed earlier, tucked away to the back of the room. Intrigued and wondering what secret places the hall will lead to, I cross the room.

When I turn the corner, I hit the jackpot. Dozens of paintings on canvases larger than most cars back home line the walls—but it's not the artists' talent that freezes me in place. The entire house is filled with beautiful paintings of random pastoral scenes, celestial beings, and biblical depictions. No, the reason my pulse is racing and my mouth is gaping open is because these paintings are of people. D'Angeli people.

My people.

Reverently, I stand before them, analyzing each brush stroke, each detail, wondering if somehow the paintings hold clues to get me home again. Could the reason I've been sent here be as simple as an ancestry lesson?

My shoes *clack* against the fired-brick floor—no soft rugs here—as I follow my family line down the hall. Generations of D'Angelis stare solemnly back and I can't help wondering what's happened to these portraits in the future. When I get home—because I *am* getting home—I'm so Googling them.

The final portrait at the end of the gallery is of three men, standing together regally and looking important. And smack dab in the middle, staring back with smiling eyes, is Uncle Marco.

"These must be the D'Angeli brothers," I whisper, running my finger along the rough, dried paint. "Which means one of these men is Patience's father."

For the first time since taking her place, I let myself imagine what it would feel like to be the real Patience. Alone in a new city, with a family I don't remember, starting over after losing both of my parents.

Mom *chose* to leave me, but I can't even think about losing Dad, too.

Another sharp pain hits my stomach, and the force of it hunches me over. The narrow hallway presses even closer, the air sucked out like a vacuum.

I frantically search the long hall for an open window, needing fresh air, and see a closed door across from me. If the rest of the house is any indication, it'll lead to yet another empty bedroom filled with windows.

Wrapping an arm around my stomach, I tear at the knob and throw the door open, and stumble into my uncle's personal chambers.

"Oops."

Uncle Marco's out of his chair and walking around his heavy wooden desk before I can bolt. "Patience, come in!"

I give him a tight smile and hide behind the large chair in front of me, fidgety and claustrophobic. I twist the frayed edge of the rug covering around my finger.

Renaissance upholstery. Interesting style choice.

"Sorry to disturb you, Uncle," I say, rocking in place and eyeing the door. "I, uh, took a wrong turn, but I'll get out of your way now."

I turn to leave but a dark head pops up from the chair in front of me, scaring the crap out of me. I thought we were alone.

Uncle Marco walks over and puts a hand on my shoulder, anchoring me in place, as he turns to Niccolo. "Patience, you remember Signore di Rialto. He will be joining us for dinner."

"I-It's nice to see you again, Signore," I stammer, attempting politeness in the midst of my panic attack, and automatically raising my hand to shake. Niccolo quirks an eyebrow and darts his gaze from my hand, to my face, and back to my hand before I realize my mistake.

Faux pas number 1,008. I'm guessing ladies didn't shake hands with gentlemen back in the day.

Niccolo winks, his icy blue eyes dancing with barely repressed laughter. "The pleasure is mine, Signorina." He takes my hand and squeezes my fingers, a slow smile stealing across his face.

The suffocating claustrophobia that's been clawing at me

dissipates by a degree, and, grateful for him covering my mistake with the handshake, I return his smile.

Despite being at least in his late thirties if not early forties, Niccolo definitely has the whole good-looking-Italian-male stereotype down. And he's certainly polite. But knowing he's an important business associate for my uncle—and aware of how badly I messed up the other night at the party—I can't help fidgeting in front of him. Homesickness has me off my game, and the perfect mask of aloofness I usually pull on in situations like this is alluding me.

He releases my hand and I twist it behind my back.

Niccolo bows his head. "Signorina Patience, your uncle has told me much about you." He looks up, his cool blue gaze cutting through me. "But he failed to tell me how charming you are."

Charming? Could that be Renaissance code for *spastic?* I glance at my uncle, hoping for a clue why they were talking about me or a sign that I ruined his negotiations, but Uncle Marco gives me nothing.

"Um, thank you," I murmur. Silently I add, *I think.*

The clanging of church bells floats through the open window behind Uncle Marco's desk, proclaiming to all of Florence that it's time to eat, but no one moves. Niccolo continues to stare at me, and Uncle Marco watches us both, a small smile on his lips.

"Um, did I interrupt something?" I ask, scrunching my nose. If the strange looks weren't enough to confuse me, their lack of urgency completely throws me. In the short time I've been here, I've learned the entire city of Florence stops on a dime when the church bells ring at this time; it's the universal signal for food. People here often skip breakfast, and suppers are usually light unless there's a party or banquet, but no one misses lunch. It's the biggest meal of the day.

The bells chime for the twelfth and final time and Uncle Marco takes his hand off my shoulder. "Not at all. We shall see you in the dining room."

Slowly backing away, I stop at the opened door and curtsy. "Uncle. Signore."

They both nod, and I quickly shut the door behind me. Rushing to my room, I know Lucia is waiting for me, fuming. So much for my declaration of never being late.

The meal they call dinner here is not the simple lunch of sushi or ham on wheat I'm partial to back home. In Renaissance times, it's an entire six-course extravaganza. And today we have company. Just the thought of how many ways I can screw this up, like the choking the other day or the handshake earlier, makes me break out in a cold sweat.

Lucia stands at my open door with a scowl on her face. "They will be waiting."

"Sorry," I tell her, plopping down on the stool and handing her a brush. I know the drill by now. "I got caught up."

Her harsh brushing tells me she doesn't care. It also clues me in to how important this business arrangement with Niccolo must be. Her nimble fingers twist my hair into a complicated, elaborate updo, and she places a jeweled wreath on my head. She then clips an ornate necklace around my neck and backs away.

Lucia nods curtly and walks out, giving me a few stolen moments alone before I face the firing squad.

"Breathe, Cat," I tell my reflection. "It doesn't matter if you mess up. No one *here* expects you to be perfect."

Maybe not, but as they say, old habits die hard.

A spritz of contraband perfume for luck, and a quick mirror check confirms I've done the best I can.

With a sigh, I begin the long walk to the dining room.

La sala dei pappagalli—quite literally "the room of the parrots"—is a huge space with walls painted in patterns of diamonds and tropical birds. It's so bright, and the shapes so dizzying, I find it hard to eat much. A good thing considering the sheer volume of food provided.

I take my place at the massive oak table next to my aunt, not finding it at all humorous that Niccolo is seated opposite me. There certainly won't be any hiding out for this meal.

Here's to hoping I at least mess up in new and creative ways this time.

The servants bring out our first course—*ribollita,* a soup made of Tuscan bread, vegetables, and beans. I scoop the steaming broth, the sweet smell of onions, carrots, and tomatoes filling my head, and slurp.

"How are you enjoying Florence, Signorina Patience?"

I nearly choke in surprise. Putting down my spoon, I smile at Niccolo. "It's beautiful. Everyone's been very nice and welcoming."

Well, maybe not everyone, I think, a vision of Antonia flashing before my eyes. But then Lorenzo's side-grin replaces it and I bite my lip to keep from smiling. Heat creeps up my neck.

"I was sorry to hear of your parents' deaths. My mother died from an epidemic as well." He leans forward in concern. "I met your brother once. He is a fine man. I am sure he is at a loss without your company."

Aunt Francesca pats my hand. "I am sure of that as well. But he is just twenty-four, and ill-prepared to take over the business as well as seeing to Patience's future, finding her a suitable match, and providing a dowry."

She squeezes my hand and I nod in fake-gratitude. As long as all that mess happens way after I *quantum leap* back to my own body and time, we're all good.

Niccolo nods at my aunt, and then turns his clear blue gaze back toward me. "London's loss is Florence's gain. Tell me, Signorina, how do you spend your time?"

The question takes me off guard. No one, not even sweet Alessandra, has asked me about *me*. For that matter, no one in the twenty-first century really ever asked, either. I start to panic, wondering how the real Patience D'Angeli would answer, before I remember that no one here really knew her. My aunt and uncle hadn't seen her in years.

"Well, I like music. And I like to dance. But my passion is art. Paintings, sculptures, jewelry, architecture—anything creative, really."

A strange sort of high hums in my veins. Back home, I tried so hard not to talk about anything personal or anything that could be used against me later. Opening up now to a table full of people, all eyes focused on me, is completely new territory. I mean, I don't even really talk about my art with Dad. It's not that he doesn't try to understand, but he just doesn't get it.

"Do you sing as well?"

From the corner of my eye, I see Aunt Francesca suck in her lips. Alessandra fidgets with the folds in her skirt, Uncle Marco looks down at his plate, and Cipriano coughs uncomfortably.

Then a snort escapes, and five pairs of eyes lock on a shocked

Cipriano.

"M-My apol—"

Another snort of laughter cuts his apology short and his cheeks flash red. He gives a valiant effort to stop, but the image of my horrendous performance floating before his eyes must be too much. He chokes, sputters, and squirms before a full-force cackle of laughter bursts from his mouth. He slaps the table and sends a spoon flying. He looks to the floor in horror.

If it were anyone else, it would be different. But Cipriano tries so hard to be stoic and reserved, at least in public. We all stare at one another; them knowing it's wrong to laugh at me, and me trying desperately to hold onto the mortification of that night. But it's useless. The dam breaks and everyone cracks up—including me—while a confused Niccolo looks on.

"Uh, that would be a negative," I explain, wiping tears from my eyes. Alessandra erupts in another fit of giggles. "I take it the Stefani rumor mill hasn't reached you yet, but let's just say you're lucky to have escaped their little soiree early the other night. My singing left much to be desired."

He shakes his head as if to wave off the ridiculous notion. "I am sure your voice is like a bird."

I catch Cipriano's eye and he smirks. "Unfortunate bird."

The silent servants enter the room again, this time carrying trays of roast beef and a strange version of salad with cooked vegetables and some kind of weird clumpy meat.

I decide to pass on that.

"How about you, Signore di Rialto?" I ask to get the heat off me for a while and hopefully to learn more about this mysterious person doing business with my uncle. "How do you spend your time?"

He takes a sip of wine and looks at Uncle Marco. "Before I answer, if I may, please call me Niccolo. I believe I am among friends here." Uncle Marco nods and they exchange a weighted glance. He then turns back to me. "As for entertainment, I, too, enjoy dancing."

"Niccolo is also a great patron of the arts," Uncle Marco tells me.

I swing my eyes back to Niccolo to catch him sit up straighter in his chair. "It is true, though I do not wish to boast. However, if Signorina Patience wishes, perhaps I could take her to see the *David* sculpture by the artist Michelangelo?"

My jaw drops. I mean, sure, I saw it a few days ago, back in my own time and at the Accademia where it was eventually moved, but not at its original location right after its completion!

I nod like a bobble-head.

Niccolo smiles triumphantly and raises his eyebrows at my uncle. Then he turns to me and says, "It would be an honor to escort you to the Palazzo della Signoria after our business has concluded this afternoon. If you are, indeed, interested?"

I slap a hand over my mouth in awe. "Are you serious? That would be amazing!" I realize I'm shouting and I wince, putting my palms up. "Sorry, I got a little excited there. But seriously, I would love to." I catch Alessandra's eye and she gives me an odd look. "Um, but can Alessandra come, too?"

With another nod from my uncle, Niccolo turns back to me. "Of course."

The rest of the meal, consisting of fish, omelets, a cheese platter, pasta, and flan for dessert, flies by as my body thrums with anticipation. I wish I could go with Lorenzo instead, but the idea of seeing *David* mere months after Michelangelo finished it with *anyone* makes me antsy. So antsy that I almost don't hear what my aunt tells Niccolo over the din of servants collecting plates.

"We must introduce her to society, and it has been entirely too long since we have held a ball in our home."

I swallow and turn to Aunt Francesca. "A ball? You're having a *ball*? When?"

She beams at me, as though she's divulging fabulous news. "*We* are having a ball. Tomorrow. And it is for you, Patience. Once word of your impending arrival spread, I was hounded like a fox about the details. It was meant as a surprise." She turns back to Niccolo, unaware of my lack of enthusiasm. "It shall be the talk of the town!"

"Mama hosts the most splendid balls," Alessandra says, every bit as excited as my aunt. She leans in to whisper in my ear, "And I am sure Lorenzo will look dashing as always."

Happy chatter springs up about dresses, guest lists, food, and music. Alessandra carries on an animated conversation with my aunt about the last ball's gossip. Cipriano and Niccolo discuss the dignitaries, nobles, and merchants they expect to attend. My uncle remains stoic as always. And no one notices my silence.

I clear my throat. "But I do not *want* a ball," I tell the table, my shaky voice growing stronger. "Or to be *introduced* to *society*."

Alessandra places her hand on my arm and wrinkles her forehead in confusion. "But it is expected. And why would you not want a ball? You said you enjoy dancing."

"Dancing I like. Being gawked at and having everyone stare at me? Not so much."

Palpable tension radiates off Uncle Marco, reminding me we

have a guest at the table. My teeth click and I hold back my next rebuttal.

Is it my destiny to have to put up with unwanted galas and to be thrust under microscopes? Is this why Reyna sent me here, the lesson I'm supposed to learn? That I just need to accept it and go with the flow? I don't think so.

Aunt Francesca clears her throat and looks at me with concern. "I can assure you, no one will be *gawking* at you." The way the word rolls off her tongue in Italian, I can tell she has no clue what it means. "But I shall be by your side when you are introduced. You will do beautifully."

Beautifully. Right. Because my previous experiences in the spotlight have led to such an obvious conclusion.

But we have company, so I nod curtly and shovel the last bite of flan into my mouth, swallowing my argument. As I devour the sweet custard, I contemplate my options. I don't have many. The only thing I can think to do is go along with the idea for now, and then claim to be sick the night of the ball. By then it will be too late to reschedule or postpone and it'll have to go on without me.

I smile at Aunt Francesca and see her relax.

I settle back in my seat and lick my spoon. I'll placate my aunt for now, but I'm still in control here. I've come five hundred years to escape a Sweet Sixteen. I'm not about to get stuck with a Renaissance Ball.

Chapter Ten

Outside, the Via della Condotta is bustling. It's smack dab in the middle of the fashion district of Florence, with most of the seven clothing guilds surrounding it. Sixteenth-century fashionistas flock here when they have money to blow on satin and velvet gowns sewn with pearls or precious jewels, or when they're in the market for the finest wool or leather tunics.

All of this I learn from Niccolo, who continues a running commentary on every single building or street we see, as if he's my newly assigned tour guide. As he pontificates about the importance of whatever building is in front of us, I completely tune him out. It's not that I don't appreciate the information he's giving—parts of it have actually been interesting—but his know-it-all aura is suddenly getting completely under my skin. I can't wait until we reach the *David* so I can teach *him* a thing or two.

The cool autumn breeze blows my skirt around my ankles

and tickles my skin, and I shiver. I rub my arm and accidently bump into Alessandra. The girl's been walking next to me the entire time, but you'd never know it. She's been uncharacteristically quiet.

I grab her elbow and let Niccolo walk a few more steps in front of us. "What's up, Less? Are you okay?"

She glances at our escort still yammering on several feet in front of us, and then back to me. "I am fine, cousin. Merely thinking is all."

I narrow my eyes. Whatever is bothering her has something to do with Niccolo. I make a mental note to ask her about it the moment we're alone. But until then, I'm still determined to shake her out of this eerie silence.

"Any more theater dreams since your fabulous performance yesterday?"

The familiar blush creeps up her neck and she checks to see if Niccolo is listening. "Shh!" she scolds. "I doubt Signore di Rialto would approve of our behavior in the meadow."

She gnaws on her lip, genuinely looking scared to death.

I can't help but smile at her nervous tizzy, and tease her a bit more. Laying on the unruly twenty-first century *accent* that always rattles her, I say, "Nah, old Nicky boy? I'm sure he'd be down with it. Maybe we should tell him, and see if he'd join us next time."

I learn forward as if to ask and she grabs my face between her palms. We stop walking, and Niccolo turns around, finally realizing we're not right behind him. In a tight voice Alessandra whispers, "Pray tell me you are mocking me for your own enjoyment, and do not intend to carry through with that ridiculous proposal!"

I roll my eyes. "Yes," I tell her through squished lips. "I was teasing you. Now unless you plan to kiss me, can you kindly let go of my face?"

"Oh!" she says, patting my cheeks softly. Her turned-down eyes remind me of a sad puppy. "I am so sorry. I do not know what came over me, acting in such a manner."

Looping an arm around her waist, I lean my head against her shoulder and start walking again. "Relax, it was funny. I teased you, you reacted. It's what friends do."

Honestly, I don't have much life experience to back up that claim, but it's what I've gotten from mass media.

A beautiful smile breaks across her face as she loops her arm around me. "Friends, cousins, and *sisters*," she clarifies in that happy animated voice I've grown accustomed to.

As we turn into the Piazza della Signoria, she glances at Niccolo again and opens her mouth to say something, but closes it when I abruptly freeze.

Michelangelo's *David* is a mere hundred feet in front of me.

Niccolo walks up and smiles at my slack jaw. "Are you ready to see the sculpture, Signorina?" he asks, offering me his arm. I latch on, excitement electrifying my veins. Next to kissing Lorenzo, this is definitely the coolest thing that's happened since I entered this time warp.

Alessandra slips her hand through Niccolo's other crooked elbow, and the three of us walk to the statue.

The piazza is the city's art center. The scent of oil-based paint permeates the air and if I listen carefully, I can hear the faint sounds of sculptors hammering bronze or chipping marble. Just being here, breathing the same air as the artists I idolize, is an inspiration overload. The square itself boasts beautiful sculptures from world-famous artists, none more striking than Donatello's gilded bronze *Judith and Holofernes* in front of me.

The sun hits the sword Judith raises high in victory, while the head of her enemy rests in her other hand. The image is powerful; the way it shines in the sunlight, breathtaking. But it still doesn't hold a candle to my man David.

I pad up to the statue, marveling at the pristine beauty. The marble is new and clean, with zero signs of damage or deterioration. It's absolutely perfect. I go into an art-trance and lose all track of time until I hear heavy footsteps walk up behind me. Assuming it must be Niccolo—Alessandra is too dainty to clomp—and without taking my eyes off the sculpture, I tell him, "Did you know that while Michelangelo obviously intended for David to be staring at Goliath, by placing it facing this direction, he's also threatening Rome?"

He doesn't say anything and after a few more moments, I continue spouting my wisdom.

"Look at how his right leg is tense and supporting him while the left one is bent, like a warrior. His scrunched forehead perfectly shows how he's facing incredible odds, yet his nostrils are flared and his eyes are fierce, showing no fear. Look at the veins in his hands and feet, the cords of his neck, the folds of skin on his upper thighs. Did you know Michelangelo wasn't even the first artist to use this hunk of marble? Dude, he was a genius."

"Am I not still a genius, Signorina?" a deep, unfamiliar voice asks behind me in lilting Italian.

No. Freaking. Way.

I turn slowly, take in Alessandra's slack jaw and Niccolo's cat-that-ate-the-canary grin, and stare at the bearded man standing behind me.

"You are quite perceptive. Has someone taught you about my sculpture?"

My sculpture.

The man standing in front of me is Michelangelo. He's looking at me. Talking to me. Waiting for an intelligent response from me.

The world goes fuzzy and I sit down in the middle of the square. Niccolo rushes to my side, then looks to see if anyone is watching. "Patience, are you ill?" He rests a cool hand on my forehead. "You are quite pale."

I wet my parched lips and manage a dazed head bob.

"Then let me assist you to your feet," he says, putting his hands under my arms and gently lifting me up.

I smile weakly at Alessandra, who stares back like I suddenly have two heads. I squint in confusion and explain, "I'm fine, really. Just got a little dizzy. Must be the heat."

Yeah, the one that's hiding behind that chill in the air.

Michelangelo tilts his head and studies me, probably wondering how a *girl* could know so much about a relatively new art work. The truth is that *many* someones taught me about *David*. Mr. Scott at school, and the contributors and authors of the stacks of art books resting on my shelf at home. But I can't tell *him* that.

"No, Signore," I finally manage to choke out, biting my lip. "No one taught me. Your work is just so flawless anyone could pick up these things." I look back at *David*, still not believing this conversation is happening. "And I have a feeling this sculpture's gonna be celebrated for centuries."

"From your mouth to Signore's ears," he says. Then he bows,

nods at Niccolo, and walks away. I watch him disappear into a nearby building before turning to Niccolo.

"You did that, didn't you?" I watch him puff up his chest, and say, "I knew it! Are you friends with him?"

"As your uncle said, I am a patron of the arts. I enjoy surrounding myself with beautiful things, and I know many artists. Michelangelo is one of the artists in my acquaintance, and I thought to surprise you with a meeting. A well-met surprise, I pray?"

The look he gives me says he knows exactly how "well-met" it was. Still, I can't help but grin. What he just did was beyond amazing, an experience I'm easily going to remember for the rest of my life.

I stand on tiptoe and throw my arms around his neck. "Are you kidding? That rocked!"

He stiffens in surprise, then wraps his arms around my waist. "I am glad you are pleased, Signorina."

I step back, too happy to worry about hugging a man in public and making yet another mistake, and say, "Seriously, that may be one of the nicest things anyone's ever done for me. Thank you."

Smiling, I glance at Alessandra and notice the two-headed look she gave me before has now morphed into a three-headed one. Her eyes are as big as saucers and her jaw is almost to the ground.

As I stare back, cold dread washes over me.

Something about the look in her eye tells me this isn't simply a reaction to my latest cultural screw-up, or about meeting a local celebrity. This look goes deeper than that. There's actual fear in her eyes—and it's directed at *me*.

Chapter Eleven

I pace in my bedroom, stop to sit on the bed, then pace again. Chilly night air blows through the open window but I can't stand still long enough to get cold.

All through supper, Alessandra remained quiet, only looking up from her plate to study me. I couldn't eat, but I did make a big show of pushing my food around. As soon as my aunt and uncle were finished, I hightailed it back to my room, waiting to see if Alessandra would confront me.

I don't know how much she's figured out, or how much I should even tell her. Again with the things Reyna failed to mention before letting me walk out of that tent. What if telling someone the truth negates the magic, and sends me back... before I even have a chance to say good-bye?

I think of Lorenzo and squeeze my eyes shut. As much as I miss Dad—and I do—am I really ready to leave tonight, and never see Lorenzo again?

A hesitant knock on my heavy door stops me mid-step and I swallow hard. The knocking grows manic and louder as I swipe my sweaty palms on my surcoat. I draw in a ragged breath and let it out slowly.

On the other side of the door stands Alessandra, looking frightened. Of me. The weight of that look is like a punch to the gut. I stick my head out to check the hall, then usher her in and close the door behind us.

She runs her hand along the sapphire coverlet of my bed, keeping her back to me. The closeness of the past few days I never thought I'd want, much less miss, is gone.

In a soft voice, she says, "Your way of speaking, the knowledge you possess, the things you do not know…I have thought these things peculiar, yet I did not allow myself to ponder them too closely. Perhaps I feared what I would discover had I done so."

She turns to me and lifts her eyes cautiously. "But this afternoon in the piazza, listening to you describe a sculpture created mere months ago, displayed in a city you have only been in for a few days, with such detail… How is it possible, Patience? Pray tell me there is an explanation that I have not yet considered." She bites on her lip and her eyes fill with tears. "Tell me, dear cousin, that you are not an imposter. Tell me I am not going out of my mind."

I hang my head and sigh. When she first began her speech, I planned to call on every acting gene I possess and lie with style. To explain everything, send her on her merry way, and go back to how things were before. But seeing Alessandra, my friend, my *only* friend, the girl who opened her life to me without question, with her heart in her eyes begging to understand? I can't do it.

I want to deserve the trust she gives me so freely.

"Sit," I tell her, pointing to the bed. She nods once and stiffly props herself on the edge, still looking scared and perhaps even calculating the quickest escape route to the door. I know I would be. I walk to the head of the bed, near her but not too close, and blow a heavy breath through my lips.

Where to begin?

"You're definitely not losing your mind. If anyone's crazy, it's me." I laugh and fiddle with the hem of my surcoat, running the smooth material between my fingers. Maybe if I don't look at her, I can pretend I'm not really telling anyone the truth. "Three days ago I was on a plane to Florence with my dad and his fiancée. When we got here, I convinced him to let me go on a tour of the city by myself, which is when I actually saw the *David* sculpture for the first time, only it was five hundred years old at that point. Afterward, I stumbled onto a gypsy tent and for some unfathomable reason, I walked in. I never do things like that. Never do things on a whim. Everything in my life is always planned out way in advance so I can control it all."

I snort. Control. That's definitely one thing I have *not* had this entire time.

Alessandra scrunches her eyebrows and swallows, but she doesn't say anything. So I continue. "The gypsy gave some bogus line about adventure in my future, but then saw my tattoo and went a little nutty. For some reason, that was a game changer. I should've left then but I didn't, and she ended up casting some kind of spell. When I walked out of her tent, I walked out of the twenty-first century and into the sixteenth."

I pause and look into Alessandra's eyes for the first time.

"My real name is Cat Crawford. And I'm from the future." Her blank look gives me nothing. I can't stand the silence. I need to know what she's thinking. I need a reaction. I throw my palms out; widen my eyes; and give a fake, cheery smile. "Surprise!"

My hands plop back in my lap and I wait. My shoulders slowly sink, releasing the tension of carrying my secret alone. Whatever her reaction may be, it feels good telling the truth for once.

Alessandra shakes her head and makes a sound that is half-laugh, half-sob. "You are mocking me again. Surely you do not expect me to believe such a fantastical tale?"

I chew on my lip, racking my brain to figure out a way to prove it to her. Then it hits me. I stand, turn to the side, and lean against the bed, gathering a section of my surcoat and linen gown in my hand. As I lift, Alessandra's eyes grow wide in shock. Modest as ever, she turns her head.

"Look, Less." She shakes her head vigorously and my voice gets harsher. "I'm not flashing you. Look!"

She slowly turns her head and immediately scoots away from me, her hand covering her mouth.

"This is my tattoo," I tell her, looking at the small patch of skin I've exposed on my hip.

Tattoos are art, and as such, I've always been drawn to the creativity involved. I know from my research that people have been using their bodies as canvases for centuries, but they haven't always had the options we have today. In the past, they were pretty much limited to henna, or a few other colors they could create from plants. Vivid colors, like the emerald green and bright white I have in mine, weren't possible.

"They're kind of popular in the future. Some people even

cover themselves completely with them, but for me, this wasn't about showing off artwork. In fact, I actually try to hide mine. Dad only discovered it a few months ago and he kinda flipped out and grounded me, but it was worth it."

"It is paint?" she asks, obviously waging an inner battle between complete fascination and feeling the need to modestly look away.

"No, it's ink. Things have just changed a lot in the last five centuries. Here, touch it." Her shocked gaze flies to my face and I roll my eyes. "It's no big deal; it's just my hip. But it'll help you understand. Maybe it'll prove to you I'm telling the truth."

I demonstrate running my finger over the small pear and she hesitantly reaches a hand out and does the same. Her eyes grow wide. "How bright the colors are!" she says, her touch growing rougher as she tries to remove the ink. "And they do not rub off."

"Ow! That's my skin, you know," I say, letting my dress fall. "It's kind of attached."

I sit back on the bed and turn to her, waiting for the onslaught of questions. She tilts her head back and forth, those same questions surely running through her head. What is a plane and where is the real Patience? How did I get here, why am I here, and how am I supposed to get back?

All the same things I'd love to know myself.

She scratches her head and then asks, "Why a pear?"

Okay, not the question I expected.

"Um, well, I actually got the idea from my favorite painting, *Madonna and Child with Apples and Pears.* It was painted by Bernard van Orley in 1530, which is actually still twenty-five years from now. Man, that's trippy to think about." I shake my head and continue. "The painting shows Mary holding baby Jesus, and in front of her on the table is an apple and two pears, one of which is sliced like my tattoo." My hand instinctively touches where my dress covers my body art and Alessandra's gaze follows. "I still remember the first time I saw it. My fourth-grade class was on a field trip at the museum and they had a print of it in the gift shop. The maternal bliss on Mary's face as she held her baby? That's the way a mother *should* look at her child."

Hot tears burn in my eyes and I wrap my arms tightly to my chest. "See, my mom never looked at me that way. All she cares about is her job, her fame, and her fans. I like to think that she loved Dad at some point, enough to marry him at least, but then how could she love him and then toss him, toss *us*, aside like that?"

Alessandra runs her fingers through my loose hair to comfort me, and I give her a weak smile as I swipe the tears falling on my cheeks. "Mom's an actress, so you'd think she could at least pretend to care, right?" At the word *actress*, Alessandra's eyes widen. I sniff and pull my legs under me. "But no, Mom's a victim of the Hollywood stereotype that says all actors are supposed to have addiction problems. But hers aren't alcohol or drugs. She's addicted to falling madly in love — supposedly — with whatever hot co-star happens to be in her latest movie."

I roll my eyes as I think back to the plane and my seatmate's tabloid cover. *Caterina Angeli Does It Again.* Another failed relationship to feed the rumor mill.

"Dad was different. He was an assistant director when they met, not an actor, and he thought he understood her so well and could make her happy. But in the end, nothing he did made a difference. He just couldn't compete with the allure of falling in love over and over again. She stayed with us until I was five—probably cheating on him the whole time—and then left without so much as a call or birthday card since."

I wipe my nose on the sleeve of my linen gown and take a ragged breath. I can't seem to shut up. I'm a blubbering mess.

Dad always tries to get me to talk about what happened, but I can't make him relive the pain she caused him. I won't. That's why he got me a therapist—he thinks it'll help me to talk about it with an unaffected third party, but I have no interest in hearing psychobabble. Talking to Alessandra is different. I trust her.

She pushes back the clumps of hair sticking to my wet, tear-streaked face. "I am sorry for the agony your mother has caused you. But the painting on your body, I still do not understand. Why a sliced pear?"

I sink to the floor and reach under the bed for my backpack. Now that she knows the truth, there's no point in hiding anything. I pull out my Body Shop Face Mist. A few sprays of the rose-scented cool mist calms my heated skin instantly.

Alessandra's eyes have grown so large at this point it's almost comical. I really have thrown a lot at her at once. I hand her the bottle and she sprays hesitantly. She sniffs, jerks her head back in surprise, and sprays again.

"In Renaissance art, the pear symbolizes marital fidelity, so it's fitting that one of the pears in the painting is sliced. Mom sliced our family apart with her cheating. She never allowed herself to look at me the way Mary does in that painting because she was selfish. She followed her fickle heart and abandoned her family. The sliced-pear tattoo is a visible reminder of what she did to us, making sure I never forget that the heart can't be trusted. Following it only leads to pain."

Immediately, Lorenzo's gorgeous face, golden curls, and hot as hell smile spring to mind. This is why I tried to push him away. My mother has taught me that love never lasts. But then, neither can my stay here. I sink into the pillows.

Alessandra's forehead crinkles and she shakes her head. "That is a sad lesson to learn," she says, wrapping her arm around me.

It feels nice, being comforted. But the catch in her voice and the way she tentatively pats my shoulder tell me she's still not buying the whole time-travel portion of the evening's confession.

My eyes land on my open bag on the floor.

"I know what will prove once and for all I'm from the future," I tell her, pulling it onto the bed and emptying the contents. She watches guardedly as I turn on my iPod and press play, hand her one of the ear buds, and demonstrate how to put it in.

A catchy pop beat blares in our ears.

First, the sound alone shocks her. Her spine snaps straight and she flattens her palm against her ear. Then, as she continues to listen, probably not understanding a word of the English but recognizing it's a woman singing, her jaw drops.

I laugh and start bouncing on the bed along with the music. My shoulders shimmy and my head swings. I grab a hairbrush microphone and mouth the words of the song. Less's eyes follow my dancing and she stiffly bops her head.

After a couple minutes, I press stop.

No need to send the poor girl into shock.

She slowly removes the ear bud and hands it to me, her gaze glued to my iPod. "Enlighten me, cousin, on what I just heard. How was *that*," she says, her voice growing in volume as she points to where I'm wrapping the buds around the iPod, "possible? Is there a tiny woman living inside that box?"

I laugh at the image and shove everything back into the bag. "Hardly. It's how we listen to music in the future. You download what you want onto here and take it wherever you go. What did you think?"

Her eyes sparkle and she giggles. "It was ever so strange… but delightful!" She pauses and stares at me for several moments, then touches my hand, which is resting on my backpack. "You speak the truth. You *are* from the future."

Hearing her say she believes me removes the last trace of tension from my chest. I collapse against my pillows in relief. "Yes, I am. But Less, I'm *also* an Angeli. That part's true. I'm still your cousin, just a little further removed than you thought."

Alessandra laughs and together we share a smile.

A loud *clank* outside the door makes us both jump and I leap off the bed, wide-eyed. "Do you think someone's out there?"

If anyone overheard our conversation, it could be disastrous. I throw open my door in time to see Lucia scamper around the corner. At my feet is a silver tray of fruit.

"Someone must have noticed your spectacular performance of shoving food around your plate at supper," Alessandra says, appearing beside me. She bends down and picks up the tray. "Perhaps they thought you would enjoy a snack."

I close the door behind us and lean against it, gnawing on

my lip. "Do you think she heard anything?"

"Doubtful." Alessandra pops a giant purple grape into her mouth and pulls me away from the door. She sets the tray on the bed and turns to look me in the eye. "Besides, who would believe such a thing?"

Her soft, open, trusting smile lets me know she does.

I'm no longer alone in this crazy, upside-down world. I have an ally. An actual friend. Alessandra is nothing like the Hollywood starlets or rich brats back home, looking for ways to knock you down. She's honest, genuine, and kind.

If only I could bring her back with me when this bizarre time trip ends.

"Well, at least you know now why I act so weird. I'm trying to fit in, but it's a lot harder than it looks." I close my eyes and play back all the mistakes I've made in the last several days. "I guess the truth is that I just don't belong here."

"That is untrue," Alessandra says, and I open my eyes. She shakes her head and smiles. "You may not be from here, or from this time, *cousin*. But I assure you, you most certainly belong."

Chapter Twelve

"Girls, once you have eaten your fill, please join me in the atrium," Aunt Francesca says, her eyes glistening. She gets up from the breakfast table and bounces to the door, entirely too energetic for the early hour. Before she steps into the hall, she turns back and wiggles her eyebrows excitedly. "The day of merriment has commenced!"

Actually, it *commenced* at the break of dawn, when the house became a flutter of ball-related commotion. Servants have been pouring out of the woodwork, dusting and polishing already gleaming furniture and bussing in candles and linens by the cartful. The kitchen staff has been a frenzy of culinary activity, bringing a crazy amount of food up the three long flights of stairs where it's supposedly more convenient to prepare it.

As for what my aunt has up her sleeve now, I have no clue, but I can only assume it also involves tonight's dreaded gala, or perhaps yet another surprise I don't want.

Alessandra turns to me and waves her arms happily. Then she takes in my lack of enthusiasm and rolls her eyes.

"Why the sullen face, Cat?" Hearing my real name in her sweet voice is about the only thing that can make me smile at this point. She grabs both of my hands and hauls me to my feet. "You heard Mama. Today is a day of merriment, all in honor of you, but you do not appear sufficiently joyous. Do they not have balls in your time?"

"Oh, they have balls all right," I tell her as she links her arms around mine and drags me down the hall. "One in particular that I *thought* I'd traveled five hundred years to avoid."

Her forehead crinkles and I lean my head on her shoulder. I exhale forcefully and explain. "In four days I turn sixteen. Besides getting my driver's permit, nothing much is gonna change when I hit that magic number. Maybe it's different in the past, but in the United States circa twenty-first century, it really is just another year. Or at least it should be."

I stop next to an open window overlooking the myriad of servants scurrying back and forth across the courtyard like happy little balls of glee. I've learned that holding a ball in one's home is a big deal, and the servants take great pride in preparing everything. Each house staff strives to outdo, outshine, and out-feed the last, letting the town's rumor mill act as judge.

Clearly, I'm the only one in this joint not in the mood to party.

"Unfortunately, it's become extremely popular in the future for girls my age to host big parties celebrating their sixteenth birthday. And that's all fine and good—I've even gone to a few and had an okay time. But I *never* wanted to have one myself."

I sigh, slither down the plastered wall, and plop onto the floor. Alessandra glances both ways to ensure we're alone, then demurely settles beside me, straightening her skirts around her. She catches me smiling at her ever-proper mannerisms, and I shake my head.

Opening up to Alessandra is as easy as breathing. Things I can't even verbalize to Dad are spilling out of me, and she's simply being her unaffected, sweet-tempered self. I scoot closer and continue.

"I told you about my parents, how they live in the spotlight? Well, I pretty much do, too, thanks to my mother's many, many, *many* mistakes. Wherever I go, people assume they know me. They expect me to act a certain way. But when they see I'm not an exciting starlet but a geek who'd rather go to an art gallery than shop on Rodeo? I see their reaction—the boredom, the disappointment, the way their gazes shift to find someone better and more interesting. The last thing I want is to be the center of a huge *internationally televised* party, with billions of people watching, so I can let the entire world down on an epic scale."

Alessandra's eyes crinkle as she tries to understand. I know she has no clue what I'm talking about—television or the concept of billions of people watching anything—but she's obviously trying. I lean my cheek against the cool stone, comforted merely by her effort, as she tilts her head and asks, "But your father does not understand your heart?"

I take a minute to consider her question. "I thought he did. And I think he still does—it's his fiancée messing everything up. The sweet sixteen was her idea, and she's the one running the show and just about everything else lately. Because this fabulous brain-child of hers didn't come until a few weeks ago, the party won't even be until at least a month after my actual birthday, so I really don't see the point. But of course, Jenna could give a crap about my opinion." I hear my voice rising, along with my blood pressure, but I can't stop. A floodgate's been opened, letting out all my frustration and anger for the past year, and it feels wonderfully cathartic. "My new step-mommy-to-be had one when she was younger and since she loved it, she naturally assumes I would feel the same way. Because you know, we are so alike." I huff. "The woman just refuses to see that I am *nothing* like her!"

The halls echo with my raised voice and Alessandra's eyes widen. I fall back against the wall and try to tame my breathing as the clanging of tools floats through the window above. If only I could explain it like that to Jenna—or to Dad. Alessandra rests her hand on my arm and gives me a soft smile before closing her eyes and leaning her head against the wall, giving me the time I need to calm down. And hopefully saving me from describing what Jenna *is* like, if she's not like me. Because truthfully, she's almost exactly like Aunt Francesca—and quite a bit like Alessandra.

But obviously different, because I actually *like* them.

Then again, when Dad first started dating Jenna nine months ago, I liked her, too. I liked that she made Dad happy and had him singing in the shower, and their relationship seemed harmless enough. It wasn't until he sat me down for "the talk" that I found out how serious it was, and by then it was too late; she'd gotten her hooks into him. She had to have, because there's no way Dad would've signed up for the pain of marriage again without coercion.

And now that Jenna's got Dad on the ropes, I'm her latest target. Coming to my room to talk about boys, and telling me she understands how hard high school can be. She just can't accept that Dad and I aren't a package deal.

A loud *thump* echoes down the hall from the direction of the atrium. An eager smile creeps up Alessandra's face and I motorboat my lips. "Guess we better go see what your mom's up to now," I say, standing and giving Alessandra a hand. I smooth down my skirt and watch the dust particles dancing in the air around us.

Looks as though the cleaning crew missed a spot, I think, and then smile in satisfaction. For some reason, this small imperfection makes me feel better about the ball—although I still have no intention of going.

As Alessandra and I resume the journey down the hall, I decide to let her in on my plan. "So you can see, Less, that while I appreciate Aunt Francesca's efforts, a ball in my honor is the last thing I want. Crowds give me hives, and we've both seen the mess I can make of social situations," I say, shooting her a sardonic smile.

Sweet as she is, she doesn't agree aloud, but she's not exactly rushing to contradict me, either. I laugh in spite of myself and continue.

"Yesterday, I couldn't argue because we had company, but I've come up with a plan to get out of tonight and avoid hurting your mom's feelings. I'm gonna say I'm sick, that I feel nauseous, dizzy, and lightheaded. All I need you to do is vouch that I look like crap and back me up when I suggest spending the evening in bed, and I think it will be a win-win for everyone."

Alessandra's eyes bug out and she pulls my arm, stopping us a few feet shy of the atrium. I hear my aunt inside, humming and moving about with an extra dose of excitement quickening her steps.

"But then they shall send for the physician, Signore Penni! You truly consider *bloodletting* preferable to wearing a beautiful dress and smiling at Mama's friends?"

I draw in a sharp breath at the horrifying image. "Bloodletting!" I shriek, then dart a quick glance around. I take a step closer and lower my voice to a terse whisper. Maybe my brain translated that wrong. "You mean, like, leeches? Seriously? That really happens?"

She nods and my wonderfully thought-out plan slips away. There's no way in Hades I'm letting some ancient barber/physician put those disgusting things anywhere near my body. I've seen *Stand By Me.*

But if I can't convince Aunt Francesca I'm sick and need to sit this one out, then I have no choice but to go to the ball as planned.

So much for controlling the situation.

My shoulders sag in defeat. "The fates win this round. Looks like I'll be smiling for my adoring fans after all. Yippee."

Alessandra's giggles bounce off the atrium's walls as we walk in, and Aunt Francesca turns around, a dazzling array of richly colored surcoats draped over her arm. Uncle Marco stands beside her, his arms behind his back and chest puffed out, looking pleased. Behind them is a large gilded mirror.

Up until today, the biggest mirror I'd seen was the small circular one in my room, and this one has to be ten times the size of that. Finally, I can actually get a glimpse of myself in full period regalia.

Alessandra squeals and rushes toward them, grabbing the olive green silk surcoat on top. "Are these for the ball?" she asks, holding it up to her body and twirling around.

My uncle beams at her reaction and my aunt nods. "Patience, your measurements were approximated based on Alessandra's, but we will send a tailor to your room for any alterations." She waits a beat and then places her hand on her husband's elbow. "These gowns are a gift from your father and uncle."

Uncle Marco slides the royal blue gown off Aunt Francesca's arm and walks toward me. "An intelligent gentleman apprehends that true happiness can only be attained when his women are happy," he says, handing me the gown. "Now that I have three women under my roof, I considered it in my best interest to indulge them."

He winks and seems so genuine that I can't help but smile in gratitude. I glance down at the gown in my hands and trace my finger along the silky brocade, drinking in the luxurious color. It's gorgeous. A vision of me in this dress, gliding across a candle-lit ballroom in Lorenzo's arms, springs to mind and my stomach flutters. Biting my lower lip, I hold the dress against me and walk to the almost-full-length mirror.

The dark blue fabric sets off my dark eyes, and my normally uninspired coffee-colored hair transforms into something exotic. My reflection stares back without a trace of makeup but I feel beautiful. My eyes sparkle and I watch as a smile stretches across my face, thinking about Lorenzo's reaction.

I want him to see me in this dress.

I nod slowly, accepting my fate. Since I'm destined to have to put up with a ball, I guess knowing Lorenzo will be waiting for me on the other side does make it slightly more tolerable.

. . .

It took three men to do the heavy lifting, four women to haul the steaming buckets of hot water, and one bottle of smuggled sample-sized bubble bath to make this possible, but it is *so* worth it. Warm water sloshes over the sides of the wooden tub as I scoop up a handful of gardenia-scented bubbles and blow gently, creating an iridescent rainbow-infused cave.

Now this is *la bella vita*.

If I'd known all it took to get a decent bath was to confess the truth to Alessandra, I'd have blabbed the first night. Though she declined to take one herself, she wrangled up a half dozen servants and got them to stop what they were doing just so I could soak. She also had Lucia bring me a goblet of wine.

"For your nerves," she told me as she lay out a white linen towel and black velvet robe.

I gladly accepted, loving the lack of a drinking age, and took a large gulp, hoping it would chill out the convulsions happening all along my nervous system. So far, it's yet to do its job.

During the dress fitting, I was fine. Good, even. Wearing that dress and imagining Lorenzo's reaction, I felt like a new person. I let myself fantasize about what it would be like to command the ballroom floor tonight, and truly become the new version of myself I've been creating the past two days.

But when I put my normal clothes on, my old self came back with a vengeance. New scenarios played alongside the other fantasies, ones where I stumble and fall, say the wrong thing, or embarrass my entire family. Again. Scenes where I hold lengthy conversations with food stuck in my teeth or horribly bad breath, and where I disappoint everyone in attendance by not living up to whatever image they expect of me.

I shake the thoughts away and take another sip of sweet red wine.

Time to switch my focus back to Lorenzo's arms.

Sinking deeper into the bubbles, I sigh as the thrill of giddy anticipation tingles across my skin, replacing my previous anxiety.

I vowed that I'd make the most of this opportunity and experience everything I could while I had the chance, leaving here and Lorenzo with no regrets. If I were back home, things would be different. I'd continue pushing him away, knowing that getting too close would only lead to pain for the both of us. But this isn't real life. This is a dream, a fantasy, an impossible situation with a beautiful boy who seems to like me, too. It would be idiotic to not immerse myself fully in this trip to the past and experience all the things a normal girl my age would. Including dancing in a gorgeous gown across a candlelit ballroom, in the arms of a sixteenth-century hottie.

A gentle knock shakes me out of the glorious vision and I look over as Alessandra's head peeks around my door. Smiling, she comes in, closes it behind her, and leans against it.

"I trust our ancient method of bathing met with your approval," she teases, looking me briefly in the eye and then bouncing her gaze above my head. She ambles over in a velvet robe that matches my own, averting her eyes and plucking the towel off my bed. "I have asked our servants to meet us here shortly to get ready. I pray you do not mind," she says, standing patiently next to the tub, looking out the window. Her fidgety foot nearly knocks over my half-full wine glass.

Before coming here, I would've said I was fairly modest, but in comparison to Alessandra, a nun could be an exhibitionist. I know I *should* climb out of the tub, quickly and wordlessly, and start getting ready. But the girl is just so fun to tease.

Gathering the remaining sudsy bubbles into a mound, I scoop them into my palms and say, "Hey Less?"

Instinct takes over and she looks, timed perfectly with my sharp exhale of blasted air that showers her with tufts of sparkling foam.

Wide-eyed, her jaw drops. Then with a laugh, she skims her hand over the top of her head and sniffs the collected suds. "Your satchel contains the most pleasantly scented items," she says, holding out the towel and averting her eyes again so I can step out. "I should enjoy exploring them more fully after the ball."

I wrap the coarse linen towel around me and run my fingers through my freshly shampooed hair. "You got it. I'd suggest a makeover tonight, but I don't think your world's ready for makeup from the future."

Cosmetics, like tattoos, have been around for forever, but luckily I've been able to avoid the look many of the girls around town are sporting. An alabaster face, neck, and cleavage, paired with bright crimson cheeks, is not a good style choice for anyone.

I slip my still-damp body into my robe, run the towel over my hair, and quickly scrunch a quarter-sized dollop of gel into my loose curls before our servants arrive. The knock on the door coincides with me sliding my bag back under the bed, and I look up at Alessandra and wink.

Lucia lets herself in, joined by a short, heavyset woman who I assume is Alessandra's servant. I compare the two while they silently lay out our garments and notice how much younger Lucia is than the other woman; in fact, the more I think about it, I realize she's the youngest female servant in the entire house, which means she's probably the newest addition to the staff.

An interesting coincidence—two newbies stuck together.

I watch the older servant manhandle poor Alessandra and smile gratefully at Lucia. She may not be experienced, and she may've been a bit rough the other day when I was late, but she's always been kind. Maybe both being outsiders has helped us bond.

Tonight I forgo the linen shirt and begin the multi-layered dressing process with a long white gown. The neck is wide, and the skirt full. I run my hands along the scratchy fabric, expecting Lucia to hand me my beautiful ball gown next. But I look up to see the most feared contraption in period clothing, a torture device I believed I'd escaped.

She sees my expression and lifts an eyebrow. "Your corselet, Signorina." Her voice carries a lilt of humor, as if she understands my shock.

From the front, it appears innocuous enough. Glancing down as she wraps it around me, I see that it basically looks like a long girdle with an attached bra. But as she tightens the laces, forcing the flat bones running throughout the cruel undergarment to expel all my oxygen, its true evil identity is revealed.

I draw a ragged breath and jerk back as she pulls another lace taut. "A man," I say, the words coming out in short, stilted pants, "had to—invent this." I grunt as her fingers climb my upper back. "No woman—would do this—to herself."

Lucia pulls the last lace and I see spots on the edges of my vision. I hunch over, attempting to re-teach my crushed lungs how to breathe.

"Is the corselet different than you are used to, cousin?" Alessandra asks, her gaze darting to the servants and then to me in concern.

I wave weakly. "I'm fine," I huff. "Just catching my breath."

Standing back up, I cup my hands around my shrunken waist. It has to be at least three inches smaller, and my boobs are pressed flat, creating mounds of cleavage where there never was any before.

At least I can look like a Kardashian while hyper-ventilating all over the dance floor.

Lucia slides my royal-blue ball gown over my new figure as I fan myself, trying to lower my body temperature. The cone-shaped skirt and long train glide over my body. Jewels edge the square neck of the bodice, and silver thread embroidery loops under my chest, swooping down the dipped waistline.

The surcoat has separate sleeves, which Lucia slides over the linen gown underneath, attaching them at the shoulder with ribbon bows. Wide and billowed at the top, tapered to fit snugly at the wrists, the sleeves mimic the silver detailing, outlining each slash in the silk fabric. Lucia pulls puffs of white gown through the slashed sleeves, adding a striking contrast of color. Then she pins a large sapphire and pearl brooch on the bodice.

I collapse onto my stool as black stockings laced with

silver thread slide up my calves, held in place by ribbon garters adorned with little silver iris pendants. My feet slip into a pair of soft slippers.

Finally dressed, I spin around on the stool so Lucia can get to work on my hair. "Well, that was fun. And it only took us, what, an hour?"

Alessandra laughs and looks over from her stool next to mine, making her servant grumpy in the process. "You look stunning, C—Patience," she tells me, biting her lip at her almost slip-up. She mouths an apology and turns her head back to the wall. "You shall surely have your pick of dance partners this evening."

I shake my head and Lucia palms either side of my face to hold it still. "I only want to dance with Lorenzo." My previous fantasy fades before it can even fully materialize, a sudden thought knotting my stomach. "Hey, Less? Speaking of dances, what if I can't?"

"Whatever do you mean? You said yourself, you love to dance."

"Right, I do, but that was, um, back in *London*," I say, emphasizing the last word in the hopes she gets my meaning. "What if I can't follow the steps here?"

Alessandra turns to me, her hair twisted in knots with a sheer veil resting on top. "Everything will be perfect. Most of the dances are effortless; you simply follow your partner. If one is deemed complex, a dance master shall lead the entire party. Do not let needless anxiety burden you so."

"Burden?" asks a bubbly voice behind me. "What is burdening my children on such a night as this?"

Aunt Francesca brushes past and turns to face me while

Lucia finishes my hair. My heart twinges. Her wine-colored dress is the perfect accent against her olive complexion, and as I smile in acknowledgement of how beautiful she looks, I can't help but see my mother standing before me.

"Patience was inquiring in regards to Italian dances, Mama. She fears she will be unable to follow our unfamiliar footwork."

My aunt shakes her head and beams at me. "With the right partner, it shall feel as though you are gliding on air. Signore di Rialto is a talented dancer and I am certain he would be honored to share a dance with you. He appeared quite impressed with you at dinner."

"Niccolo?" I ask in surprise. It's a shame to admit, since he did hook me up with meeting my idol, but I haven't thought about him since we said good-bye yesterday.

"*Sì*, Niccolo. He is a good man, Patience. Did you not think so?"

"No, yeah, he's great," I say, trying to get a glimpse of what Lucia's creating on my head. When her hands tighten, effectively holding me in place, I sigh and smile at my aunt. "It's just that I plan to have my dance card filled by Lorenzo."

A wave of confusion passes over her face.

Lucia pats my head, letting me know she's done. I lean down and the small mirror perched on my stand reflects a sheer, shimmering veil draped over a crown of braided hair. "It's beautiful," I tell her, skimming my fingers over the filmy veil. "Thank you."

She nods and curtsies, then scurries out the door. I turn back to see my aunt and cousin exchanging a weighted look. But before I can ask what I missed, Aunt Francesca opens her arms and throws them around my shoulders.

"You are both visions of loveliness. Tonight, the D'Angeli women shall show Florence how one properly throws a ball!"

She steps out of the embrace and stoops down, making it so she's even with my stool, and gently runs the back of her finger along my cheek. Her smile is eerily reminiscent of Jenna. "Patience, I will do all that is in my power to minimize your distress this evening, though I have every confidence you will shine with the utmost grace and poise. Nonetheless, I shall remain by your side for as long as you need me."

Nodding, my aunt taps my chin and stands up. Alessandra joins her and they gaze down at me, still seated, unable to move.

My heart hammers. It's show time.

Chapter Thirteen

The rumble of voices, clinking silver, and soft music swells the landing as we stroll toward the ballroom. With each step taken down the stone stairs, my legs tremble more. I bunch the silk fabric of my dress in my hands and then smooth it back down again, breathing in shallow, quick gasps that strain against the unforgiving bones of my corset. I pause at the last step and close my eyes.

It'll be over soon. Lorenzo is waiting for me.

I meet Alessandra's concerned gaze and nod as I lean in to whisper, "Let's do this."

We enter the crowded room and my aunt pulls us to the side where we can watch from a shadowed corner. Servants in white frocks brush past our hiding space, carrying trays of delectable treats and extra candles. The immense room is aglow in candlelight, showering down from the rows of golden chandeliers hanging from the ceiling. Near the front of the room is a makeshift stage where a quartet of musicians stand, playing a lively, lilting tune. A flute, mandolin, harpsichord, and drum provide the soundtrack to what could end up being the best night of my life or my worst nightmare.

I'm seriously hoping for the former.

Another servant walks by carrying a tray of wine glasses and I reach out and snag one, hoping to rekindle the warm buzz that faded during the long and painful dressing process. The sickly sweet aroma tickles my nose as liquid courage pours down my throat. When that doesn't immediately calm my nerves, I pluck a pastry off the next passing tray. Fried dough, shaped like a pinecone, tasting of honey. If nothing else, the sugar rush should at least give me some happy endorphins.

The cool night breeze blows through the wall of opened doors to my right that lead out into the courtyard, ruffling the hem of my dress. I devour my calorie-packed treat and stand on tiptoe, twisting my head to search for Lorenzo's golden curls among the crowd. Just a glimpse of that side-grin of his will replace all my anxiety with nervous energy of a completely different sort. But the only thing I see is an endless row of bodies.

My aunt squeezes my hand and I pull my eyes away from the terrifying den I'm about to enter. She scrunches her nose and wipes her now-sticky hand on her dress. "It is time."

I sneak one last sip from my still-full wine glass before she pries it from my fingers and hands it to a passing servant. Cipriano and Uncle Marco join us and my uncle offers his elbow. I close my eyes, count to five, and exhale. When I open them, my uncle is smiling down at me. "Signorina, shall I escort you into your ball?"

With a weak nod, I thread my arm through his and take a shaky step. Then another. The crowd turns to watch as Aunt Francesca and my cousins fall in behind us, and we float to the makeshift stage. At least it feels as though we're floating because I cannot feel my feet. They are moving forward without my permission. I dare a glance into the crowd and see smiling faces sprinkled throughout a sea of appraising ones. It's just as I thought. They're watching, waiting for me to mess up.

I channel my inner-blasé, straightening my shoulders and pasting a sunny smile on my face as we turn at the front of the room.

"It is with great honor I present my niece, Signorina Patience D'Angeli," Uncle Marco says in a loud, booming voice. "Although she has been abroad for many years, she has come home to Italy. Let us welcome her this evening."

The crowd breaks into applause and I curtsy in lieu of standing frozen like a statue. My family remains by my side as a wave of people rush us. I stand silently as they talk over me, almost as if I'm not standing right here in front of them, sharing memories of when Patience was younger, and stories about her parents. Alessandra looks behind my aunt and rolls her eyes.

When the people do acknowledge me directly, my aunt actually helps me through it. She whispers names under her breath before they reach us; coaches me on what to say; and directs the conversation to safe, comfortable topics. I keep waiting for the other shoe to drop, for me to say the wrong thing or embarrass myself, but with Aunt Francesca's guidance, I don't even have the chance to "pull a Cat."

The last one to greet us is Niccolo. As he talks with my uncle, I lean back and grab Alessandra's hand. "Have you seen

Lorenzo?"

She shakes her head. "He is known for his unpredictability. I am sure he will arrive shortly." Her eyes dart in front of us and she bolts back in place.

"Signorina Patience," Niccolo says, bowing over my hand, "you are breathtaking this evening. A vision that would make even the esteemed Michelangelo weep."

A bit of an overkill, but sweet nonetheless. Understanding the rules of society better now, I curtsy in reply. "Thank you, Signore."

He continues to hold my hand and every eye in the room zeros back in on me. Alessandra watches through squinted eyes and my aunt nods at me encouragingly.

Um, okay. Confused, I give my aunt a small smile and nod back.

Uncle Marco waves to the seated quartet and they stand, conferring with one another.

"The first dance of the evening shall be *Branle des Lavandieres*," my uncle announces, and an excited hum bubbles from the crowd.

As couples pair up, I move to clear the dance floor, but Niccolo steps in front of me, blocking my path. He bows again and says, "Signorina, may I have the honor of the first dance?"

I quickly scan the room, hoping to see Lorenzo making his way toward me. But he's not here. My aunt gives me a not-so-gentle nudge and I shrug. What harm can a dance do? Besides, I still don't know what kind of business associate he is. *Not* dancing with Niccolo could very well cause a problem. I curtsy again—really getting the hang of it now—and say, "I'd love to."

The crowd parts for us as Niccolo guides me to the center

of the floor. He pulls me next to him in line and grabs my hand. The music begins and just as he did on the way to *David* yesterday, he spouts his wisdom, explaining the steps to me like I'm an idiot. The man really does love the sound of his own voice, but at least in this case it's warranted, since I *am* clueless.

Standing side-by-side and holding hands, we take two steps to the left and then two to the right. We do that again before Niccolo spins to face me, and we take turns wagging a finger at each other. I know I have to look ridiculous, but I can't help a small laugh at how silly Niccolo looks, staring at me so intently while shaking his finger at me like I'm a naughty five-year-old. At the sound of my laugh, the woman next to me glances over and gives me a meaningful smile.

My eyebrows furrow when Niccolo takes his place again at my side. As I clap along with the crowd and jump in a circle kicking my feet, I notice other women giving me the same smile or winking like we share some kind of secret. If we do, I wish they'd let me in on it.

With the staring completely unnerving me, I decide to make small talk so I can focus on anything else. Niccolo returns to my side and I say, "Um, thanks again for yesterday, introducing me to Michelangelo. That was amazing."

His blue eyes reflect back the lit candles above as he wags his finger at me. "The pleasure was mine. I enjoyed witnessing your enthusiasm for the art." He pauses and leans his mouth near my ear so I can hear him over the music. "I look forward to discovering more shared passions in the future."

My step falters at what his words could imply, but luckily the notes fade and the dance ends. I turn and study him with narrowed eyes. Niccolo's serious, icy blues stare back before he breaks into a smile. I shake off the weird vibe and take a step, only to jump as he places a searing hand on the small of my back.

He nods to the trays of goodies set up along the wall. "Shall we partake of the refreshments?"

Across the room, my uncle watches us intently, probably hoping I don't find a way to mess up his business arrangement. Refusing to go with Niccolo will cause my uncle embarrassment, so with still no sign of Lorenzo in the dispersed crowd, I sigh and let Niccolo escort me to the tables lining the far wall.

As we walk, I watch the way others respond to him. Especially women. Nodding, following him with their eyes, posing and lighting up in his presence.

Apparently, I'm the only one getting a bit of a creeper feel rolling off him.

We stop at one of the four buffet tables covered with white tablecloths and trays of delectable food. "You're well-respected in Florence," I tell him, stepping quickly from his hand. I get a good foot away and continue, "Everyone seems to love you. I'm curious what it is that grabs their attention. You're not royalty, are you?"

I wave my hand at the adoring crowd and catch a glimpse of Antonia a few feet away. Her eyes are slits of death directed straight at me. Why, I don't know. I've failed to insult Italian wine or pierced any eardrums so far this evening. I turn back to Niccolo and he chuckles.

"No," he says, motioning toward a tray of radishes carved into animal shapes. I wrinkle my nose, and he plucks a duck and hands it to me anyway. "But it is my belief that one gets back what he puts out. The only way to truly earn regard is to conduct oneself with the utmost honor and respect."

I stare at him, trying to figure him out. If his goal is to gain public respect, then he does a good job. Everyone here seems to worship him—including my own family. Maybe our problem is a century barrier. What comes across as patronizing and chauvinistic to me may be perfectly acceptable to women from his time.

I nod and look back over the crowd, grateful to see Antonia no longer there. "That is a good belief, Signore di Rialto. You are a smart man."

"Thank you, Signorina." He pauses, perhaps to watch the crowd as well, and then says, "And please, call me Niccolo."

His husky whisper is at my ear. I flinch in surprise and turn to see he's covered the distance I put between us. He takes the radish from my hand and replaces it with a pear, grinning at me as his finger traces a lazy circle across my palm. I yank it back, my heart pounding in my chest. I shakily lift the fruit to my mouth and turn back to the crowd, frantically searching for Lorenzo.

But he already found me.

"Lorenzo!" I squeal, surprised and relieved to see him suddenly appear at my elbow. "I was looking for you. I am *so* glad you're here."

I drink in his dark green doublet jacket, shockingly set off against his golden curls, and all the worries of the night and the creeptastic vibe rolling off Niccolo disappear. Lorenzo looks dashing and regal and all those other adjectives used to describe heroes in classic novels—but as I grin into his chocolate brown eyes, I notice he's not equally enamored with *my* presence. In fact, he's not even looking at me. He's nailing Niccolo with a lethal stare.

Niccolo's previous grin vanishes as he meets Lorenzo's hostile glare.

"Um, Niccolo was kind enough to instruct me in my first Italian dance," I say, trying to break the tension. "*And* I only managed to step on his toes twice—okay, maybe a little more than that, but considering the public debacle at Antonia's house, I'd say that's an improvement."

Not even a twitch of a smile from Lorenzo at my rambling self-deprecation.

The two of them remain locked in their silent challenge. Having a guy act jealous over me, ready to defend my honor, is not an experience I ever expected. And honestly, it sucks. If the two of them break into a brawl right now, it'll ruin my aunt's night. Not to mention whatever deal my uncle's working on.

Lorenzo's nostrils flare and I put my hand on his tense arm. I don't get it—Niccolo *was* acting skeezy and inappropriate, but he's way too old for Lorenzo to honestly think of as competition!

Niccolo breaks the standoff and puts his hand on my elbow, narrowing his eyes when he sees my hand on Lorenzo's arm. "Patience, I shall leave you now." The words are directed at me, but he's speaking straight at Lorenzo. "I have business to discuss with your uncle, but I will see you again *tomorrow*."

He delivers that last word with a weird twinge to his voice and a sardonic smile. Then with a light squeeze on my elbow, Niccolo walks away.

Lorenzo's chest rises rapidly as he watches Niccolo make his way alongside the edge of the dance floor to my uncle. Tension stiffens Lorenzo's shoulders as Uncle Marco enthusiastically greets Niccolo, clapping him on the shoulder like an old friend.

This is so not how I envisioned the night going.

"Lorenzo?" I ask, trying to regain control of the situation. "Are you mad at me for something?"

His eyes, a stormy, roiling sea, snap back to me and a shadow crosses his face. He shakes his head and closes his eyes, breathing in deeply. When he exhales audibly, his eyes open — sad but softer, the storm within subsided. "I am the one acting disagreeable. Nothing is your fault." He takes a step back, his head hung low. "If you'll excuse me for a moment."

After a few more steps, he attempts a smile. Then the crowd swallows him.

I stare dumbfounded at the space he disappeared from, and then play back the last few minutes.

Did that really just happen? I blink and shake my head, but nothing changes.

"You certainly know how to keep things entertaining, cousin," Alessandra says, walking up beside me.

"Less, did you see that?" I tear my gaze from the dance floor and throw my hands up in confusion. "What the heck just happened? Did I miss something? I mean, Niccolo's flirting was borderline gross on a massive scale considering his age and all, but I don't think Lorenzo even saw that. What is his deal?"

She wraps her arm around me. "I believe this is where your unfamiliarity with our time is most evident," she says, casting a glance around to see if anyone is within listening distance. "Niccolo is held in high esteem by all of society. He is quite wealthy and pays his servants more than their share." I raise my eyebrows and lift my shoulders, not seeing how any of that connects to what just went down, and she heaves a sigh. Leveling me with an exasperated look, she explains, "Cat, Niccolo is at the age where he is ready to be married. A fact of which our young Lorenzo is quite aware."

I laugh—hysterically. I can't help it. It's probably from exhaustion as much as mystification.

"Lorenzo cannot think Niccolo would really want *me*. I'm, like, less than half his age! That's just…disgusting," I tell her, wiggling my shoulders at the thought.

Alessandra shakes her head. "You are not thinking like a maiden from the sixteenth century. Niccolo has known my family for years, and I have secretly wondered if he would find me an agreeable match. But I am only fourteen, and so not yet the age for marriage."

I decide to let that revolting thought slide for now and ask, "Surely I'm not marriage age yet, either, right?"

In reply, Alessandra lifts her chin toward the open courtyard where the Stefani clan stands together. "Antonia is sixteen as well, and I believe she and her family have had designs on Signore di Rialto for quite some time." My jaw drops, and she grins. "So you see, while it may not be the way things are done in the future, in my world you are a perfectly acceptable age for matrimony."

"Yeah, well," I sputter, scanning the dancing crowd again, this time seeing the age differences among the couples. My gaze lands on my aunt and uncle. I never really noticed or cared, but Uncle Marco's easily into his fifties and Aunt Francesca can't be older than mid-thirties. I swallow and turn back to Alessandra. "You're right. That is *not* how things are done where I come from."

The song ends and a horde of people rush us at the refreshment table. We step to the side and I throw my pear on the tray for trash. I can't eat. My appetite left with Lorenzo.

A young man separates himself from the group and walks up to Alessandra, looking shy and awkward. "Eh, m-may I have the pleasure of this next dance, Signorina D'Angeli?" he asks, his voice squeaking at the end.

Her pale white neck turns crimson as she nods. She turns back to me and widens her eyes. I raise an eyebrow and mouth, "He's cute." She flattens her mouth in a nervous grimace, and I give her a push. With a squeak, she lets him escort her to the floor.

A new dance begins, this one mostly involving a lot of walking back and forth and pausing before turning in a circle. To keep from thinking about Lorenzo, I watch the couples dance in unison. The circular patterns they make and the array of colorful skirts swishing across the floor are interesting at first, but as they repeat the same steps over and over, I grow incredibly bored, incredibly fast. My thoughts turn back to my Renaissance hottie, as they have so many times the last few days. I wish he'd come back. Now that I know why he reacted the way he did, I can *kind of* understand.

He was still a hothead, but at least an understandable hothead.

Near the end of the song, I get my wish. I spot him making his way toward me and he bites his lip, looking sheepish. Any annoyance I still held vanishes instantly. I smile at him and the etched lines in his face disappear.

"You are an angel, a vision sent from Signore," he says, repeating the line he gave me at the marketplace. He grins and looks at the ground. "When we first met, I thought you could never be more beautiful—but I was wrong." He lifts his head, and warmth pools in my belly. "Tonight, you shine brighter than any diamond."

Now this is more like it.

A passing couple bumps into Lorenzo from behind, and the two men share apologies. He waits until they have walked away before saying, "I must apologize for my reprehensible behavior earlier. I thought—" He breaks off and shakes his head, then meets my gaze. "It matters not what I thought. I acted dishonorably toward your guest and it is my prayer that you can forgive me."

I place my hand on his arm. "There is nothing to forgive."

The intense look he gives me makes my breath catch. "I would ask for the honor of the next dance, but I must confess I have never been very good at it. I fear Signore graced me with two left feet."

I look out at the dancers as they repeat the same boring, silly steps again and shake my head. "You know, back home we have a much simpler dance." I stop as a crazy idea takes shape in my mind. Stepping closer, I whisper, "Meet me outside by the garden."

He furrows his brow and I smile, then I take off through the crowd.

Outside, the cool air is a welcome relief to the crowded room fueled by body heat. There are pockets of people milling about, but I know the perfect spot. Tucked away to the back of the courtyard is a garden filled with large shrubs and fragrant flowers, where the sound of the music still hangs in the air. The glow of the candlelight just reaches it, but it is dark enough so we can avoid discovery.

As I wait for Lorenzo, I consider which dance to teach him. One option is the good old "press your bodies together and sway" bit that most couples do at school dances, but as much as Lorenzo flaunts society's rules when it comes to flirting with me, that may just scandalize the poor boy. So instead, I decide on the waltz.

Dad taught it to me when I was a little girl standing on his feet and since then, it's been our thing. He loves putting on his old records—yes, the man still owns records—and coaxing me off the comfortable sofa to dance around the living room. And although I don't believe in falling in love or getting married, as we dance, I always pretend it's my wedding day. When I was younger, my groom was always my dad, and as I grew older, the groom morphed into whatever teen celebrity was hot at the moment. But waltzing with Lorenzo won't be a game of pretend.

My heart pounds in excitement.

"Patience?"

Lorenzo's cautious voice cuts through the night air and I step out from the darkened space. "I thought we agreed you'd call me Cat," I tease in a playful voice, suddenly feeling a bit seductive.

Back home, I've never trusted a guy's motives for approaching me. It's always been about my parents—who they are, the connections they have, and what people assume I'll be like because of them—so if and when a guy did approach me, I pushed him away with witty comments or casual indifference. I assumed that if I *had* been built with the flirtatious gene everyone else seems to have naturally, my non-use made it die a slow and painful death.

But being with Lorenzo has woken something inside me. When I'm with him, I feel nervous and giddy, desired and *sexy*. I don't want to push him away—I want to pull him closer and closer.

Maybe I inherited a bit of that temptress side from Mom after all.

Lorenzo's perfectly shaped lips kick up into a smile. "My apologies, Signorina." He looks around my secret rendezvous spot and lifts an eyebrow. "Whatever do you plan to do with me in such a hidden place, *Cat*?"

I stare at those perfect lips, remembering our kiss.

Oh, I have a few ideas.

Aloud I say, "I'm all dressed up and I want to dance. With you."

He starts to squirm and I can't help but giggle. I grab his right hand and wrap it around me so it rests on the middle of my back. He's so close I can feel his warm breath fan across my face. My eyelids flutter, and I inhale his woodsy male scent and get drunk on his nearness.

It's funny. I tried all day to get a good buzz to take the edge off my nerves, and all I needed was Lorenzo. This natural buzz doesn't relax me, however. It electrifies me.

Lorenzo pulls me closer, then looks at my mouth and bites his lip. My knees go weak and all I want to do is grab the back of his head and kiss him until I can't see straight—but I'm determined to have my vision play out. There will be plenty of time for *that* later.

"I thought I'd teach you a dance from where I come from," I tell him. "One that's much easier than that multi-step mess inside."

I place my left hand on his shoulder and slip my right one into his. I pause to listen to the music floating over the tinkling voices and bubbling fountain, and begin counting the three-beat tempo. "One, two, three. One, two, three."

I stand still, only my head moving, slowly nodding with my words so he can hear the rhythm.

When his head begins subtly bobbing with mine, I show him how to add his feet. He takes a tentative step forward with his left while I step back with my right, then we side step, close, and repeat the steps with our other feet, all while I lightly whisper the beat count.

The breeze picks up, blowing my skirt and skimming my veil across the back of my neck. Chills run down my spine, but the warmth coursing through my veins from being in his arms provides a delicious contradiction.

Lorenzo continues nervously darting his eyes to our feet, but he *is* dancing. As he relaxes into the movement, his shoulders rising and falling with the steps, the confidence he always seems to exude creeps back on his face, and he tightens the hold around me. Our faces are kissably close, our lips a hairs breadth away from touching.

I stare into the chocolate depths of his eyes and the rest of the ball fades away. The only music guiding our steps is my light whisper and the erratic rhythm of our breathing. Time slows. Lorenzo grins.

"I think you got it," I say breathlessly, running my hand along the soft fabric of his shoulder, feeling the rock-hard muscles underneath.

My body curls inward, pressing against his. The proper form for the waltz is a straight spine and shoulders back, but if there was ever a time to break the rules, this is it. I lay my cheek against his chest, hearing the staccato beat of his heart. My hand slides up the length of his arm, over his shoulder, and around his neck. His breath catches, but he slips his other arm around my back, pressing me even closer. Longing makes my stomach swirl, and I'm lost in unprecedented *want*.

Our steps slow until we are standing still, holding onto each other. I raise my head and Lorenzo's gaze travels from my eyes, to my mouth, and back again, asking for permission.

I lick my lips and he draws in a breath.

One of his hands travels slowly across my waist, inching up the soft silk of my bodice to my chin. His other hand skims along my arm and he cups my jaw in his hands, the tips of his fingers buried in my hair. Tilting my face toward his, he leans down and trails a line of soft kisses from my forehead, to my feathered closed eyelids, to the tip of my nose, and finally my mouth.

Our second kiss is gentle and passionate, tentative and hungry, all at once. My fingers thread through his curls and clasp around his head, tugging him to me. He tastes like the wildflower honey pastries inside, sweet and intoxicating. I explore his mouth, starting with his soft lips, and when he deepens the kiss, the warm cavern inside. I sigh against him and a tremor rocks my body. He breaks away from the kiss, his dazed eyes meeting mine, making sure I'm okay before he kisses me again and again—our lips settling into the rhythm of a different dance.

His thumbs draw light circles along my cheeks. I suck on his lower lip and the moan that escapes his throat makes me ache.

A rough cough breaks our trance. Lorenzo rips his lips away

from mine and pulls me behind him, shielding me with his body. He looks out into the darkness, searching for anyone who could be spying on us. After a few moments, and after my breathing has almost returned to normal, he slowly turns to look at me. His lips are swollen and flushed crimson. I lean on tiptoe to kiss him again, but he steps back with pain in his eyes.

I shiver, instantly colder without his body heat. I wrap my arms around my chest and look at the ground.

Did I do something wrong?

"I could not live with myself if we were to be discovered," he says, his fingers lacing through mine. "Your reputation could be ruined." I shake my head, not caring about reputations or discovery, and he presses a gentle kiss to my hand. "Cat, trust that I do not wish to leave your arms tonight. Not ever. But this is a ball in celebration of you, and I will not be the cause of your ruination. Now, make haste back to the ballroom. I shall wait a moment then follow so we will not appear to have been together."

The whole cloak-and-dagger scenario seems ridiculous, but I see the determination in Lorenzo's eyes, along with the fear. Nodding regretfully, I smooth down my dress to make sure I don't look rumpled. I pat my hair and breathe deeply. I take a step and turn back, leaning in to press a final kiss against his lips.

Then I flee to the party, running away while I still can.

In the candlelit courtyard, I make my way to the crowded ballroom with my head down. As I pass the fountain, my thoughts are on Lorenzo and the amazing feelings shooting throughout my body, and I fail to pay attention to my surroundings.

"Having an agreeable time, Patience?"

I look up into Antonia's smirk and for the first time, I get what Lorenzo was so worried about. Did she see where I came from? I quickly glace back, telepathically begging Lorenzo to stay hidden just a little while longer.

"Of course; everything's perfect," I say, walking away and hoping she'll follow.

The smirk never wavers as she slowly falls in step behind me. We are almost to the wall of doors leading inside when she looks back, just as Lorenzo scampers out from behind the garden. He sees us standing together and freezes, eyes widened.

Bowing uncomfortably, he says, "Ladies." When he stands back up, I see the panic in his eyes. Of all the people to discover us, Antonia has to be the worst.

She chuckles as she watches him dash inside. "My, my, my. Tonight has certainly been enlightening. It's a pity so few have come outside to enjoy the fresh air—you *could* say the real night's entertainment is here."

Antonia's eyes cut back to me, laughter dancing in her brown irises. But I refuse to squirm. Controlling my face, I meet her amused expression with one of my own, realizing she could totally be bluffing. "I assure you, I don't know what you're talking about."

I lift my chin and take a step, nearly tripping as she says, "Patience, if I may, let me give you some advice."

Advice. *Right.* Because the shrew of Florence is probably great at that. And would obviously have my best interests at heart.

I turn my head, incredulous, but the glint in her cool gaze stops the rebuttal I had formed on my lips. Strangely intrigued to hear what she could possibly offer as advice, I nod stiffly, totally poised to cut her off at a moment's notice.

Antonia purses her lips as she scans me from head to toe, the combination of the night breeze and her blatant disapproval making me shiver. "Unfortunately, we cannot all fashion ourselves into true ladies. And while I do not even begin to comprehend the foolish workings of the male mind, the truth is this: you would do yourself good to focus your romantic attachments on Signore di Rialto."

She pauses as I reel back, absorbing that absurd bomb with about as much grace as an elephant, and a pitying smile replaces her previous smirk.

Somehow, the effect is even crueler.

She wiggles her fingers in a dismissive gesture and sighs. "Go. Enjoy your little *dalliance* with young Lorenzo tonight. Get the boy out of your system, soak up every glorious minute…and then in the morning, wake up from this dream world you both seem to inhabit."

My head spins from her unique mixture of stinging insult and pure insanity. I open my mouth wanting to laugh, and instead brilliantly say, "Excuse me?"

Looking past the enormous *ick* factor of the older man thing, Alessandra just got through telling me that Antonia wants Niccolo for herself. Why on earth would the girl be trying to pawn him off on me?

I tilt my head and examine her, searching for her angle, knowing there has to be one.

Antonia shrugs her dainty shoulders. "Making a good match with a respectable man is about all we can ask for in this life. And if that man happens to love you, all the better. Anyone can see the way Signore di Rialto watches you. Marry him; give up the fantasy of Lorenzo."

This night has simply been too much. First, the anxiety over standing before a crowded room while everyone scrutinizes my every move. Then Niccolo's creepy flirtation, not to mention the showdown between him and Lorenzo, followed by the most amazing moment of my life, and now this. I roll my eyes.

Antonia's arm juts out to stop me from walking away.

"You are no better than the rest of us, Patience D'Angeli," she spits at me, her eyes narrowing into slits. "This is how real life works. It is time to abandon playthings and the ways of childhood and step into womanhood. Accept the blessings you are being given, or someone else *will*."

And with that parting bit of wisdom, she gives me an enraged once over and sashays away. At the door, she casts a final pointed glance in my direction and then disappears.

By the time I finally make it back inside, I'm emotionally drained. I just went from elated to seething in a nanosecond and my tired brain cannot keep up. The party's still raging, with couples dancing merrily on the dance floor and chatting on the sidelines. I don't see Lorenzo in the crowd, but I do spot Niccolo near the front of the stage.

I duck into the shadowed corner my aunt showed me earlier.

Sinking down the wall to the floor, I hold my head in my hands to process. All I want is to be alone in the seclusion of my room so I can replay the magic of the Lorenzo portion of the night and forget everything else.

I stand, trying to think of the best way to escape the party, when tidbits of a nearby conversation catch my attention. Mostly because it's about me.

"London must be worse than we thought," a shrill voice says. "The girl is completely ill-bred. She cannot sing or play music, and she is entirely too headstrong and free spirited. Francesca, you certainly have your work cut out for you if you expect to land her a decent match."

Francesca? My aunt is out there?

I lean closer toward the sound of the voices. I knew I couldn't trust her.

"Shut your mouth, Filippa." I shrink back at the venom laced in my aunt's usually chirpy voice. "I shall not tolerate you disrespecting my family in my own home. Patience is a beautiful, lovely, intelligent girl. Any man would be blessed to have her by his side. And anyone who does not agree can leave. In fact, they must. *Lucia.*" My aunt's voice raises and I hear scampering feet along with shocked intakes of air.

"Signora, do you require my assistance?" Lucia's familiar voice is added to the floating headless movie playing in my mind.

"See to it that Signora Benedicti and Signora Cacchioni have everything they require. They are leaving us."

No one could ignore or mistake the tone of finality in my aunt's voice.

Wow. I close my mouth and feel the prick of tears behind my eyes.

I wait until the *click-clack*ing of shoes disappears before I step out of the shadows. Aunt Francesca's still standing there, silently fuming. Her cheeks are flushed, her lips taut.

"You showed them," I say, walking up beside her.

She jerks her head in surprise and gnaws at her lip. "You overheard that horrid woman?"

I nod and she glances back at the door, her kind eyes hardening into shards of ice.

"I also heard you kick some Italian butt," I tell her. "Who knew you had a vicious streak?"

Her eyes widen but when she sees my teasing smile, she laughs.

Pulling me into a hug she says, "It is not common knowledge. However, if someone disrespects my children…" She trails off and leans back, her soft gaze traveling across my face. "Patience, I pray you realize how much I consider you to be my daughter. I could never replace sweet Maria, Signore rest her precious soul, but it would be a great honor to be a mother to you."

She stares at me, waiting for a response. The look in her eye is so serious, so believable, but the smile on her face is back, reminding me again of Jenna.

My aunt is asking me to trust her, to let myself believe in the love she's offering me. A big part of me wants to say yes, to use this time as an experiment in what it would feel like to have an actual mother who cares about me.

But I don't know if I can take another rejection.

So I smile and hug her again in response to the silent question in her eyes. It may not be the answer she wants, but it's the only one I can give.

Chapter Fourteen

I spend the morning tucked away in my room, staring moony-eyed at my rumpled ball gown and running a finger over the wrinkles, remembering with a smile how they got there. Every caress of Lorenzo's fingers, every brush of his lips in the darkness. The way he held me in his arms while we danced, the way he looked at me before leaning down to kiss me.

And I spend a whole lot of time wondering when I can see him again.

The morning has been quiet, with everyone sleeping in after the late-night revelry. Even the servants are hushed, probably under strict orders not to disturb our sleep. Left to my own devices, I grab my sketchpad and box of pastels and attempt to recreate the magic of last night. The dappled moonlight filtering through the trees, the way Lorenzo's curls danced in the light breeze. I chew on my bottom lip as I try to capture the perfection that is his grin and the slightly crooked tooth it exposes. Then I lean back and compare it with Lorenzo's drawing of me.

The beauty of the memory, and my Italian subject, has added a new quality to my work. There is a lightness, a wistfulness to the strokes that I've never before been able to achieve. I'm not too proud to admit Lorenzo's is better—but considering the fact he's been soaking up the mojo in the Renaissance air for eighteen years, second place ain't too shabby.

With a grin, I roll them both up and put them in my backpack. Then with Lucia still not beating down my door, I break out my toiletries from home. After brushing my teeth, washing my face, and running my boar-bristle brush through the ringlets running down my back, I slip into a sea-foam-green surcoat and waltz around my room to the rumbles emanating from my empty stomach, pondering the likelihood of anyone getting up any time soon to feed me. I haven't eaten since the cast-aside pear at the ball.

Lucia's distinguishable knock, rapid fire and purposeful, beats against my door just as I reach inside my backpack for the peppermint I shoved to the bottom last week.

"Come in," I call, pushing the bag back under the bed.

Please be here to tell me food is coming.

My always serious servant sticks her petite head inside and appraises my outfit. "Your uncle has summoned you to his *studiolo*. He says he has an urgent matter to discuss."

"An urgent matter?" I ask, shooting to my feet. I wonder if people use that word as casually in the past as they do in the future. At certain times of the month, I've considered chocolate consumption an urgent matter.

Lucia nods and I follow her out into the hall. She points a finger toward my uncle's private chambers and then briskly takes off in the opposite direction.

Okay, then.

I walk down the winding hallways between the two rooms, my slippers a soft whisper along the rugs, and consider all the possible things my uncle could need to speak with me about.

I come up with nothing.

Outside the heavy wooden door to my uncle's *studiolo*, I stop and listen, hoping to hear Alessandra's chirpy voice inside or coming up the corridor behind me. But all I hear is silence. Suddenly feeling as though I've been called to the principal's office, I brace myself. I take a deep breath and knock.

"Come in, dear!"

Not my chirpy cousin, but my cheerful aunt—that has to be a good sign. If she's inside, I couldn't be in too much trouble, right?

Relieved, I relax my shoulders and let myself in.

Aunt Francesca beams at me from her position next to Uncle Marco on the other side of his massive desk. Both of them look euphoric, as though they just won the lottery. And since I know they're in no way hurting for cash, I can only assume it means one thing. I'm in for another surprise. My shoulders tense right back up.

"You wanted to see me, Uncle?" I ask, holding tightly to the memory of dancing in Lorenzo's arms. *Not all surprises end badly.*

Uncle Marco waves me in and claps his hands together. "*Sì, sì!* Please, Patience, come in and rest yourself." He indicates the large rug-covered chair opposite him, the one Niccolo sat in the last time I was here, then strides to close the door, testing the knob once he does to ensure it's shut.

My aunt rounds the desk, takes my hands in hers, and says, "Your uncle and I have *glorious* news of your future to share with you!"

The Jenna-like enthusiasm scares me. The cords of her neck bulge in a barely contained reaction to whatever earth-shattering information she believes she holds, and when my uncle joins her, they both stare at me with matching smiles of glee.

Not all surprises are bad, I tell myself again. Maybe when she says *future* she means later today, when she'll be taking me clothes shopping or to an art gallery. Or maybe we're going on a trip somewhere, like Rome or Venice, or somewhere equally as cool.

Wringing my hands together, trying to hold on to a shred of optimism, I repeat to myself: *Lorenzo, Lorenzo, Lorenzo*. "Okay," I say, forcing a smile. "Lay it on me."

My aunt lifts her eyebrows at my uncle. He adds his hand to our joined ones, puffs his chest with pride, and says, "Your betrothal has been arranged."

Muted voices from the street float through the open window behind the desk. I blink and stare at my uncle, noting his expectant expression, and wait for my brain to comprehend what he really just said. Clearly, the message scrambled in translation.

Am I losing my Italian decoding skills?

A nervous jolt shoots through me. Maybe the gypsy magic is wearing off. If so, does that mean I'm going to be leaving soon?

My aunt squeezes my hand, jiggling it up and down, bringing me back to the *urgent* news they have to discuss. She widens her eyes and nods repeatedly.

Squinting, I tilt my head and scrunch my nose. "I'm sorry, what did you say?"

Her delighted smile lessens by a degree, and this time she's the one who speaks. "Your betrothal, dear. It has been arranged."

The same message as before but this time delivered in a different voice. Aunt Francesca's words slowly sink into my gray matter…and I bust out laughing. I never took my aunt and uncle for practical jokesters, but I'm pleasantly surprised to see they have a sense of humor.

They exchange a look of confusion, and Aunt Francesca frowns. "I do not understand your response, Patience. Is it from merriment that you laugh so?"

I wait for their masks to crack, for them to laugh and call an end to this strange form of teasing. But if anything, their faces just become grimmer. My laughter trails off and I shift my gaze back and forth between them. "Wait, you guys are serious?"

Her eyes fill with concern. "Very much so."

Perplexed, I open my mouth, then close it, then open it again. "And who, exactly, would I be marrying?"

A muscle in my uncle's jaw jumps. "Signore di Rialto, of course." Horror locks my spine and the world tilts as he folds his arms across his chest. "Niccolo made his intentions to take you as his wife quite clear. Surely you suspected as much last night."

I grip the sides of my chair, realizing this time there was no translation error. "*Niccolo?* You're telling me that Niccolo wants to marry me. He actually said those words?"

Uncle Marco nods. "As soon as an approval from a notary is obtained, though I dare say that shall take no longer than a few days."

Blood rushes from my face. My heart pounds faster as the world closes in around me.

A few days?

I've already been here a few days. A few days are nothing. Who's to say gypsy magic will swoop in and save me in a few more?

My lungs feel as though they've collapsed inside my chest. I struggle to catch my breath as a cold sweat breaks across my upper lip. A deep chill runs down my body from head to toe and my legs tense.

I spring from my chair on autopilot and tear through the door, faintly hearing Aunt Francesca call out after me. I don't stop running until my knees scrape against the marble steps of the fountain in the courtyard.

Wrapping my arms tightly around my mid-section, I close my eyes and rock. This isn't happening. This isn't real. I'm gonna open my eyes and wake up, and realize this whole thing has been one really, really long dream.

One, two, three, open.

Smooth white marble shimmers up at me, reflecting the almost noonday sun, and I gingerly touch it.

I'm still here. And this time travel thing has officially become real. I need to get home. Whatever voodoo curse that gypsy put on me has to end. Now.

Before I become someone's wife!

Niccolo's wife.

I pull at my hair and shake my head over and over, the icky feeling of Niccolo's finger trailing across my palm last night washing over me.

Be sure to keep your mind open to the lessons ahead.

That's what Reyna said. Somehow, those words hold the key to getting me back to the twenty-first century. I stare helplessly into the depths of the fountain and replay those words over and over, hoping my brain can figure out the message's meaning while the rest of me drifts in a state of numbness.

A hand rests on my shoulder, and I dazedly look up into my aunt's concerned gaze. "It was our hope this news would be met with an entirely different reaction," she says with a sigh, sitting beside me. She stares into the fountain for a long moment before saying, "I am aware of your attachment to the Cappelli boy."

I stay quiet, trying to quell the trembling in my limbs, fearing that if I say anything it'll make this real.

Aunt Francesca lifts her head. "I had a romance of my own when I was your age, before I met your uncle." She pauses and chuckles softly at the memory. "Like Lorenzo, he was shy of the age of marriage, but my heart did not care."

Lorenzo.

The pain in my gut twists again as I think about him. My shoulders curl to my knees, my chin burrows into my chest, and I draw ragged, shallow breaths. I feel her rub the top of my head, running her fingers along my hair.

"It ended, of course, as your entanglement must, and that is when my father arranged my union with Marco. He was older than I, and much wiser. In all honesty, I was scared to death. But together, your uncle and I have created a wonderful life. Two beautiful children and years of memories."

After a moment, I hear her get up, but she doesn't walk away. She simply stands there silently, perhaps waiting for me to say something. When I don't, she sighs again. "That is the life we want for you, Patience, and you can have it with Niccolo. Open your heart to him; see what a good man he is. Do you understand how rare that is to find? As his helpmeet, you shall be cared for and protected. In this world, that is more than most can ever hope to achieve."

But I'm not from this world!

Of course, I don't say this aloud. Even if she would understand, the thought of speaking right now seems impossible.

My aunt presses a kiss on the crown of my head, and from my semi-fetal position, I watch her tiny feet disappear up the stairs. I hold out for as long as I can before I dash upstairs myself, peering around the corner to make sure the coast is clear, and darting inside my room, slamming the door behind me.

In the safety of the now-familiar four walls, my legs give way and I fall to the floor. Crawling over to the bed, I realize I haven't cried or screamed or done any of the things a normal person might do when faced with something like this. It would appear all the years I spent living behind a mask have dulled my senses.

Instead, I yank my beloved backpack from under the bed, rip it open, and dump out the contents. I pick up each item, holding them and remembering little details—where and when I bought them, times I used them—reminding myself they are real. That I don't belong here. That I'm not crazy.

My gaze lands on my iPhone and my heart jumps. I turn it on and my screensaver springs to life, a picture of Dad and me sitting in front of a monitor on one of his sets. With shaking fingers, I scroll through my contact list and tap on Dad's name.

For a split second, I fool myself into thinking it'll work. That he'll answer and come riding in to save me. But of course, that doesn't happen. They don't have service towers in the 1500s. Dejected, I fling the phone and watch it crash into the painted chest in the corner of the room.

Hanging over the chest is my wrinkled ball gown from last night. Another wrenching pain twists my stomach and I hurl myself facedown onto the mattress.

• • •

The Piazza Mercato Vecchio is crowded, and everyone is watching us. Somehow, without the use of Facebook, Twitter, or text messages, word has already spread about our *betrothal*. Just the word makes me shiver. I look at the man walking next to me and narrow my eyes.

It doesn't even faze him.

Grinning at the people gawking, Niccolo puts his hand on my elbow and leads me past the beggars on the stone steps asking for alms. I want to stop and help them, but I don't have any pockets or a purse, and let's face it—at this point, I'll be lucky to help myself.

"Patience," he says, leaning close so no one can overhear us, "I understand if you do not yet love me, but you will learn to do so in time."

I stop walking so I can laugh incredulously—any concern I had about messing up his business arrangement with Uncle

Marco went out the window with the words *your betrothal has been arranged*—and Cipriano crashes into me. My cousin is acting as my chaperone again this afternoon, but this time I'm eternally grateful. Hours after barricading myself in my room, Niccolo showed up all smiling and ready to "discuss our future." My aunt and uncle practically pushed me out the door, but the only thing that really got me to leave was Cipriano offering to tag along as guardian.

My cousin apologizes for running into me and takes several steps to the side to give us privacy. I really wish he wouldn't.

Niccolo's lips flatten into a straight line and he sighs in annoyance. I'm sure this isn't how he thought our talk would go. With the way women usually act around him, he probably expected me to fall at his feet and thank him for deeming me worthy.

But yeah, that's not happening.

With a quick look to our audience, I fist my hands on my hips and attempt to control my voice. "Niccolo, *why* do you want to marry me?"

The question, as weird as it feels rolling off my tongue, has to be asked. There's still a chance we can stop this whole thing from happening if I can just talk some sense into him.

His eyes narrow. "Because you're perfect."

I snort at his haughty tone and throw my hands in the air. "No, I'm not!"

A group of men passing by us abruptly stops. They smirk at one another and step closer in the obvious hopes of eavesdropping better. The sound of Niccolo's jaw clicking is magnified with the now-hushed crowd around us, and for a moment, I consider making a big old scene—throwing a temper tantrum, flinging a few insults, and putting all my trashy talk-show viewing to good use. A man who worries so much about honor and respect wouldn't want the *little lady* mouthing off in public. But my behavior would also mortify Cipriano...and my aunt and uncle. They don't deserve that, even if they do want to marry me off to an old geezer.

So I close the distance between Niccolo and me by a fraction and lower my voice. "You don't even know me."

Niccolo's gaze flicks over to Cipriano as if he can't believe I have the audacity to challenge him. Cipriano stares stonily back—and I don't even attempt to hide my smile.

Ha ha. He's on my side, Big Guy.

Niccolo huffs in exasperation. His nostrils flare as he pastes a tight-lipped smile onto his face. "You are mistaken, my dear. I'm aware of your love for art, your light feet on the dance floor, your clever mind, and your occasional sharp tongue, though I dearly hope that last quality grows tempered with time."

He smiles at the crowd now straining to listen and lifts his chin in acknowledgment, rolling his eyes as if to say, *Women, whatcha gonna do?*

Then those cool blue eyes bore into mine and he lowers his voice so only I can hear. "You are but a young girl with much left to learn, though soon you will come to your senses. We have common interests as well as family connections, and we will make a good match. It is what is expected. And it *is* what will happen. It would behoove you to accept it."

He exhales and his face relaxes as though we've merely been disagreeing about the weather or what color curtains to put up in our future love nest. I throw my head into my hands, my mouth open in a silent, humorless laugh. I'm aware of the women in the crowd shooting daggers at me, pulling their daughters close to them as if to shield them from me. That's the worst part—well, no, potentially being stuck here and marrying this guy is the worst part, but it definitely sucks that if I were a normal Renaissance teen, marrying Niccolo would probably seem like I hit the jackpot. Girls here grow up expecting to hook up with an older man, and they have no clue that in healthy relationships, one where the dude isn't old enough to be your father, a man and a woman get married because they both want to, not because she's been handed over like some kind of prized cattle.

Not that I actually know anything about healthy relationships personally, but Dr. Phil certainly seems to.

Inhaling a slow breath, I turn to tell Niccolo this marriage is only happening over my dead body, but no words come out. Because at the end of the square, Lorenzo appears. He intently scans the crowd as if searching for something—or someone. We lock eyes, and that devastating smile crosses his face.

Then he sees who stands beside me.

"Cat!"

I bite my lip from calling out to him. Cipriano, though he doesn't understand the name, recognizes Lorenzo's voice and immediately sets off toward his friend, calling a belated "Excuse me" over his shoulder.

"Whatever is he…" Niccolo's voice trails off as he looks in the direction Cipriano charged and sees Lorenzo approaching us. A vein in his temple pops as he works his jaw back and forth. A low growl emanates from his chest.

Antonia.

As Niccolo's eyes narrow into slits, I know she saw me with

Lorenzo. And maybe it was a last-ditch effort to win him for herself, or a simple act of vindictiveness for when I didn't jump to take her advice last night, but when pure hatred washes across Niccolo's face as he stares at Lorenzo, I know without a doubt—she told him about our dance. Possibly even our kiss.

His lips turn up in a cruel smirk as Lorenzo struggles against Cipriano's hold. Their two heads—one dark and tousled, the other golden and curly—lean together as Cipriano confirms what is plainly obvious to the rest of the gathered crowd. Niccolo and I are betrothed.

Even the thought makes me nauseous.

Lorenzo's gaze snaps to mine, and a murmur rises among the patrons as they realize the real-life soap opera unveiling before their eyes. Niccolo grabs my arm and starts pulling me in the opposite direction.

"Get your hands off me," I say through clenched teeth, still not wanting to make a scene even though that ship has long sailed. I lean back and try to pry my arm out of his grip, but he tightens his fingers around me and I wince in pain.

"Patience," Niccolo growls at my ear, "a future bride of mine does not engage in public exhibitions. You *will* hold yourself together, remember who you are, and act like a lady."

"And if I'm not a lady?" I spit back, fully aware I'm acting like the exact brat he thinks I am.

When Niccolo stops and turns around, my victorious grin dies before it can even begin. His cold eyes bore into mine. "Then your uncle will be quite displeased. And disgraced."

The truth of his words sinks in. The only thing he could've said to get me to walk away with him now. I give up the struggle.

Running across the piazza to Lorenzo will do nothing but

humiliate my Renaissance family and make everyone believe Patience is the uncivilized foreigner they believe her to be. I'll just have to find another way to explain to Lorenzo the insanity of the last few hours…and hopefully discover a way out of it.

As Niccolo guides me farther and farther away, my mind reels over one appalling fact. When I first stepped out of Reyna's tent and then met Alessandra, Cipriano, and Lorenzo, I actually let myself believe the gypsy transportation was the perfect way to get out of my Sweet Sixteen.

But now, as I hear Lorenzo's voice call my name again, I realize that an unwanted party is *nothing* compared to an unwanted betrothal.

Chapter Fifteen

The clanging church bells sound different inside the Cathedral Santa Maria del Fiore. The Giotto bell tower—the massively tall white-and-green structure that houses the seven thundering bells—stands just to the left outside, yet the warm sound floats through my ears dull and muted. The early morning sun filters through the dazzling stained glass windows, hitting the marble tiles of the floor and reflecting back onto the breathtaking paintings and frescoes. Any other day, I'd be spellbound.

Today I can barely summon the energy to look.

The past twenty-four hours have been a blur of activity and conversation about wedding feasts, trousseaus, and dowries. Aunt Francesca has been keeping me busy, operating under the delusion that all this planning will get me excited about becoming a blushing bride. Church seemed like the only place I could go without her hovering. Where incessant chatter about a future I don't want can't follow me. A place where I can think, crack Reyna's code, and figure out just how the heck I'm gonna get back home before I end up someone's wife.

Surprisingly, even with the countless lists and things to prepare, my aunt allowed me to come here—probably in the hopes that God will talk some sense into me. And I have to admit, if ever there's a person who can help me now, it's Him.

As I drift across the cold, hard floor and peer up at the domed ceiling, I pray silently for divine intervention. More than anything, I'd love to find a way to stay a little longer with Alessandra, Cipriano, and Lorenzo—but if staying here means marrying Niccolo, I need to get the heck out of Dodge. Whether it's through the form of gypsy transportation, a huge guardian angel swooping down and carrying me back home, or one of those crazy portal things like in the movies, I don't care. I just want to be back in my own time again, where life makes sense.

The heady scent of incense tickles my nose and I sneeze. Behind me, Lucia—the chaperone Aunt Francesca sent with me on my pilgrimage—provides a constant stream of muttering that joins the hushed murmurs of the other patrons as the soundtrack for today's excursion. I glance behind me and watch her lips move, noticing they're forming the same words over and over like a chant. A thought tickles the back of my mind.

Turning around, I walk backward and ask, "What are you saying? Is that a prayer?"

She lifts her wide eyes and throws a palm up, a moment before I collide into something hard. When arms circle around me, I realize it's a some*one*.

"Cat."

At the sound of Lorenzo's voice, I sink back against his chest. Just like that, the fog I've been in lifts, my numbness fades, and the clanging bells roar to life. His arms tighten around my waist and I feel his sigh against my neck. Lucia coughs repeatedly—reminding us where we are—and with obvious reluctance, he lets me go.

My shoulders sag in relief as I turn to face him.

"Lorenzo." His eyes soften as I say his name, and even though the world around us is completely nuts, I smile. "How did you find me?"

The grin he gives me back lacks its usual confidence, but it's just as sexy as ever. "One of my servants has been stationed outside your palazzo since sunrise." My eyes widen in surprise, and I can't help but grin at the sweet, romantic gesture. He laughs once before his face falls. He quickly scans the area around us and soberly whispers, "I needed to speak with you."

I nod and grab his hands. "I know. Lorenzo, I'm so sorry." I take a breath and wet my lips, my heart going about a mile a minute. "The piazza yesterday was so messed up—you shouldn't have found out about Niccolo like that. You have to believe this is *not* something I want. My uncle totally ambushed me after the ball, and it's been a living nightmare ever since."

He closes his eyes tightly and lets go of one of my hands to run his fingers through his disheveled hair. It's then that I notice how miserable he looks. His doublet is rumpled, there's a purple tint under his eyes, and his skin is ashen and lifeless. The glow he normally exudes is gone.

"It has been for me as well. I have not yet slept, for I have been formulating a plan." He steps closer, darts an appraising glance at Lucia, and grasps my shoulders. "Cat, you must fight this betrothal. You do not love Signore di Rialto. You care for me, just as I care for you."

A half laugh, half whimper bubbles from my chest. "Of course I don't love him, Lorenzo." Shaking my head, I *want* to tell him he's right—that I do care about him. Want to *be* with him. But even now, I can't bring myself to say the words. Instead, I shrug my shoulders. "But it doesn't matter how I feel."

His tired face transforms into a mask of determination. Lorenzo skims the back of his knuckles across my cheek, and the gentleness in his gaze makes my stomach twist.

Closing my eyes, I lean into his touch.

I hear him draw a shaky breath and hold it, and when I open my eyes, he lets it out in a rush. "But it does matter. It means everything. Cat, I am fighting my father for permission to marry now. I have promised to take my place in the family business if he allows me to have your hand in marriage. He is… *considering*"—his voice is a growl as he says the word—"my proposal. And if he denies it, then we will run away together." Lorenzo's jaw tightens and he swallows hard. "Either way, you are *not* marrying di Rialto."

For one long moment, I let his words sink in. And when they do, my world tilts for the second time in as many days. What is up with the men around here? Is something in the water? Then I remember they don't even drink the water, and I'm left clueless again.

For a girl who doesn't even believe in the institution of marriage after the string of exes her mother's left behind, I'm certainly racking up the proposals.

But then I shake my head, realizing none of this is funny. "Lorenzo, all you would be doing is playing right into your parents' hands, giving them what they want. You said it yourself

that day in the country—you can't be a banker. You're an artist."
I see the rebuttal forming on his lips and I throw my hand up to
stop it. "No. Even if we run, you *know* there's no better place to
be an artist than Florence. This is your dream, Lorenzo—and I
won't be the reason you give it up!"

The last word echoes off the stone walls, and the church-
goers around us turn to sneer in disapproval. Behind me, Lucia
stamps her foot. "Shh!"

Lorenzo gently places his hands on either side of my face,
lowering his head to stare directly into my eyes. His voice is
barely above a whisper as he says, "Patience D'Angeli—*Cat*—
you are my dream now."

His gaze is steady and confident, and something inside me
sinks, leaving me weak. I rest my forehead against his chest and
wrap my arms around his narrow waist, not caring if I'm causing
a scandal. What's the worst they can do to me? Force me into a
marriage I don't want when I'm severely underage? Oh yeah,
they're already doing that!

Lorenzo presses a kiss on the crown of my head and
whispers so only I can hear, "Find a way to meet me tomorrow
for evening vespers. I will be waiting."

I look up and stare into his hope-filled eyes, failing to
find the energy to argue anymore. Slowly, I nod in agreement.
The smile of victory he gives me in return is nothing short of
beautiful. Lorenzo winks, and then dashes out the door.

• • •

My steps are lighter on the way back to the palazzo. Seeing
Lorenzo has given me hope again, enough to see through the
fog at least. It's not that I'm actually planning to run away with

him, but now I have hope that another solution may be out there. I exhale audibly and lace my arm around Lucia's as we round the corner in front of our house. She rolls her eyes.

"You are in better spirits, Signorina," she says, shaking me off and taking a step back.

Lucia motions for me to take the lead into the courtyard, and as we enter the coolness of the inner square, I look up to see Alessandra watching us. She gives me a cautious, tight-lipped smile, and I wave.

"I *am* in better spirits, Lucia. But you know what I need? A girls' night. I've never really had one before and besides, shouldn't the bride at least get a bachelorette party?"

While the joke is forced, the sentiment isn't. I know none of this mess is Alessandra's fault; she's been all kinds of awesome from the moment I got here. But ever since my uncle dropped the Niccolo bomb, I've been too wrapped up in my own misery to let her in.

Lucia raises an eyebrow at the unfamiliar word but nods, somehow getting my meaning. Just in case, I explain, "I need a night away from all the drama, a night of pure, unadulterated fun. You think you can get the kitchen to whip up some of those awesome pinecone pastry things—and whatever other medieval goodies you guys have going on up there—and bring them to my room?"

Lucia nods again and asks, "Will you be alone?"

I smile up at Alessandra's window and say, "Not if I can help it." Cupping my hand around my mouth, I call out, "Hey, Less, you're sleeping in my room tonight! I'm gonna show you what a girls' night in *London* looks like!"

She catches my wink and beams down at me. "I shall meet

you in your room!"

Her dark head disappears from the window, and out of the corner of my eye, I see Lucia's mouth twitch before she dashes up the stairs. As I follow behind her, I try to remember all the chick flicks I've seen that had sleepover scenes, considering I haven't had one personally since I was seven. Though the products in movies might be better, I think the basic ingredients are still the same: beauty treatments, makeovers, and lots of girl talk.

Thanks to my handy dandy contraband backpack, I got all the bases covered.

Alessandra is already waiting for me in my room when I get there, sitting poised as ever at the foot of my bed. I close the door behind me, thread my fingers behind my back, and lift my nose in the air as though I'm about to impart some important wisdom.

"The first rule of a sleepover is you must be willing to loosen up." She nods her head solemnly and then crinkles her forehead in confusion. I smile, grab a pillow off my bed, and bonk her on the head. Her eyes widen into saucers.

"Second rule, anything said here will be held in the strictest of confidence. But with us, that's pretty much a given anyway, unless you want people to think you're a nut job. And the third rule, well, I don't really have a third rule, but things just sound better in groups of three."

A rapid, purposeful knock sounds on my door. "Come in," I call, flopping onto the bed beside Alessandra. I turn to her and point to the tray Lucia's carrying. "There we go, rule number three. Caloric consumption. Thou must not thinketh or worry about the circumference of one's thighs while at a sleepover."

Alessandra eyes the tray and repeats the phrase, "Caloric consumption," over and over.

Lucia sets down the tray of pinecone goodness and mini pies, and I nod in approval. "Excellent work, Lucia."

She quickly turns and closes the door behind her, and I reach under the bed. "Now, girl," I say, dropping my backpack onto the mattress between us, "I believe you expressed some interest in 'exploring my satchel of pleasantly scented items'?"

Alessandra claps her hands spastically—well, as spastically as Less gets—and bounces on the bed as I dump everything out. After a few spritzes of perfume and sniffs of my various floral- and fruit-smelling body creams, she reaches for the battered copy of *Us Weekly*, running her fingers almost reverently over the glossy cover picture of Taylor Swift.

"That's a magazine—practically a tabloid, actually. It dishes the dirt on celebrities. In fact," I say, taking the magazine and flipping to the picture of Dad at his premiere, "this is my dad. And that right there is my elbow. I'm pretty photogenic, don't ya think?"

She picks up the magazine and lifts it to her face, eyeing the picture closely. "Your father is very handsome. And the beautiful Signora beside him, is she the betrothed you spoke of?"

I roll my eyes and start rifling through my toiletry kit. "Yep, that's the evil step-witch-to-be."

"Evil? As in my role in the play you taught us in the meadow?"

Pulling out a tube of neon green facial mask, I sigh and meet her gaze. "No, she's not that bad. And really, I'm no Snow White, either. Jenna just bugs the crap out of me." I wiggle the tube in front of her face, not wanting the thought of my dad's fiancée, or anything else depressing—like impending marriage to skeezy older men, or handsome guys giving up their life dreams for me—to ruin my first-ever girls' night. "Time to make ourselves gorgeous, darling."

Once our faces are covered in the sticky goop, I pick up my digital camera, lean my head against hers, and snap a picture for posterity. I don't know why I haven't tried to take more. I'm still clinging to the hope that somehow I'll find a way back home, and when I do, documented proof that this wasn't just a dream will be nice.

I glance down, smiling at how silly we both look. Having this picture will also help when I'm all alone again and desperately missing her.

"Is it expected," Alessandra asks, twitching her nose, raising her eyebrows, and working her jaw simultaneously, "that I should find it difficult to move my face?"

Sniffling, I laugh and hand over the camera so she can see how she looks. "Yeah, that's part of the charm."

Her jaw drops to form an *O* when she looks at the photo. "How marvelous, an instant painting! Just as in your colorful magazine. Does this magic box contain others?"

"Not many of people. I'm not exactly what you'd call social back home, but I do have a lot of pictures of buildings, bridges, sunsets, that sorta thing." I reach over and scroll through the gallery, stopping every few to explain. "That is from one of Dad's movie sets. The blonde next to him is Carlie Williams, second only to Mom in box-office popularity and divaness," I tell her with a roll of my eyes.

She sits up and holds the camera higher. "That lovely woman

is an actress?"

I smile when her eyes widen as much as her tightening facemask will allow, absorbing everything she can about the picture. It's so easy to forget how our contemporary views on acting and women in general can shock someone like Alessandra, especially since she's so passionate about theater. Suddenly I snatch up my iPhone and battery pack, remembering that I downloaded *Kisses and Disses* off iTunes last month.

"Yep, and if you want, I can even show you the movie," I say, thumbing through the icons on my newly juiced phone. "I have no plans to follow my parents' footsteps into the business, but I like downloading Dad's movies and breaking them down. I visit his sets a lot, so it's fun remembering when they filmed each shot and trying to figure out why he chose a certain angle."

I find the movie, tap the thumbnail, and the bright green rating system screen appears. Alessandra is immediately lost in the wonder of "moving pictures" and female actors, and I plump a pillow behind my head to watch her. Here sits my great-great-great-great-great-great aunt or cousin, watching one of my dad's movies from the future, sporting a funky green beauty mask. I have to be breaking at least a bazillion time-travel laws, if such things even exist, but seeing the look of rapture on her face is so worth it.

A memory springs to mind before I can squelch it of Jenna buying me that tube of facemask, hoping for a girls' night just like this. It was a couple of months ago, not too long after they got engaged. Dad was out of town shooting on location and I came home to find beauty products laid out on the counter, piles of pillows and blankets on the sofa, and the coffee table overflowing with chocolate gooeyness. There was a weary, cautious look in her eye, but when she presented the idea, her voice was as bubbly as ever.

Of course, I declined. I didn't know what trick she had up her sleeve, but I wasn't gonna fall for it. So instead, I locked myself in my room listening to music and reading, bored out of my ever-loving mind. When I went to the bathroom later, I nearly tripped over the plate of brownies she left by my door.

But as I pinch a corner off one of Lucia's pastries, I can't help but wonder…if I had stayed, would I've had a night like this? Fun, silly banter and pampering that Dad could never get, regardless of how hard he tries? Dudes don't seem to understand the inbred desire—a desire I'm only just fully realizing—that girls have to pour our hearts out, eat sweet treats, and cover ourselves in high-priced goo in the name of beauty.

Is it possible I could've been having this all along with Jenna?

I look up at my painted ceiling and reflect over the past nine months as Alessandra giggles at the movie. Besides Jenna's misguided attempt to throw me the Sweet Sixteen, she's never actually done anything *that* bad. Dad adores her— as does almost everyone else she comes in contact with—and Alessandra and Aunt Francesca honestly do remind me of her a lot.

I glance over at my cousin sprawled out on my bed, her mask now dry and crusty, her hair pulled up on her head in one of my clips, and I make a vow. If—no, *when*—I get back home, I'm gonna give Jenna a break.

Heck, if I get back, I'll even agree to the stupid Sweet

Sixteen and MTV coverage.

Sitting up, I grab the magazine and flip back to the picture of her and Dad. Jenna's smile holds all the qualities I've grown to love in my Renaissance relatives. Maybe if I can find a way to break the magic, I can grow to love her, too.

Chapter Sixteen

The streets are cold and quiet as I make my way to the church, my heart pounding in rhythm with my steps. I've had almost twenty-four hours to think about Lorenzo's proposal, and though I've waffled a few times, scared this is my only out, I know what I have to do. Staying here and marrying Lorenzo isn't an option…not that I'm exactly itching to get hitched anyway. Even if his parents go for his offer to become a stuffy banker, my aunt and uncle will never agree to let me marry him. Marco and Francesca think Niccolo can rope the freaking moon.

The only other option I have besides sticking around, keeping my mind open for Reyna's lessons, and/or praying I'm suddenly struck with an epiphany to get me out of this mess is to run away with him.

But can I really let Lorenzo give up his dreams for me? Leave my aunt and uncle without a word or an explanation?

With zero guarantees that the gypsy magic will even work if I leave Florence?

I turn the corner and see the Cathedral Santa Maria del Fiore ahead. Out of habit, I glance both ways before crossing the street, wondering if Lorenzo's already inside waiting for me and praying I make up my mind before he asks. I wrap my arms around myself tightly for warmth and pick up the pace, putting my head down despite the empty streets, not wanting to take the chance that anyone will recognize me.

"Signorina D'Angeli."

I gasp at the low hiss, and the cold evening air causes my breath to form a puffy white cloud. A few feet away, Niccolo steps out from the shadows.

"I must confess that I am surprised your uncle allowed you to wander the streets without a guardian. If I did not know better, I would assume you were here without his permission."

I suck in my lips and bite down to keep from screaming. Every single instinct I have suddenly goes on red alert, screaming that perhaps meeting this creeper unchaperoned on the dark empty streets of Florence isn't a good thing.

Niccolo circles me like some kind of wild animal. "And the only reason I could think of for you to go out without permission," he continues in a steely voice that makes me shiver, "is if you have ill-advised intentions."

I don't blink, and I don't open my mouth. With my heart hammering in my ears, I straighten my spine and meet the challenge in his eyes, refusing to rise to his bait. He's just jealous and lashing out—the only thing I can do is act calm.

He stops in front of me and gives me a tight, fake smile. He wraps an arm around his chest and fingers his lip. "Patience, I believe I should share a story with you. It's a sad story, one you probably have not heard, but it is regrettably quite common with the youth of our city."

His eyebrow quirks as if asking for permission to keep yammering—a first for him—before he settles into lecture mode. "You see, our young women seem to fall victim to an unfortunate habit when they reach your age, a habit of disobeying their families when it comes time for them to marry."

My eyes narrow in suspicion. Alessandra has filled me in enough over the last few days to know the scenario he's describing is anything but *common*. Most girls—all of them, actually—seem to go along blindly with whatever their family or society tells them to do.

Which means Niccolo's story is not about women at large—it's about me. And if the cold gleam in his eye is any hint, things are about to get ugly.

He nods as if I asked him a question. "*Sì*, it is a sad story, is it not? But I fear it gets worse. These same women also often choose to accept the propositions of young men." He leans closer and whispers, "Offers to run away."

A deep chill runs through me. My heart sputters, and then pounds.

He can't know. There's no way that he knows about Lorenzo's plan—unless Niccolo had spies follow me and listen to our conversation at the church yesterday. I think back, trying to remember if I saw anyone suspicious, but there were too many people and too many faces for any one person to stand out. And I'd assumed that with the bells clanging and the hum of whispered prayers, no one could hear us anyway.

Apparently, I was wrong.

The set of Niccolo's jaw and the arrogant look in his eye leaves no mistake about it—regardless of any decision I have or haven't made, he knows what Lorenzo offered me. I break away from his cruel gaze and the possessiveness radiating off his stance and glance around. We're alone.

Okay, all I need to do is get inside the church. Lorenzo will be there.

I clear my throat. "That is a sad story, Signore," I say, forcing false confidence into my voice. "And I thank you for sharing it with me. But if you don't mind, I'd like to go into the church and pray."

I take a step forward and he matches it, blocking my path.

I swallow, take a breath, and give him a tight-lipped smile.

"Signore, if *I* didn't know better," I say, turning his words back on him, "I'd assume you were trying to keep me away from God. Now that doesn't seem very *honorable.*"

Niccolo's lips twitch and I even hear a slight chuckle. I pull myself up and take another step, but his arm shoots out and knocks me across the chest.

"Of course, you must pray. You will be my wife soon, and I expect you will come to me unblemished. But before you go, I thought you would like to hear the end of my story."

I close my eyes and count to three, the whole idea of running away with Lorenzo and never having to see this guy again seeming awfully tempting. When I open them, Niccolo is practically standing on top of me, looking down his long, pointed nose. I jerk back.

"What is the end?" I whisper, inwardly kicking myself for showing weakness.

"The young men who promise safety and dreams of running away? They all seem to meet the same disastrous end." He lowers his voice and leans his head close to my ear. "They are never heard from again."

. . .

"You came."

Lorenzo's relieved whisper in my ear gives me chills. Ever since escaping Niccolo's clutches, I've been kneeling near a painting of the Virgin Mary. I collapsed here among the flowers and gifts left behind from others in hope and gratitude for answered prayers, my shaky knees refusing to carry me any farther. Just moments ago I calmed down enough to place my own offering beneath the frame, a ripe green pear from the kitchen.

If ever a symbol characterized me, it's that fruit. It began my love affair with Renaissance art, it inspired my tattoo, and once Reyna saw it on my hip, it somehow led me here. I intended to leave it with the other tokens, hoping it will grant my prayer for a miracle that'll send me home or a sign to make my decision easier.

But after speaking with Niccolo, my only prayer now is for Lorenzo's safety.

Turning my body toward him, I notice the haggard look still in his eyes. I push past the lump in my throat and say, "Of course I came."

The right side of his mouth lifts in an attempt at his usual smile as he sinks to the floor beside me. He closes his eyes and breathes deeply, his shoulders rising and falling with the effort. When he looks at me again, there is hope mixed with panic in his gaze.

"My father has agreed to my proposal. I am to leave in a fortnight for an apprenticeship with his associates in London."

I can't help but notice the way his eyes tighten when he mentions leaving his beloved Florence, the mecca for art in his world. If I hadn't already decided not to accept his offer, that look in his eye would have done it.

My stomach twists at the thought of leaving him. But regardless of whether we run away tonight or not, we'll have to say good-bye eventually—because I *will* make it home one day—so better to do it now, while I can make sure that he's safe.

Closing my eyes, I draw up the strength to do what I need to. Growing up, I'd watched my mother's example and believed that love could only lead to hurt—and here I am, about to hurt the guy I've come to care about more than I ever thought possible. But at least this time, unlike all the times with my mother, it's not out of selfishness.

In this case, caring about Lorenzo means letting him go.

I reach into the top of my dress, watching his eyes widen, and pull out my camera. "Lorenzo, before we talk about the future, will you do one thing for me?" He nods slowly, eyeing the slim plastic box in my hand, and I fight back a sob. Clearing my throat, I say, "Can you give me one of your breathtaking grins? It seems like forever since I've seen it."

He furrows his eyebrows and stares at me a moment, and then laughs. "Anything for you, Cat."

And then it's as though someone lifts a veil, because the somber, anxious, frantic look about him vanishes, leaving behind the confident, happy, sexy boy I'd started to fall for. I snap the picture before reality hits again, sending him back into hiding, and stuff the camera into my dress.

His eyes narrow in question and he opens his mouth, but I shake my head. I don't want to waste a second of my remaining time with him explaining gadgets from the future. With tears building, I ask, "Can I ask one more favor?"

Lorenzo's grin grows wider as he nods. "But of course."

"Can you kiss me again?"

His head jerks back and then he looks around, reminding me we are in church. I bite my lip, understanding that kissing here definitely wouldn't be appropriate, but unwilling to deny myself this last request. I grab his hand and pull him up and out the double doors of the Cathedral, not stopping until we are around the corner and away from prying, gossiping, *spying* eyes.

"Now?" I ask, not caring that I sound pathetically desperate at this point.

He nods, the passion in his eyes turning into liquid pools of melted chocolate, and wraps his strong arms around me. "Now."

Lorenzo's kiss is full of the desperation and longing of the past two days, along with the hope of what he thinks is our future. We pull at each other, needing to be closer and neither of us getting close enough. He deepens the kiss, and I shudder against him, exhaling a half sigh, half sob. The taste of salt fills my mouth and I realize tears are pouring down my cheeks. He breaks away to look down at me.

With hands softer than silk, he wipes the tears away and presses a kiss to the tip of my nose. "Do not cry, angel of mine. We shall be together now."

Pain shoots through my stomach. Even though I desperately want his words to be true, I know this is it. It's time to say good-bye.

Closing my eyes, I stand on tiptoe and kiss him one last time. I run my fingers through his soft golden curls, nibble on his full lower lip, and drink in his woodsy scent. I leave a trail of kisses on the slight bump of his nose, his bronzed cheeks, and the indentation above his upper lip. And then, with regret, I stand back and gaze into his dazed, smiling eyes.

"Shall I escort you home and request an audience with your uncle?" he asks, skimming his hands down my arms and interlocking our fingers.

I shake my head and watch the confusion cloud his gaze. I slowly inhale, count to three, and then five, before exhaling.

"No. Lorenzo, I'm so sorry, but I can't marry you. Or run away."

He bolts back in shock, his mouth opening and closing. Confusion, doubt, and pain all flash across his face and before he can argue or I can lose my nerve, I press on.

"You need to follow the plan you had before you ever met me. You're an amazing man, and your father will see that eventually, regardless of your career. He'll be proud of you as an artist. And one day, when the time is right and you have your life in order, you're going to fall in love. Truly, deeply, and passionately. I just know it."

Lorenzo grabs my arms, his breathing shallow and rapid, and searches my eyes. "You do not mean what you are saying. You want to be with me; I know that you do."

I let the tears fall as I twist my arms from his grip, not because he's hurting me like Niccolo did, but because it hurts to be near him. He looks down at his hands in horror and releases me.

"I *do* want to be with you, Lorenzo," I say, backing away.

"But I can't let you throw away your life for me."

Then, before he can beg again or my resolve to do the right thing crumbles, I spin around and grab the hem of my dress. As I race back home, heartbroken, the sound of my cries joins the pounding of my footsteps against the cold cobblestone road.

Chapter Seventeen

Lucia's *thump*ing on my door shakes me out of a restless dream. Sleep eluded me most of the night, allowing me to watch through swollen eyelids as the dark sky outside my window turned orange and pink and purple. Exhaustion must have consumed me shortly after dawn.

"Come in already!" I scream, shoving my balled-up fists into my eye sockets.

She does, but her purposeful stride halts when she takes in my appearance. I can only imagine what a night spent crumbled in the fetal position on my bed, dry heaving and weeping, has done for my complexion. Her familiar eyes turn sad as she tries to coax me out of bed. "Today is an important day, Signorina."

For a moment, I don't know what she means. And then I remember. Today is my sixteenth birthday.

The whole hurting the first guy I've ever cared about and being stalked by a maniacal sociopath distracted me from such a monumental occasion. Now, according to ancient philosophy, I'm old enough to be married. Let the celebration begin.

I nod at Lucia as I stumble toward my stool. "Yeah, thanks for remembering. I guess sixteen is a pretty big deal, huh?" I ask, my voice hoarse and scratchy.

She tilts her bonnet-encased head in confusion and grabs the brush. As the rhythmic strokes lull my heavy lids closed, she clears her throat. "Your uncle should return any moment, so we must make haste in dressing."

My eyes pop open and an uneasy feeling steels my spine. I lick my dry, cracked lips and ask, "Return?"

The brush stills. "*Sì*, from the notary."

My already labored breathing grows harsher as a fresh wave of panic washes over me. I turn and unclench my jaw to repeat, "The notary."

Lucia stares at me, sees the question in my eyes, and nods once. "He accompanied Signore di Rialto at sunrise. Your aunt and cousin have been preparing for the wedding feast. Today is your wedding day."

NO!!!

The one word screamed only in my head bounces around my brain, eclipsing the next thing Lucia says. Through dazed eyes, I somehow register her lips moving.

I put a shaky hand to the table and force myself to stand. "I-I'm sorry. What did you just say?"

Surely, I heard her wrong. There's no way my aunt wouldn't have told me something this important. But then, I did pretty much tune out all the planning stuff, refusing to believe this day would ever really come.

Lucia thrusts her hand under my arm to steady me. "It is

your wedding day," she says again, as if she's addicted to the freaking sentence. She nods her head toward a large trunk near the door. "And your counter-trousseau just arrived."

I lurch forward and Lucia catches me, her eyes narrowing in concern as she guides me over to the door. Sinking to my knees, I lift a shaky hand to unhook the lock and pry open the latch, not really knowing why, other than the need to prove somehow that this isn't happening.

The trunk is filled with jewelry—bracelets, brooches, rings, and pendants—and gowns of every color and fabric. Silk, satin, taffeta, brocade, and on top, a crimson cut-velvet surcoat. Lucia takes it, along with the matching slippers underneath, and drapes it on my bed.

"This is the gown you shall wear for the wedding."

The pretty, innocuous, Italian words float in my ear and I dumbly nod in acknowledgment. I blink and swallow hard, then look to my bed for my backpack. I don't even care if Lucia sees it; I need to hold it. I crawl over and reach out, but stop when my fingers brush across a folded piece of paper on the floor. Right below where Lucia hung the gown.

Gingerly, I pick it up, almost as if it'll bite. I know who it's from. Forgetting about my backpack for now, I grip the letter in my fist and let my feet carry me back to the stool, where I stare at the wall before me.

The passage of time ceases to hold meaning as I retreat within myself again. On some distant level, I feel Lucia's hands work my hair, then lift me up and dress me for the day. I still feel the paper in my hand, now cutting and breaking the skin due to my death grip. Lucia finishes and clears her throat.

I blink unseeing eyes and focus on her petite frame. She

hands me a mirror and I nod at my reflection.

"Thank you," I say, my voice void of any emotion.

As I passively hand her the mirror back, a surprising image registers in my mind and my grip tightens around the gilded frame. I tug it back, my eyes boring into the glass.

For a fleeting moment, I see myself as I did the day I arrived in Florence with my dad. Full makeup, hair down, fake-confident smile.

I glance at my crimson surcoat, then back at my reflection, watching as the image fades into the sixteenth-century version of me, veil skimming over an elaborate hairstyle adorned with flowers. But that hallucination is enough to wake me from my trance.

Trotting horse hooves outside my window catch my attention and I glance out to see a line of carriages arriving. Niccolo stands near the fountain, talking with a guest.

I open my hand and unfold the letter, knowing it's from him. The words are few, but they were obviously crafted to pierce my heart.

Signorina Patience D'Angeli,

I look forward to making you mine. Young Cappelli is safe. You chose correctly.

N.

I lift my head, and as if he senses my stare, Niccolo looks up, meeting my gaze with an icy look of superiority and triumph.

Uncle Marco's voice reaches me from below, and I shift my eyes to watch him greet the guests in turn. Pride radiates off him even from this distance as he surveys the growing crowd. Almost the entire guest list from the ball appears to be in attendance, whether to celebrate Patience's wedding or to mourn the loss of the town's most eligible bachelor, I'm not sure. What I do know is this:

Running will cause a scene.

A scandal.

I should know; it's what my mother excels at. And because of that, because of her, I've always done exactly what I think is expected of me. Always tried to make up for her failures.

I look back at Niccolo and shake my head.

But not this time.

"I can't do this anymore." Exhaling sharply, I turn to Lucia and bunch the sides of my soft velvet dress in my hands. "I have to get outta here."

Lucia stumbles back as I barrel past her, through the door, and down the hall—the smell of the wedding feast's roasted peacock assaulting me. I pass Alessandra near the dining room, but I refuse to stop even when she screams after me. I can't. I won't stop until I'm down the stairs, through the courtyard, and out the arched doors leading to the street, far, far away from this nightmare.

The astonished crowd in the courtyard parts and I tear through, pausing only long enough to shout a tearful "Sorry" to my uncle. Behind me, Niccolo screams in rage. But I'm already gone.

After a few blocks, my lungs and thighs burn, and I have a painful stich in my side. Reluctantly I slow my frantic pace, hearing footsteps slapping the road behind me. Leaning against the sandstone building next to me, I close my eyes and draw ragged, searing breaths. The trailing footsteps slow and come to a sharp stop.

"I'm not going back," I tell whoever it is, shaking my head with my eyes squeezed shut. I'm almost certain it's Alessandra. Maybe even my aunt or uncle. But I'm scared to death to open them and see Niccolo. I don't care what he threatens to do to me; I'm not becoming his wife today. I'll run away on my own if I have to.

"You don't have to go back, *Caterina.*"

The eerily familiar Russian-accented, English-speaking voice breaks through my panic and my eyes snap open. Another pair of clacking footsteps rounds the corner and I turn and lock gazes with Alessandra, all wild eyes and bright red cheeks.

Then I turn back to Lucia.

"Reyna?" I ask in disbelief, watching her drab servant uniform vanish and a voluminous outfit of purple veils and layers of multicolored chiffon skirts replace it.

At least this time, more than just her eyes are exposed. She smiles at me and nods. "*Arvah.*" She takes a step back and motions to a tent that has materialized behind her. "I believe the two of us should step inside."

Alessandra's slowed steps finally reach us and she wraps her hands around the top of her head, squeezing it in confusion. She looks from me, to Reyna, to the tent, and back again. "I do not understand."

Reyna nods at her, and then her familiar eyes pierce mine. "I'll leave you two to talk, but make it quick. I will see you inside, *tatcho*?"

I nod, relief and joy competing for which emotion I feel most. A laugh echoes off the building next to us before I even realize it came from me.

I'm going home.

The flap of the tent closes behind Reyna and I turn to face Alessandra. The joy transforms into grief in a nanosecond.

"Um, so that was my gypsy lady," I say, forcing a smile. "It looks like I'm heading back to the future now."

As much as I want and *need* to get away from Niccolo and unwanted betrothals and people who eat roasted peacock to celebrate anything, the thought of leaving Alessandra tears at me. I reach for her hand and pull her into a tight hug. I breathe in the scent of my floral shampoo clinging to her hair and choke on a sob. "I'm never gonna forget you, girl."

Alessandra sniffles and stays quiet for a minute. Then she says, "Nor I you. You have taught me much about life and the future." She rubs her forehead on my shoulder. "I shall forever miss my dear sister."

My grip around her neck tightens as I shake my head. "Your family is the one who taught me, I assure you." I pull away to swipe at my tears. "Geez, you people turned me into a freaking crybaby."

She smiles softly and laughs once. "Mama will miss you, too, as will Father. They love you, you know."

I hiccup and blink away a fresh batch of tears. "Take care of them for me, will ya? Your mom and dad, Cip, *Lorenzo*." My voice breaks on his name, and I have to take a steadying breath before I continue. I squeeze her hand for strength.

My gaze falls on the tent and a thought suddenly dawns on me. "Less, I don't know what kind of mess I'm leaving you with here. I don't know if I'm gonna walk into the tent and the real Patience will step out, or if she does, if she'll even know or understand anything that's happened. And what if no one steps out?" I ask, the horrifying image playing in my mind. "What if Patience no longer exists, or if she never shows up? I mean, it's great that she won't have to marry Niccolo, but people will think she ran away! That'll devastate Aunt Francesca!"

I remember all those guests back there. They'll think I jilted Niccolo on our wedding day. With his arrogance and need for public approval, something like this will shame him.

The thought actually brings a smile to my face.

Now that, I like.

Alessandra puts a hand on my elbow and smiles confidently at me. "Do not worry about what will happen next, fair cousin. I will take care of everything."

I tilt my head and study this new girl standing in front of me. "You will? How?"

Her smile grows wider as she lifts one delicate shoulder. "I do not yet know, but I *am* an actress."

She giggles and I just stand there, watching her embrace her passion—even if it's only with me. Maybe my being around did help in some small way after all.

I wrap my arms around her for one last hug. "Yes, you are," I say, burying my head again in her soft hair. "A gifted one at that."

The flap of the tent moves as Reyna sticks out her head. "We really must be going. Everything is ready."

I nod and step away from Alessandra. Heat floods my cheeks. My chest tightens in a steely grip as I blink rapidly and choke out, "I love ya, girl."

Her doe-eyes fill with tears again as she says, "I love you, too, Cat."

She squeezes my hand, then gently shoves me toward the

tent, and with a heavy sigh, I walk away from my cousin and the past, and head toward Reyna and my future.

• • •

Inside the tent is just as dim as I remember, but this time nowhere near as spooky. The patchouli incense still tickles my nose, the dotted candlelight makes the same dancing shadows on the ground, but at the back, Reyna is perched on top of the black-sheathed table, drinking a can of Coke.

She sees my smirk and shrugs. "I missed carbonation."

I roll my eyes and laugh, the English language and the bright red can a welcome sign of normalcy. Remembering the drill from before, I slide my slippers off my feet and promptly freeze.

"I need to go back!" I shriek, causing Reyna's eyebrows to shoot up in surprise. She folds her arms and, scared I'll say the wrong thing and end up being stuck here forever, I take a breath and lower my shaking voice. "You don't understand. I forgot my backpack in my room. My phone, my camera, my wallet, hundreds of dollars' worth of products. My art supplies. Lorenzo's drawing. *My* drawing… My life is in that bag!"

As she watches me, a small smile twitches her lips. Figuring that's as close to permission as I'm going to get, I turn to put my shoes back on, fear tightening my muscles as I imagine running into Niccolo again. A gentle breeze whips strands of hair in my face and when I push it back, I see my backpack lying on the floor.

I jump about a foot and shoot her an open-mouthed look of disbelief.

Reyna snickers. "Did you not think I could perform such a

simple trick? I transport you five hundred years into the past, and *this* is what you do not buy?"

Relief coursing through my veins, I grin. "Touché."

Sinking to the ground, I run my hand across the rolled-up drawings poking out the top. Pressure builds behind my eyes, but I refuse to cry. I'm going home, where I need to be. I can blubber like a baby once I'm in a cushy bed back in the twenty-first century—and far away from Niccolo. I slide my backpack onto the reserved space on the shelf and push myself to my feet.

In the back of the tent, I take a seat opposite Reyna and lean my elbows on the soft silk sheath. With a nod to the purple votive candle, jar of oil, and dish of red powder sitting beside the large sapphire candle and red Coke can, I say, "Looks like you're ready for another session of hocus pocus. Well, this time I am your more-than-willing vessel, Gypsy girl. Work your magic."

Reyna's mouth twitches again. "Are you not curious to know why all this happened?"

Honestly, the need to get home and see Dad again is almost overwhelming. But so is finally getting the answers to my bazillion questions. I lean my chair back and bat my eyelashes. "You mean to say that you don't do this to every random tourist who walks into your tent sporting a pear tattoo?"

But she doesn't laugh. Reyna's luminous eyes glaze over as she stares at a point just above my head. And when she speaks, her rough voice is unusually gentle. "Since I was born in Romania twenty years ago, I have always known that I had a particular destiny, one that lives outside my own. I spent the whole of my childhood preparing for my sixteenth birthday, when the goddess Isis would grant me my magical powers at my *patshiv*, along with a special assignment to use them for good. The morning of my sixteenth birthday, I awoke from a vivid dream of a painted pear. And every night since, it has been the same vision. Occasionally with flashes of more, but always the pear."

Reyna falls quiet, trapped in her memories, and I try not to break the eerie silence. But I can't help scrunching the fabric of my skirt as I impatiently wait to hear more.

It's not every day I learn I'm someone's destiny.

Finally, Reyna inhales deeply and lowers her eyes to mine, though they still look a little misty. "About a year ago, I wandered into a museum, searching for a glimpse of the pear in my waking hours, and I stumbled upon an ancient book. I cannot explain the magnetic pull I felt to that book. The woodcut illustrations fascinated me, and though it was written in Italian and I could not understand a word, it was impossible to look away. Having never been interested in art, or history, or even Italy before, I knew there had to be a connection. I noted the printing was from Florence, somewhere around the early 1500s, and I threw myself into learning about the Renaissance, devouring all I could, hoping it would lead me closer to my destiny. Eventually I traveled here. And when I saw your tattoo that afternoon in the tent, I knew my destiny had finally arrived."

Wow. I stare into the flame from the sapphire candle, realizing that as unbelievable as her story is, I totally believe it. How could I not after everything that's happened this past week? But as I replay her words in my mind, my eyes narrow, one piece still not quite making sense. "I think I understand why *me*…and why *then*, the Renaissance. But I don't understand why

I had to become someone else? Why Patience?"

Reyna nods, fiddling with the pop-top of her can with a small smile. "The Goddess did not reveal that part until the final spell. As I called upon her to show me your destiny, she lifted the veil and your story unfolded like a film. Your aunt, so much like the women you struggled not to think about during the tea ceremony. Your cousins, the ones to teach you to open your heart again. Lorenzo"—my stomach clenches at his name—"to show you how love can be if you trust yourself. And Niccolo, so you can discover that some things are beyond our control. If we are to fight them, we cannot be consumed with the need to be perfect, or to always do what is expected. We need to be willing to chance failure in order to succeed."

I collapse against the back of my chair, amazed. The cryptic message to "keep my mind open to the lessons ahead" had haunted me since the moment I woke up and realized there was more to this trip than a simple twenty-four-hour immersion, but I wasted so much time trying to riddle it out that I forgot to pay attention to the things that really mattered. All the elusive lessons surrounded me the whole time.

As if reading my thoughts, Reyna leans forward, her marble-like gaze hypnotic in its intensity. "Caterina, what have you learned from this experience?"

Taking a deep breath, I consider her question.

"Well, for starters, I learned that having a sweet sixteen is *not* the worst thing that can happen."

Gratified with her snort in reply, I purse my lips and concentrate on remembering all the amazing bits and pieces of my Renaissance vacay. The horrid dinner at Antonia's and my even-worse performance. My countless blunders and the craziness with Niccolo.

"This experience definitely showed me I can't control everything, as much as I want to. And I guess I realized it's okay if I occasionally make a few mistakes. I'm *not* my mother."

Shocked by the conviction in my own statement, I laugh—then as a strange lightness enters my chest, I put my hand over my heart and do it again. I take another breath, finding it easier this time, and close my eyes, energized by my self-discovery. Behind my veiled eyes, I see the faces of Alessandra and Aunt Francesca, Uncle Marco and Cipriano, and finally, Lorenzo. I let the hurt come, along with the engulfing sense of love and comfort.

"And I've learned that letting people close to you doesn't always lead to pain. Some people are actually worth the risk."

As I think about Jenna, and how different things might be if I give her a chance, I hear Reyna laugh, a surprisingly soft tinkling sound. I open my eyes to see her shaking her head.

"*Misto!* I believe my work here is done." Picking up the purple candle, she smiles and asks, "So then, Caterina, are you ready to go home?"

I throw my head back and sigh. There's so much I'll miss about the sixteenth century, but in the end, it's nothing compared to Dad and home. When I lift it again, I feel lighter than air. "Yes. Definitely, yes."

Reyna nods, pleased, and I watch as she inscribes my name on one side of the candle. She then draws an infinity symbol above and below it. With one hand, she grasps the wick and rolls it first in the oil, and then in the red powder, while handing me a piece of parchment paper with the other.

"Back to business," she says in her usual rough voice. "Write down what it is you need control over and place it under the candleholder."

Control.

It's crazy to realize how important that word has been in my life the past sixteen years. But now, after going so long without having any shred of it, I realize all I really want control over is getting home. I grab a sparkly pen off the shelf lining the wall, write HOME on the stiff paper, and then slide it under the holder as instructed.

Reyna strikes a match and the candle's flame begins to dance. She closes her eyes and chants, "Wax and herb, now bring me power that grows with every passing hour. Bring control back into me. As I will it, so mote it be!"

This time, there's no creepy parlor trick to accompany the magic. A strong wind rattles the outside walls of the tent, but inside is relatively calm. A subtle electric current runs up my spine and down my limbs, and my stomach clenches—a tickling feeling close to the kind I get from a roller coaster. But that's it.

The candle burns completely down and Reyna grabs a second dish to incinerate the parchment paper.

I have to admit, I kinda missed the crawly skin and crazy voodoo. But I'm not the one running this ship. And as long as she gets me home, Gypsy girl can do whatever she wants.

The last particle of the paper disintegrates and Reyna lifts her gaze to mine. "It is finished."

The sides of the tent still and I hear an angry car horn blare in the distance. The sound of home.

I jump to my feet and circle the table, pull her up, and throw my arms around her neck. "Thank you so much for everything. Seriously, now that I'm back—and not married—I have to tell you that this whole experience completely rocked!"

She laughs and pats my back, and I pull away to look down at her. "Now that it's all over, what will you do?"

Reyna shrugs. "Some gypsies get another assignment; others carry on their lives as they did before. I guess I will have to wait to see which camp I fall into." A wistful look passes over her face, and then it clears.

"Will I ever see you again?"

Her eyes sparkle as if she has a hidden secret. "It is possible."

Realizing I'm not going to get anything more than that, I gnaw on my lip and eye the front of the tent. Dad is just a twenty minute walk away. But then I turn to her once again. "And the real Patience—my however-many-once-removed cousin or aunt. What happens to her?"

It's the only question that's been nagging me since I entered the tent, and the one I'm most scared to hear the answer to. My stomach immediately knots a hundred different ways, wondering if she ended up with Niccolo or was lost forever somehow.

Reyna closes her eyes and bows her head, circling slowly once to the left, and then again to the right. She chants softly under her breath, and when she lifts her head, she smiles. The pressure in my chest lightens a smidge.

"She returned to your aunt's house, with your memories intact as if they were her own. She approached your uncle with Niccolo's letter and together, they confronted him. The betrothal was broken."

I sink against her, collapsing in relief. "And Niccolo?"

Reyna's lips twitch. "Married Antonia Stefani." I slap my hand over my mouth and she nods. "I believe that's what they call poetic justice, don't you think?"

We share a laugh, which after the stress of the morning feels freaking amazing. My laughter trails, giving way to the fading roar of a Vespa, and I turn my head to follow the sound. When I look back, Reyna spears me with her perceptive stare. I force loose hair behind my ear and shake my head.

I can't ask about Lorenzo.

I'm back where I need to be, where I'm meant to be, but I'm not ready to hear how he married a gorgeous Florentine woman—or even that he remained alone the rest of his life, screwed up after meeting me. Either possibility is just too painful to consider.

Reyna presses her lips together and nods once, understanding. Grateful, I hug her tightly one final time, and then smile in spite of myself.

The family of huggers rubbed off.

Reyna steps back, hesitant and almost shy. She squeezes my arm in a rare show of affection, and then promptly turns me to face the front of the tent. "Upon walking outside, you will find that no time has elapsed since you left on your adventure. When you see your family again, nothing for them will have changed. But hopefully that will not be the case with *you*."

"I can say with almost complete certainly, Jenna will flip her pancake over the change in me."

She snorts and with a gentle shove, says, "*Kushti*. Then I believe your father is waiting."

A surge of excitement and longing shoots through me and I race to the front. I slip my feet into slippers that I know will change the second I step outside, and slide my arm through the shoulder of my beloved backpack.

With a wave at Reyna, I pull back the flap, pausing for a moment to close my eyes and savor the smells and sounds of the twenty-first century. Who knew that the rhythmic rumble and buzzing of Italian traffic could be so beautiful? I take a step, and then another, basking in the warm, pollution-filled sunshine. I open my eyes to gaze down at my familiar Seven jeans and Abercrombie top and with a kick of my Steve-Madden-gladiator-encased feet, I walk out into present-day Florence.

Chapter Eighteen

The lobby of our hotel is quiet. More importantly, it is Dad and Jenna free. The shiny golden clock hanging above the concierge desk confirms it's a quarter till two, which means that despite my nine-day absence, I'm actually early for our lunch date.

I plop down on a plush sofa, the floral fabric wrapping itself around me, and lay my head on the silk-covered arm. Hugging an envelope-style pillow to my chest, I rest my eyes and try to sneak in a quick catnap while I wait. Time travel can really take a lot out of a girl.

"Signorina, are you all right?"

No catnaps today, I guess. With a sigh, I open my eyes and see an older, middle-aged man with thick-rimmed glasses and a gentle smile. In clear English he asks, "Is there anything I can get for you?"

I lift my head and smile. "No, I'm good. Really good, actually, but thanks. I'm just waiting for someone, and I couldn't resist diving into this super-soft sofa, I guess."

"I don't blame you," he says, sitting down in the matching love seat. "They are quite nice, aren't they? All the hotel's furnishings are inspired by the Renaissance, but this level of luxury isn't exactly authentic to the sixteenth century," he says, his eyes shining with humor and wisdom.

I bolt upright, suddenly excited about the opportunity to share my experience with someone else. Even though I just got back, I feel like if I don't talk about it as soon as possible, the memories will start to fade or seem less real. I look at his shiny gold nametag. "So, Henry, you know a lot about the sixteenth century, then?"

He nods, running his hand along the soft upholstery. "You have to know at least a little to work in a hotel that was once a sixteenth-century palace, but it's also a hobby of mine. I taught Italian and Renaissance history at Northwestern and moved here when I retired. It's about as close as you can get to actually living in the past, don't you think?"

I bite back a laugh and nod instead. A movement near the door catches my eye and I twist my head around, hoping to see Dad, but it's just another white-socked tourist. My shoulders slump and I turn to look away when I notice a huge painting hanging to the side of the glass doors.

A strange tingle runs through my left arm and my eyes narrow as a peculiar sense of déjà vu hits me. I have to see that painting. I get up, the weird prompting drawing me closer, and the man follows.

"Do you know anything about this painting?" I ask him as we cross the hardwood floor toward it. "There's something about it that seems familiar, but I don't think I've ever seen it before."

"Ah, yes, it is our hotel's most prized possession. A Cappelli original."

My feet stop.

I turn and ask, "Did you say Cappelli?"

Henry's smile grows wider with pride as he answers, "Yes, a Lorenzo Cappelli." My jaw drops as he points to the painting and steers me closer. "This particular one is of great value due to the speculation as to what the pear on the hip of the Goddess of Victory means. Oftentimes in Renaissance art, the pear is used to symbolize fidelity in marriage, but Victoria was not married in the mythology."

I stare wide-eyed at the small plaque below the painting that says, GODDESS VICTORIA WITH PAINTED PEAR, LORENZO CAPPELLI 1506.

A year after I was there.

The memory of our day in the country comes flooding back as I gaze with wonder at the goddess Victoria standing before a rushing waterfall, a crown of daisies in her hair and white linen draped around her body in such a way that it exposes a pear tattoo on her right hip.

Yep, I think, a giddy giggle busting out of my mouth, *he definitely copped a look.*

"You said it is a prized possession," I say, tearing my gaze away. "Are there other Cappelli paintings in existence?"

Henry eyes me with a perplexed frown and my heart rate increases. I wet my lips and swallow, my head buzzing with possibilities. I couldn't handle knowing Lorenzo married someone else, but *this* is different.

Suddenly I have to know—and I'm kicking myself for not

asking Reyna when I had the chance—did Lorenzo become an artist like he wanted, or did his parents finally win?

A noisy tour group enters from behind us and a harried-looking clerk barks Henry's name from the front desk. Thankfully, he hesitates, shaking his head and flashing the universal signal for *give me a minute*. He tilts his head, as if he can't quite figure me out, and says, "But of course there are other paintings. Lorenzo Cappelli is one of the Renaissance's most beloved artists...as celebrated as da Vinci, Raphael, or even Michelangelo."

A gasp of astonishment, followed by an impressive round of choking on air, is my eloquent response to this bit of unbelievable news. I slap my hand over my mouth, waving away his concern, and turn back to the painting.

Lorenzo followed his dream.

Minutes pass and Henry leaves, but still I stand there, completely captivated by Lorenzo's artwork. It's not just that he painted me, although if you know what you're looking for, you can clearly see it's me on the canvas. But his artistry, the paint strokes, his use of color. He truly was a brilliant artist.

And somehow, something I did in the midst of my many, *many* screw-ups changed history.

I helped make this happen.

A hand closes around my shoulder, breaking the painting's spell. "Cat?"

My knees buckle at the sound of Dad's voice. His grip tightens and I collapse into his arms, throwing mine around his neck and inhaling the comforting scent of his spicy aftershave and Armani cologne. "Daddy, I missed you so much."

He laughs and kisses the top of my head. "You weren't gone

that long, Peanut. But a few hours without dear old dad can feel like a lifetime, right?"

I squeeze him tighter and whisper, "You have no idea."

When we finally break apart, I see Jenna standing a few feet behind us. She gives me a cautious smile and as I walk toward her, it turns into one of confusion. I wrap my arms around her neck and I hear a startled intake of air, and then a happy giggle, before she hugs me back.

"That tour of yours must've been some kind of awesome," she says, running her fingers through my hair. "All we did was window shop. You'll have to show us everything you saw."

I step back, nodding, a smile on my face as I realize I can't show them *everything*, and say, "Sure thing."

Jenna's forehead crinkles, still flabbergasted from my open display of affection, so I decide to go for the kill and really freak the girl out.

"And, you know, Jenna, I've been giving a lot of thought to the whole Sweet Sixteen thing."

Her tentative smile falters and she bites her lip.

I scrunch up my mouth and furrow my eyebrows—trying to draw out the suspense—but when deep grooves form in her poor lower lip, I smile.

"Let's do it—the ball, the napkins, MTV, all of it. Why not, right?"

Her eyes grow as large as saucers and her hundred-watt grin restores to its full glory. Dad squeezes my shoulder.

I continue. "It'll probably be fun to do together, although this is definitely more your domain and I'll bow down to your mad skills." I glance back at Lorenzo's painting and smile. "But, I do have one small request."

• • •

I stand on the balcony overlooking the ballroom of the ginormous hotel Jenna booked for the party. Pseudo-candlelight cast by rows of golden chandeliers shine on hundreds of costumed dancers, and cameramen snake through the crowds to interview party guests. They've already gotten me several times, and the entire experience has been surprisingly painless. Jenna's been by my side the whole time, coaching me on what to say and telling the director what he can and cannot ask.

Hayley sidles up beside me, bopping her head to the music. "This was such a fun and unique idea," she tells me, leaning in to be heard over the booming music below.

"Thanks." I turn my head to give her a smile before looking back to crowd watch. "I've always had a soft spot for the Renaissance."

My friendship with Hayley is new and we're still feeling each other out, but it's definitely been one of the best developments since I got back home last month. She's a loner like me who prefers hanging on the fringes of our school's social order. We're both art nerds and Hayley's also really into fashion. The sixteenth-century-inspired gown she's wearing for the night is her own creation, and while the design isn't completely authentic, it still looks incredible.

Jenna waves to me from below and begins ascending the steps to the balcony. While she climbs the spiral staircase, my gaze sweeps across the crowd again, landing on a dark green doublet.

My breath hitches as I follow the guy's golden hair across

the floor and out the side door leading to the pool.

It's not Lorenzo, Cat. It can't be. You have to stop looking for him.

I know it's ridiculous, but I haven't been able to stop. Ever since Dad shelled out the big bucks to buy his painting from the hotel as an overly expensive birthday present (hey, you only turn sixteen once, right?), I've kept it by my bed, rehashing every minute Lorenzo and I spent together. The way he found the beauty in the ordinary. The way he made *me* feel beautiful. The way he smiled, the way he held me. The way I was actually able to be myself around him.

I have this creeptastic feeling that Reyna's out there watching me, waiting for me to take all the lessons she taught me and put them into practice…and I have for everything else. I've branched out and made friends with Hayley. Jenna and I have had several girl nights, complete with goopy masks and calorific goodness, and I even gave her control over this entire shindig.

But guys? They are totally different animals.

Hayley keeps trying to hook me up, even trying to pawn me off on a few different guys tonight, but I'm just not ready yet. It feels like it's too soon, like even thinking about *thinking* about another guy is wrong.

The glass door leading to the pool shakes but fails to open and I clench my jaw impatiently. I need green-doublet boy to reemerge so my tap-dancing heart can see he isn't Lorenzo. But before he does, Jenna reaches us, her perky smile in full effect, and I exhale audibly as I turn to my future stepmother.

"You sure know how to throw an awesome party," Hayley says, moving over to give her room near the railing.

Jenna beams at the compliment and smooths her emerald surcoat down over her hips. "Thank you, Hayley. Everything turned out exactly as I imagined it would. Once Cat suggested the Renaissance, it just all came together!"

I smile at her enthusiasm and nod in agreement. Everything did flow together once we decided on the theme. Throw in a few touches from my personal experience and you get a pretty kick-butt gala.

"Hayley, do you mind if I steal Cat away for a minute?"

Hayley shakes her head and grins. "Nah, I'm gonna go shake it. See you in a few, Cat."

I nod and lift an eyebrow at Jenna. "More interviews?"

"Oh, no, nothing like that," she tells me, worry lines creasing around her eyes. "It's just that because we had so much room here, I invited a potential client and her family tonight so they could see some of my work. The parents are music execs who just moved back from Milan. I thought maybe you could come down and say hello?"

Her mouth flattens into a grimace and I hold back a smile. I get why she's nervous. This is exactly the type of thing that would've bothered me before my trip to the past, but honestly, now it doesn't bother me at all.

The more the merrier, right?

"Sure, lead the way," I tell her.

We walk down the stairs side by side and she wraps her arm around the waist of my amethyst gown, leaning in so I can hear her. "They also have a son who I think is around your age. Pretty cute, actually," she tells me with a wink.

I shake my head. Although I'm sure the boy's cute, I doubt I'll have any interest in him. No modern-day guy can hold a candle to Lorenzo.

We cross the shiny hardwood floor and stop in front of an older couple and young girl, all fully decked out in Renaissance costumes.

"Cat, this is Angela. She's planning a Sweet Sixteen of her own next year," Jenna says, introducing me to the family. Out of curiosity, I look around, but I don't spot the son.

Angela is pretty…and terribly shy. She gives me a stilted wave and then casts her eyes back to the ground. Her parents, on the other hand, more than compensate for it, immediately wrapping me up in a conversation about all the planning.

"Yeah, it's actually been a lot of fun," I tell them, smiling at the girl and trying to draw her out of her shell. "And Jenna's a pro. You'll be in very capable hands."

Angela nods and grins, exposing a dimple in her cheek. She's freaking adorable, and she completely reminds me of Alessandra. I reach my hand out and ask, "Not that your parents aren't great and everything, but do you want to come hang with me for a bit? There's some pretty good grub at the back table."

Her eyes widen and she looks at her parents, who nod encouragingly. Then she turns to me with a huge smile and places her hand in mine. "Thank you," she says softly.

I wink at Jenna and her parents, and then lead Angela along the edge of the dance floor.

"So is this Sweet Sixteen idea more your parents' thing or yours?" I ask once we make it to the refreshments.

I hand her a glass of raspberry lemonade and she takes a sip, continuing to watch the dancing mob. "It was mine originally, back before we moved. But I don't have any friends here. My parents think it'll be a great way to meet people, but I don't know. I mean, who would even come?"

I smile and crook a finger at her, looking around in a mock-stealthy way. She mimics my serious expression and leans in as I tell her, "I'll let you in on a little classified intel. See these people? Hardly know any of them. I mean, they go to my school so technically I do, but we never hang out or anything. But the secret to LA is, if you throw a party—especially one of Jenna's parties—all you need to do is put the word out. If you build it, *they* will come," I say, pointing to the crowded room.

She laughs at the corny movie reference and takes another sip of lemonade. I turn back to the table to snag a cookie and hear her say, "Oh, there he is."

"Who?" I ask, torn between double chocolate chunk and macadamia.

"My brother." Then quiet Angela cups her hand around her mouth and belts out, "Lucas! Over here!"

Intrigued by her unexpected exuberance, I grab a macadamia, turn to follow her gaze, and promptly forget how to chew. Or even breathe.

The guy making his way through the crowd toward us is my age, maybe a year older. He's tall with broad shoulders and a muscular build—I can tell because his authentic green doublet is contoured to his chest.

The boy from the balcony.

Her brother's golden blond hair is styled in a sexy, messy, "this is on purpose" sorta way. And when he smiles, like he is now, a dimple flashes in his bronzed skin. He stops in front of us and the entire ballroom seems to disappear.

"Cat, this is my brother, Lucas."

Wetting my suddenly parched lips, I raise a shaky hand. "N-nice to meet you. I'm Cat Crawford, birthday girl."

Molten chocolate eyes glance first at my hand and then back at me with an amused glimmer. "Lucas Cappelli, party crasher."

The hand he wraps around mine is warm and strong, and it takes a second for the name to register. When it does, my hand clenches within his grip.

Cappelli.

I jerk my head around, looking for Reyna or one of my Renaissance relatives, my heartbeat faltering at the thought of Niccolo being here, but I'm surrounded by a sea of modern teens. In shock, I turn back.

The smooth skin between his eyes wrinkles. "Your mom throws a good party," he says, still watching me.

"Stepmom," I say distractedly. "Future stepmom." I shake my head to clear the fog and realize I'm still clutching his hand. With an awkward laugh, I release my hold—and bite my lower lip when he tightens his.

As his eyes roam over my face and I squirm under the scrutiny, I notice the freckle under his eye and the scar on his chin. Both alterations to his sixteenth-century look-alike and obvious ancestor. But then Lucas winks, and it's as though I'm right back in the shadowed garden of the palazzo courtyard.

Angela clears her throat and heat rises to my cheeks. Again, I try to release his hand, but this time Lucas tugs me closer. The fresh scent of soap mixed with mint fills my head as he leans down to ask, "Care to dance, birthday girl?"

This close up, it's hard to remember this isn't Lorenzo. My gaze falls to the dark doublet stretched across his shoulders and

I nod. One dance—one chance to relive the night of the ball—can't hurt, right?

Lucas laces his fingers through mine and leads me to the center of the floor, threading us among the dancing bodies. He stops, turns, and the slow, sultry beat of the music works its magic as he glides his hands over the satin of my surcoat, resting them at the small of my back. With a hard swallow, I slide mine up the hard muscle of his arms to clasp them behind his neck.

Is this really happening?

I blink, trying to clear my suddenly fuzzy head, and look up into Lucas's dark brown eyes. A side-grin steals across his face, and my stomach clenches.

"I hear we're going to be classmates soon," he says, his warm breath fanning the loose hair around my face. "Angela and I are transferring in January. It'll be nice to have a friendly face there."

I give a noncommittal nod and force a smile at Hayley, dancing behind us with a guy I recognize from bio. She waggles her eyebrows, giving Lucas the eyeball equivalent of a thumbs-up, and I shake my head. *It's just a dance.* Then Lucas begins rubbing small circles on my back, and my eyelids flutter.

I want to tell my giddy heart to chill.

Inwardly I waggle a finger at my internal organs doing a jig and scream, *This isn't Lorenzo. You do not have permission to swoon!*

My fuzzy brain ignores the message.

I lift my head again and Lucas rakes a hand through his golden curls. The same deep brown eyes I've thought about so often this last month stare back. A soft smile plays across Lucas's lips and he ducks his head, the trace of his Italian accent growing stronger as he says, "You know, I'm really glad I came tonight."

A dancer bumps me from behind and I stumble. Lucas cups my elbow to steady me, and a low-wattage, yet still noticeable hum slides up my arm. My chest actually hurts from how hard my heart pounds.

Nothing about this makes sense. The strange pull between us, him being Lorenzo's doppelganger, or the fact that after a month spent declaring no boy could ever measure up to my Renaissance hottie, my entire being completely relaxes in Lucas's arms.

It's the last thing that terrifies me.

Lucas continues to watch me and I watch him back, wondering if he, too, feels the mysterious pull or if it's all just in my head. Finally, I bring myself to tell him, "I'm glad you're here, too, Lucas."

The bemused wrinkle on his forehead eases and he pulls me closer, mimicking Lorenzo's hold from the night in the courtyard. But tonight is different. The lilting, live quartet has been exchanged for perfect, studio-recorded music, and Lorenzo's familiar woodsy scent traded for mint with a subtle hint of aftershave.

My head spins, filled with both excitement and a guilty feeling of doubt. I lower it to rest on Lucas's solid chest, and his arms close tighter around me. With his heartbeat pounding beneath my cheek, matching the rhythm of my own, I close my eyes and let the music wash over me.

Epilogue

I jiggle my key in the door and let myself in to an empty house. The *click clack* of my heels reverberates off the tile in the entryway as I beeline for the kitchen, dropping my heavy suitcases along the way. After the way-too-early, six-hour plane ride from Mississippi, all I want is to tear into a bag of Oreos and drink my weight in soda.

As I pop the top on a can of Sprite, I read the note Dad left me on the fridge. Another apology for sending the car to get me at LAX, a reminder that Jenna won't be back from New York until tomorrow, and a promise to pick me up for dinner promptly at seven.

My *Love Story* ringtone plays within my bag and I dig it out with a sardonic smile, assuming the night's plans have changed already. Thanks to Dad's temperamental/blockbuster star, production is seriously behind schedule. But when I look at my phone, it's not Dad calling with a prolific apology after all.

It's Lucas.

Taking a deep breath and rubbing the back of my neck to relieve the throbbing tension, I tap my finger and accept the call. "Hey there, stranger."

"So you do know how to answer your phone." Even though the words are sarcastic, I can hear Lucas's smile over the phone. I can also hear his slight Italian accent, which makes my betraying stomach do a flip.

Apparently, my body is nothing if not fickle.

"Hardy-har-har," I reply, trying not to smile.

For three weeks, I've dodged Lucas's calls and texts, even spending most of Winter Break with my grandparents to avoid temptation. But with school starting back tomorrow, and Lucas transferring into my class, *Project Evasion* has officially hit a snag.

Lucas chuckles on the other end and a yummy warmth pools in my belly. I squeeze my eyes shut in self-condemnation.

"Just wanted to make sure you got back home in one piece," he says in a flirtatious, teasing tone. "I'd hate to have to walk the halls tomorrow without a friendly face."

Immediately my mind fast-forwards to the reaction I know he'll get in the school halls and I inwardly sigh. *Yeah, I don't think you'll have a shortage of those.*

"I'll be there," I say, shooting for a breezy tone and having no clue if I make it there or not. "All spiffed up and shiny in my new semester finery."

I smack my head against the granite counter.

Can I possibly be any lamer?

On the other end, Lucas laughs under his breath, and I decide no. I can't.

"I look forward to seeing what you Americans consider appropriate high school fashion," he says, his sexy/bordering-on-arrogant smile evident in his voice, and I melt a little bit more.

Even though I've spent the last three weeks ignoring most of Lucas's calls, it doesn't mean I haven't thought about him. I have...a lot. But I still don't have any answers. I don't know if it's wrong to like him, or if I should go for it. If he even likes me, or if he's only interested because of my mama drama and who my dad is, just like everyone else. Then there's the whole look-a-like weirdness. I can't decide if it's just a freaky coincidence or a cosmic sign from Reyna.

Where the heck's a gypsy girl when you need her?

Lucas clears his throat on the line and I rack my brain for a topic of conversation. I've never had a boyfriend or anything close besides Lorenzo, so all of this is unchartered territory. Restless and fidgety, I grab the huge stack of mail beside me and begin flinging pieces across my counter.

Junk mail, bill, junk mail, Vogue, *junk mail…*

My flying fingers freeze on the thick, stiff envelope in my hand. Tossing the rest of the mail aside, my entire body suddenly electrified, I flip the envelope over and then back again.

"Cat, you still there?"

It's not the lack of a stamp in the corner or return address that has me shell-shocked—I know who sent it. It's not even the fact that the envelope is sealed with red wax, straight out of some historical novel. No, what stops me is the name written in perfect calligraphy on the cover.

Signorina Patience D'Angeli.

"Yeah, Lucas, I-I have to go. I'll see you tomorrow?"

He pauses before saying, "Sure, no problem," in a tone much less playful then earlier. "See you tomorrow."

We hang up and I hesitate a moment, staring at the icons on my phone, wondering if I just completely blew it with Lucas. Then a prickle of unease works its way down my spine, along with a creepy feeling like I'm being watched, and I cast a quick glance around the kitchen. Gingerly, I lift the back flap and slide out a small card. The words on it are few but powerful in their mystery, and my hands tremble as I read.

> *Dear Caterina aka Patience,*
>
> *The night after our return, I began having another vision. It took me some time to decipher the message, but I finally have. A delivery will be arriving at your door at one o'clock. It is in capable hands; I trust you will know what to do.*
>
> *Latcho Drom,*
> *Reyna*

My gaze snaps to the digital clock on the microwave. According to Reyna, a delivery of some kind will be here in thirty minutes and I have no doubt it will arrive right on time. Ignoring my grumbling stomach, I snatch up my bags and tear through the house to my room, my mind an endless wonder of questions. Am I going back to the past? The future this time? Do I have a quest to fulfill? She said she trusts that I'll know what to do, but how can she be so sure?

Unsure of how or what to prepare for the delivery, I jump in the shower and try to pass the excruciating waiting time by getting ready for anything.

A delivery. What could that mean?

I blowdry my hair and put on makeup, my mind still racing with ideas. A quick check of the clock shows I have less than five minutes. I throw on a pair of dark wash Kent 5 jeans and a Blu Moon top, then race down the stairs to wait by the door.

My fingernails drum on the granite countertop and my knees pound a rhythm against the cabinet. Then, finally, as the grandfather clock in the foyer strikes the hour, my doorbell rings.

My palms slicked with sweat, I hesitantly walk to the door and stop with my hand on the knob. The sound of my pounding heart echoes in my ears and I take a calming breath. Who knows how my life can change once I turn it?

When I do scrounge up the courage to open the door, my eyes bug out, my jaw drops, and I shake my head in disbelief.

"Alessandra?"

Acknowledgments

This book wouldn't exist without the push and inspiration from my gorgeous niece Hayley and her best friend, Katie. My equally gorgeous other niece, Desiree, advised on all things lingo, clothing, and general cultural whatnot. Without the three of you, I'd still be dreaming of 'someday.' Girls, thank you for rocking so hard...and for letting me use your names!

Thanks to the Houston YA/MG Writers Group for teaching me so much, and Mary Lindsey for your constant encouragement. Nancy Bowden and Natalie Markey, thanks for being my first-ever critique partners, and Rose Moriarty, thanks for the awesome critiques, yummy margaritas, and much-needed girl talk.

My critique partners are my sanity, and nothing feels complete without their stamp of approval. Trisha Wolfe, the queen of steam, thanks for teaching me to trust my instincts, putting up with my constant need for techno help, and taking me under your wing. Victoria Scott, thanks for always keeping it real, challenging me to dig deeper, and making me laugh. And Shannon Duffy, thank you for your unflappable faith in this story, confidence in me, and boundless friendship. It's because of you three that I found my voice.

So many writers have pored over these pages, offered their friendship, and/or given much-needed guidance. HUGE thank you to: Hope Collier, Demetra Brodsky, Kelly Hashway, Vicky Dreiling, Sophie Jordan, Debbie Wentlein, Elizabeth Isaacs, Mindy Ruiz, Tiffany King, Brandi Kosiner, Julie Brazeal, Stacey O'Neale, Lisa Schroeder, Holly Schindler, Lisa T. Bergren, Sarah MacLean, and everyone at West Houston RWA. And a special shout out to Crystal Waters for her gorgeous artwork on my swag tattoos. You have mad skills, girl!

Tara Fuller, Melissa West, Lisa Burstein, Chloe Jacobs, Cindi Madsen, Nicola Marsh, and Diane Alberts: you ladies make writing an absolute blast. Thanks for the virtual giggles, friendship, and support. I LOVE being your pub house sister!

Entangled really is a family and I'm truly honored to be a part of it. Massive shout out to Lea Nolan, Laura Kaye, Stephanie Thomas, Rachel Firasek, Cari Quinn, Brooke Moss, Lisa Kessler, and Katee Robert. You ladies inspire me. *jazz hands*

To our captain, Liz Pelletier, thanks for the tireless work you do and for my beyond-gorgeous cover. I bow down to your awesomeness. Heather Howland and Misa Ramirez, thanks for sharing your infinite wisdom and humor. Danielle Barclay, you are my angel. You make me laugh, calm me down, and encourage and inspire me. Knowing you are in my corner as my friend and publicist has made this journey amazing. I heart you so much!

Stacy Cantor Abrams, what can I say? Your enthusiasm is contagious. You understood the story I wanted to tell and then took it and made it shine. Thanks for saving me from the slush pile and putting up with my many e-mails and occasional, inexplicable lapse into being British. You made this entire process a joy.

Lauren Hammond, the agent of awesome, thank you for believing in me and always making me smile. I get giddy whenever my phone plays "Girls Just Wanna Have Fun" because I know you're calling. I'm blessed to have an agent who is also my friend. #GoTeamHammond.

To my mother-in-law, Peggy, for being the first to buy this book and your constant cheerleading. To my amazing parents, Ronnie and Rosie, for passing down your love of the written word and reading every book I've written. To my brother, Ryan, for going after his dream and inspiring me to do the same. And to my two princesses, Jordan and Cali, for the wonderful talks about black moments and turning points, your handmade covers for my books, and understanding when Mommy needs to work.

And finally, to my husband, Gregg, for never doubting this could happen. Thanks for going to conferences with me, hashing out plot points and character arcs, cooking dinner, and always bragging about me. You are my rock and without you, none of this would be possible. SHMILY!

Keep reading for a sneak peek of Allessandra's story in the companion book
A TALE OF TWO CENTURIES
by Rachel Harris

When her time-traveling cousin returned to the future two years ago, Alessandra D'Angeli was the only one in her family who remembered the truth. Now, still haunted with visions of the future, Less finds it difficult to live the quiet life her parents expect.Dreaming of a gypsy adventure of her own, Less cries out for help.

The stars hear her plea.

One mystical spell by the gypsy Reyna later, Less arrives on Cat's Beverly Hills doorstep five hundred years in the future. Surrounded by confusing gadgets, talking boxes, scary transportation, and scandalous clothing, Less experiences the modern world for the first time. High school halls and community theater productions have never held so much magic.

Now, torn between a past with her family and the world she knows, and a future filled with love and possibility, Alessandra fights fate to figure out what to do, knowing she belongs in the sixteenth century and cannot stay in the twenty-first. Or can she?

Chapter One

I close my eyes against the gentle breeze and twirl, my silk celadon surcoat swishing around my ankles in glorious abandon. The warm sun seeps into my skin, and it is as if the very air I breathe is saturated with happiness. Fourteen years groomed to become a wealthy merchant's wife, two years toiling to suppress my sinful desires, and it all culminates in this moment.

Pray, let it be today!

Five long days ago, Matteo—as he allows me to call him in private—asked me to meet him here so we can discuss our future. A future I am eager to begin. Every dutiful prayer and every wistful thought since has been spent in anticipation.

The scent of fresh cut flowers from a merchant's stand fills the air as Mama's wise words float in my mind: *Nature is but a sign of Signore's provision, Alessandra.* My eyes open to the vibrant blue of the iris petals, a certain premonition of good things to come, and a giggle springs from my throat.

"The sun's light holds not a candle to your radiance today, Less."

With a smile even the dreaded Antonia could not temper, I turn to the only person besides my beloved cousin Cat who refers to me by the peculiar name. "You and your flattering tongue are agreeably met, dear friend," I tell Lorenzo, maintaining one eye on the crowded piazza. "Care to keep me company while I await Signore Romanelli?"

My brother's best friend sets down his easel. "It would be my pleasure." He props his foot against the sandstone building behind us and rakes a paint-stained hand through his golden curls. "Last week you believed he had intentions of betrothal in mind. Have you seen each other since last we spoke?"

An inkling of disquiet blooms, but I whisk it away. "No, but it is my suspicion he has spent the time in preparation to meet Father."

Lorenzo nods and we fall into a companionable silence, taking in the bustling life around us. The Mercato Vecchio is as noisy as ever, a cacophony of yelling, laughter, babies crying, and donkeys braying. A group of children race past, bumping into a nearby servant and jostling the basket she carries. A single red apple rolls to a stop by my feet.

A vision of the day in the countryside plays before me, unbidden and poignant. The poisoned apple, the evil hag, the chance to shuck my dutiful daughter role and become someone wicked. I adore my cousin for many reasons, but the gift of that afternoon most especially. Despite the church's strident opposition to female actresses, Cat gave me the opportunity to experience the rush of performance. To live the dream I once thought sinful.

Unfortunately, it was after my dear cousin departed that agony adhered to the memory as well. When Cat returned to the future, she left three powerful words in her wake: *passion*, *equality*, and *freedom*. Maidens of the twenty-first century may hold these ideals dear, but they are most unacceptable in the sixteenth—as much as I wish it otherwise. As a result, I have spent the last two years in turmoil, battling between my expected duty of propriety and my newfound desire for passion.

Lorenzo kneels to pluck up the apple and I meet his gaze.

He, too, is remembering.

Cat's implausible time travel did not leave me solely affected. As the only two who know the Patience living among us today is not the girl we all once knew, Lorenzo and I bonded in our commiseration. He used the pain of Cat's departure to fuel his art, studying under a variety of masters, earning public commendation, and creating masterpiece after masterpiece.

I stuffed it into reinvigorated attempts at matrimony.

Lorenzo returns the apple to the woman and gives me a tight-lipped smile. When he looks away, his smile becomes genuine. "I believe your suitor has arrived."

Giddiness bubbles inside as I follow his gaze.

Matteo.

He has yet to spot me, so I take the opportunity to drink in the sight of him. The broad line of his strong shoulders displayed in his dark doublet. The enticing tilt of his mouth I can see even from this distance. Absent are the lines of worry that often mar his handsome face, and I watch as he laughs with someone to his right. My heart hammers.

He is truly *yummy*, as my fair cousin would say.

At twenty-eight, Matteo is eleven years my senior. He is a bit young for marriage, but our families are old friends and a union will bring increased prosperity. We will make a good match. Being with him will quiet the rage inside me, the need for more. It has to.

The crowd between us parts and I spot a young woman beside him. I tilt my head and squint.

"Novella de Amico," I say, my voice barely above a whisper. Formerly Novella Montagna, daughter of one of the wealthiest families in Florence. Courted and desired by all the men of marriageable age last year, she married a Venice nobleman and moved away last winter. I turn to Lorenzo, my ribs an iron vise around my lungs. "Why has she returned to Florence?"

He shakes his head, his eyebrows furrowed. "I am not sure. But I shall find out."

Lorenzo marches over to a band of women pretending to shop, obviously using the pleasant fall day as an excuse to prattle incessantly. As he approaches, Signora Benedicti, Signora Cacchioni, and Signora Stefani turn and graze over his features as if he were a piece of Venetian glass or a new onyx cameo. Completely undignified, but sadly, not uncharacteristic.

If gossip is desired, Lorenzo could not have chosen a better group.

I look away in disgust and fix my gaze on Matteo, willing him to glance my way. A few minutes later, I get my wish. My insides squeeze but I force a smile, pushing every stolen moment and whispered promise into the gesture.

He does not return it.

Matteo reaches to clasp Novella's hand, his once warm eyes now emotionless stones.

All excitement and hope drain away. Air ceases to be a necessity. Time stops and cold dread washes over me. The market fades away, and my gaze locks onto their interlaced fingers.

From the corner of my eye I see Lorenzo turn away from the gossiping horde, his handsome faced etched with pity. But I already know.

When he reaches me, he looks down and scowls. "Signora de Amico returned home a widow last week, her full dowry intact."

He inhales sharply and I close my eyes, steeling myself for the truth to come. This is not how I envisioned this day unfolding.

"They met with the notary just yesterday."

Good begets good.

Somehow, the lesson from my childhood does not fit this new reality. I always do—have always done—the right thing, the proper thing. I do my duty. There should be a reward.

He's supposed to love me back.

Lorenzo clears his throat and I know he's waiting for me to meet his gaze. With burning tears threatening to escape, I compel my eyes open.

He places a gentle hand on my shoulder. "Alessandra, Matteo and Novella are married."

• • •

The *click clack* of footsteps on the cobblestone road muffles my sobs. After pleading with Lorenzo not to follow, I made my faltering escape from the piazza, away from the prying eyes of Mama's friends and the smirk of triumph on Novella's contemptuous face. Tearing through the streets of my beloved city, my gaze blurred, I prayed my feet would somehow find their way home. And as my eyes alight on the familiar four-story, tan stone building, my knees nearly buckle in gratitude. Fate may not have ruled in my favor in matters of the heart, but it appears to have taken pity on my sense of navigation.

My toe catches in the cracked stone floor and I stagger through the arched opening of my courtyard. I set myself to rights and press on, the quiet solitude of the garden beckoning me forward, and sink to my knees in a corner covered in shadow. This was Cat's favorite place, the spot where she followed her heart with Lorenzo the night of her ball. Whenever I need to feel close to her, to imagine her words of strength and wisdom, and remember her assurance that my desires are not sinful, I find myself here.

But today, the darkened retreat does not soothe. The scent of fragrant flowers, the recall of bittersweet memories, and the melodic bubbling of the nearby fountain do nothing to ease the stabbing pain of Matteo's betrayal.

I still cannot bring myself to believe it. Months of secret assignations and declarations could not end in such a way. Surely, I must be in the midst of a nightmare. At any moment I will wake up, get ready again, and leave to meet Matteo, where he will whisper words of our future, and how much he loves me.

I blink rapidly, but nothing changes.

With a trembling hand, I wipe at relentless tears. I cannot help but think that Cat would be stronger. In my place, she would have stormed across the crowded piazza, flung a cutting remark at Novella, and demanded an explanation from Matteo. Then, she would have kicked him.

The image of my near-betrothed's eyes popping out of his head eases my spirits a little and I hiccup a laugh. Cat had been a storm of unquenchable vigor, challenging the rest of us to either match her in vivacity, or be left in the dust.

But alas, I am not my dear cousin.

In Cat's world, in the future, a girl is free to live with passion and blatant disregard for propriety. She can ignore the rules of etiquette and society, and follow her dreams—even when they lead her here, five hundred years into the past. Fate, mixed with a little gypsy magic, granted her the opportunity to experience the impossible. Cat glimpsed another way of life, and for a short while was given respite from the worries of her own.

Crumpling to the ground, for once not caring if my surcoat gets soiled, I close my eyes and let fresh tears fall onto the damp earth beneath my cheek.

"How I long for a gypsy adventure of my own."

As I lay there, unmoving, willing the world to end, a faint tinkling sound rings near my ear, yanking me from my despair.

A slow shiver creeps from the base of my spine. It quickly gains speed before bursting across the rest of my body. My eyes spring open to branches and petals dancing around me in a sudden breeze. A few snap and flutter away as the winds grow stronger. Ribbons of my auburn hair slash across my eyes. I clamor to my feet, fighting against the abrupt gust stealing my breath, and hold down the hem of my gown. The wind shoves me forward and the storm swallows my shriek.

Then, as suddenly as it began, everything stops.

I finally find my voice. "What, in Signore's name, was *that*?"

Unsurprisingly, the now calm and quiet courtyard does not reply.

Glancing down, I brush away the debris clinging to my surcoat—but the sharp crack of a twig behind me causes my hands to still.

"*Buna ziua,* Alessandra."

I spin around and my gaze lands on a girl near my age. Her long raven hair is unruly and tousled, her costume one of brightly colored skirts and sheer veils. Her arms are bare, as is a slice of bronzed skin around her midsection. Averting my eyes, a whisper of a memory taunts the edges of my mind.

How does she know my name?

A small smile, unnatural and amiss on an otherwise somber face, plays upon the girl's mouth as she says, "The stars have heard your plea."

Made in the USA
Charleston, SC
03 August 2012